Also by Christopher Barzak

ONE FOR SORROW

The
Love We Share
Without Knowing

A Novel

Christopher Barzak

BANTAM BOOKS

THE LOVE WE SHARE WITHOUT KNOWING
A Bantam Book / December 2008

Published by
Bantam Dell
A Division of Random House, Inc.
New York, New York

Book design by Melissa Sutherland-Amado

Library of Congress Cataloging-in-Publication Data

Barzak, Christopher.
The love we share without knowing / Christopher Barzak.
p.   cm.
ISBN 978-0-553-38564-9 (trade pbk.)
1. Psychological fiction.   I. Title.

PS3602.A844L68   2008
813'.6—dc22
2008026623

Printed in the United States of America
Published simultaneously in Canada

www.bantamdell.com

BVG 10 9 8 7 6 5 4 3 2 1

For Tadashi Mizuno,
who opened the door for me.
When I walked through,
this is what I saw.

My loneliness, what makes me really lonely,
Is that I can't feel by my side a single will to halt this drift to ruin,
To get to the root of loneliness, to join the rest of the world.
That's all.

—Kaneko Mitsuharu, "Song of Loneliness"

I had no doubt you'd cross my path one day. I waited for you
calmly, with boundless impatience. Devour me. Deform me to
your likeness, so that no one after you will ever again understand
the reason for so much desire. We'll be alone, my love. Night will
never end. The day will never dawn again on anyone. Never
again. At last. You're still destroying me. You're good for me.
We'll mourn the departed day in good conscience and with
goodwill. There'll be nothing else for us to do but mourn the
departed day. Time will pass. Only time. And a time will come
when we can no longer name what it is that binds us. Its name
will gradually be erased from our memory until it vanishes
completely.

—Marguerite Duras, *Hiroshima, Mon Amour*

The Love We Share Without Knowing

Realer Than You

Everything you think you know about the world isn't true. Nothing is real, it's all made up. We live in a world of illusion. I'm telling you this up front because I don't want you thinking this story is going to have a happy ending. It won't make any sense out of sadness. It won't redeem humanity in even a small sort of way.

My name is Elijah Fulton, and unlike so many things, this actually happened. It happened in Japan at the beginning of the twenty-first century, when I was sixteen and my parents forced me to leave America. It happened in Ami, a suburb an hour away from Tokyo, on a trail in a bamboo forest.

I was running that day, as usual, because running and biking were the only ways I could get anywhere. You had to be eighteen to drive in Japan, so all of a sudden I was a kid again. Without a car, I was stuck in our tiny house with my thirteen-year-old sister and my mom as they learned how to cook Japanese food with Mrs. Fujita, the wife of my dad's boss. Mrs. Fujita was always calling from the kitchen for me to come taste whatever weird thing they were making in there, like, "Come taste this delicious eel, Elijah!" and I wasn't having any of that. So I ran to get away from everything. From my parents and their friends, from my little sister. From Ami. If I could have, I would have run away from Japan altogether.

When I first started running, I didn't know where the roads led to or even in which direction they traveled, so to be safe I'd circle the apartment complex next to our house, and every day I'd run a little further. By the end of my first week I made it to the end of our road, and a few days after that I crossed over to a road that ran over a hill, into a forest of bamboo and pine trees. The road twisted uninterrupted through the woods for a long time, like a stream flowing through the trees, but I kept going, and eventually I reached a place where the road split off in two directions. One way curved out of the forest, opening onto a cabbage farm and, beyond it, the sloping red- and blue-tiled roofs of town. The other way deteriorated into a dirt trail that wound further into the forest.

I took the trail that went into the woods, where under the gray-green bamboo shadows locusts buzzed and sawed, carrying on a strange conversation. As I ran I listened to the thud of my feet as they fell on the path, and the rise and fall of my breathing. Safe rhythms. They let me know my body was still the same, even though nothing else was familiar.

As I ran, a dragonfly big as my hand flitted back and forth around me, circling me but never leaving. It was bigger than any dragonfly I'd ever seen in America. I could see all of its details, its metallic body and bulbous head, its knobby joints and how its wings sparkled in the shafts of falling sunlight. It's no wonder why people once believed they were fairies. But people will believe in almost anything, really. Sometimes you don't even have to try very hard to convince them.

I was so distracted by looking at anything other than where I was going that I didn't notice the trail I was running on had ended at some point. And when I did notice, I found myself in a cleared circle deep in the woods, where a tiny unpainted house, like the sort people back home put up on poles as bird mansions, stood pressed into the shade at the back of the clearing.

This house had little stairs leading up to a doll-sized door bolted with a rusty lock, and coins and braids of colored string lay scattered across its steps. As I walked closer to examine it, I started to think someone very small would unlock that door at any moment, swing it open, and step out. Maybe it was the dragonfly and all those thoughts of fairies that made me think that. Maybe it was my mood that day in general. Whatever the reason, no one opened that tiny door to ask what I was doing there. Instead, a rustling startled me, and when I looked up, I found a red dog stepping out of the trees behind the house.

It looked more like a fox than a dog maybe. Not like a real fox, though, all skinny and dirty. More like one that just stepped out of a storybook. It had a rich coat of red fur and a bib-shaped patch of white down on its throat. Lifting its nose to sniff the air, cocking its head to one side, it inspected me like I'd inspected the house.

While it circled, I stood still like you're supposed to, careful not to provoke it. I mean, storybook or not, it was some kind of canine and I was obviously on its territory. It must have decided I was okay, because eventually it lowered its head, uninterested, and walked away. I let a breath out, but only a second later I realized my troubles weren't over. The dog was leaving, but it was taking the path I needed to leave by.

I could have waited until the path was free of strange animals, but instead I decided to walk a little ways behind it. It was getting dark, and I couldn't help but wonder what other creatures might come out to meet me if I was still lost in that forest after the moon rose.

As I followed, the dog kept moving, only stopping to look over its shoulder occasionally, its black nose gently nudging the air in front of it. Whenever it did that, a little pang went off inside my chest and suddenly I wanted to pet it, to wrap my arms around its neck and hold it like I used to hold my girlfriend back in the States before we broke up because I was leaving. The fox felt that familiar.

And that's when the really weird thing happened. That's when I got the idea that our meeting wasn't an accident. As we left the shade of the forest, I thought, *It's leading me. It's taking me home again, isn't it?*

But then it didn't lead me home after all. Well, not all the way, that is. When we reached the path to the intersection where I needed to cross over, it stopped, looked at me once more with its bright green eyes, then dashed back into the woods we'd come out of. I stood there watching it slip through the poles of bamboo for a while, a flash of burnt orange amid the gray-green. And afterwards, when all I saw was green again, I ran the rest of the way home.

The name Ami officially has no meaning, but I think it has a secret one. In the Dictionary of Secret Meanings, the word *Ami* means "the most boring town in the world." With its Catholic-school-uniformed boys and girls walking the sidewalks, with its 1950s-looking housewives wearing aprons as they zoomed down the street on mopeds, it was like living in some surreal *Leave It to Beaver* rerun. Unfortunately, they have those in Japan, too.

It wasn't just the apron-wearing housewives on mopeds or uniformed Japanese students wandering the streets, though. Those things were all a part of it, but it was more than that. It was the strange symbols on billboards instead of the Roman alphabet, it was the radio announcers spewing streams of incomprehensible chatter, it was the TV shows that made no sense, it was the way my family took everything in such stride. It was all of those things together that made me feel dizzy.

My dad's boss, Mr. Fujita, got my dad used to the place pretty quickly, so I don't think he ever felt the same kind of vertigo I did. And Mrs. Fujita and my mom were dead set on becoming best friends. With Mr. Fujita, my dad bought a car. With Mrs. Fujita, my mom learned which stores had the best groceries, which restaurants the best sushi. So both of my parents had interpreters helping them make everything easy.

Liz and I, on the other hand, had been put in a school for kids of English speakers. Mostly Australian and British kids went there, but it was still cool to be able to speak English, even though there were differences between our English. Like what the hell's a *jumper*? How about *arse* and *bloke*?

Words like that always made the few American students snicker and look at each other smiling. Then the Aussies and Brits would laugh at the Americans snickering. It was all a friendly sort of making fun of one another, I guess. I had a Japanese class, but just being there sounding like an idiot as I tried speaking Japanese with a bunch of kids who really spoke English made me feel like I'd stumbled into some kind of government brainwashing program. When I told Liz how I felt after our first few weeks, she said, "Classrooms and government brainwashing programs *are* the same thing, Elijah. That's how they are everywhere, though. Not just here." I seriously have no clue where she comes up with these things.

My dad works for an electronics company, a big name brand in America that rhymes with *phony*. And that's the word I want to talk about. Phony. Because that's what I thought about most of the people I met in my first few weeks. They were phonies. Fakes. Or as my English teacher back home would have said, what I was dealing with was a "culture of charlatans." Everyone seemed to always be bowing and apologizing, saying how they should have been the one to thank you for giving them the opportunity to present you with a gift, which to me seemed like the biggest guilt trip ever. I couldn't really believe anything they said, because it all seemed so absurdly polite. I thought they had to be lying.

I wanted the bluntness of America. I wanted someone to lean on a car horn and shout out the window, "What the hell's the holdup?!" I wanted someone to say what they were *really* thinking. Stuff that helps you know where you stand with a person. But the Japanese are all about subtlety. If they're mad, they'll just keep smiling, saying "please" and "thank you." If you want to know what they really think, you can forget about it unless they're thinking something nice.

When I got back from my run that day, my sister, Liz, was watching one of those weird Japanese TV shows. The host kept saying, "*Hontooo*?" and the audience laughed whenever he said it, like he was the funniest guy ever. Liz laughed with them, as if she understood. Actually, she did understand. It was me who didn't get it. Liz was only thirteen, but she'd spent the last three months before we moved studying Japanese, learning two of its three alphabets. When Mr. Fujita had come to pick us up at the airport, she'd been able to introduce herself in Japanese. I like my sister a lot, but sometimes I feel like she's the one who should be getting ready to graduate and go to college, not me.

When she realized I was in the room, she looked up, still giggling, and said, "*Konnichiwa*, Elijah. *Genki desu ka*?"

"Okay," I said, sighing. "I guess." Usually I refused to respond if she spoke Japanese, but I didn't have the energy that day to deal with it.

Liz looked at me suspiciously, and her laughter faded. "Are you okay?" she said again. "I mean, really?"

"Yeah," I said. "It's nothing."

I went back to my room and fell on my futon, thinking hard. The air was thick with moisture, and my small fan didn't do much but stir it around. There was air conditioning, but after our first week here we'd stopped using it. Some Japanese friends from Phony International had come over and freaked out when they saw it running. "This air is expensive!" they'd gasped, and of course my mom had hopped to, like she does when any Japanese person suggests anything.

"When in Rome," she was always saying. But we're not in
Rome. We're in Ami.

I breathed in that wet air now and thought about what
had happened. Something big, but I didn't know how to explain it. I already knew I wanted to go back to the clearing,
though. To that little house. To see that red dog or fox again.
To feel the calm it gave me. It was the first time I'd felt that in
months, and after having it for just those few moments, I
was already desperate to feel it again.

I was still lying on my futon an hour later, face down
in the rice-filled pillows my mom had bought us on Mrs.
Fujita's recommendation, when I decided to go ahead and
talk to Liz about what I'd seen in the forest earlier. I hadn't
really paid my little sister much attention before we left
America, but here she seemed like the only person I could
talk to.

She was still stretched out on the couch in the living
room where I'd left her, but now she was watching the international news hour. American soldiers in beige camo were
standing with their guns pointed at some Iraqi people
spread out on the ground around them, shouting at them to
not move. If it wasn't the funny Japanese talk shows, Liz was
watching stuff like this, which was thoroughly depressing,
and even Mom and Dad would sometimes tell her to turn
the channel to something less grim. Liz always obliged, but
not without some snotty comment. "Yes, why on earth
would we want to watch *real* reality TV?" she'd say snobbily.
Sometimes she was like this really old British woman
trapped inside the body of a thirteen-year-old American
girl.

Anyway, when I sat down on the couch by her feet and said, "Hey, I saw something strange today," Liz muted the TV with a flick of the remote.

"Go ahead," she said, sitting up and turning to me like an encouraging psychologist, her eyes wide and alert, prepared to understand me. By the time I finished telling her everything, she was nodding in this knowing way, curling her long brown hair in a loop around one finger. "You saw a shrine, Elijah," she told me. "They put them in different places. Probably the one you saw was private. Like a family put it there, or maybe even just one person."

"It looked old," I said. "You know, in disrepair."

"Probably it's abandoned," said Liz. "Maybe the person who made it died."

I thought about that for a second, then asked, "So what's it for?"

"For gods to live in," said Liz. This was totally one of her things, apparently. I got up and went to the kitchen for a glass of the iced barley water my mom said Mrs. Fujita swore by as the perfect late summer drink, and Liz followed, eating up my interest. "That's why there were things on the steps. They were offerings."

"Really?" I said. "That's sort of cool."

"Yeah," said Liz, "and what you saw is a small one. We should find out where the big nearby shrines are and go. Those are huge and lots of people visit them."

"Maybe," I said. But I liked my shrine without all the people. It felt like it was just for me and whoever had built it. And for the red fox. For the red fox, definitely. I don't think I would have had that feeling if I went to a shrine with lots of people. And even though I was behaving in general, I didn't want to give anyone the impression I was settling in. That would have felt too much like I was losing something.

I went back to the shrine a few more times after that day, but I never saw the red fox again. I sort of liked that the fox wasn't there—it made our first encounter feel more special—but at the same time I was disappointed. I wanted to feel that eddy of wonder again. I wanted to know what it meant. And after a while, I started to get anxious again, like I'd been before I found the shrine, and a sort of longing began to grow inside me. Sometimes I could feel it, like a solid thing pressing, swelling in my chest. At those times, when the weight of wanting was heavy, I imagined a shrine being built inside me—a shrine like the one in the forest—and then, somehow, I'd feel a little better.

❖

I tried to fill the empty space the best way I knew how. All of the kids at the English school were stuck in this place because of their parents, like me, and I thought maybe one of them might understand. So I asked this kid Colin if he wanted to hang out and do something, and we went to a game center after school one day and talked about all the whack games they have. Pachinko parlors in particular puzzled us. They seemed to be everywhere—their neon billboards flashed on every corner of every town you found yourself in—but neither of us could figure that game out. It was sort of a mix between pinball and a slot machine, from what we could tell. Colin said, "You must have to be Japanese to fully understand it."

"It's probably a joke on the gaijin," I told him. "The Japanese in these pachinko parlors are really just actors paid to look like they know what they're doing, but what's really happening is the game is a complete fraud and they have cameras on us, and we're being laughed at by a studio audience and fifty million Japanese viewers sitting at home."

"Like a Philip K. Dick novel," said Colin, laughing. "You know, the guy who wrote the story about that guy whose life was really a TV show?"

"Oh yeah," I said. "I think I saw the movie. Philip K. Dick could have been Japanese. He seemed to know a lot about how the world is never what it looks like. That's pretty much Japan through and through."

"What do you mean?" asked Colin.

"You know, how everyone here says one thing and means another, how no one ever says what they really feel, how they're always complimenting you for speaking good Japanese. I mean, seriously, I accidentally said 'Chicken *kudasai*' to this waitress once and she practically melted all over me, she thought it was so cute."

"I dunno," said Colin. "I think it's like that everywhere, maybe."

"Have you ever been to America?" I asked. Colin shook his head, busy shooting zombies. "You'll be in for a big surprise if you ever go," I said. "People there say whatever they think."

"Really?"

I nodded. "Yeah," I said. "Hey, watch out for that zombie coming out of the grocery store."

"Sounds a bit dangerous," said Colin.

"What?"

"I mean, there are a lot of things I think that wouldn't be good if I said them. Sometimes it's better to only say what's important."

I nodded and said maybe he was right, but I was really thinking he'd already been brainwashed by the program, and right then and there my attempt to connect swirled round and round, circling the drain between us. Don't get me wrong, Colin was mostly cool, but I wanted someone to understand where I was coming from. I didn't want to argue about whether my feelings were wrong or right. They were just feelings, you know? Here I'd been thinking that just because someone spoke English we'd understand each other. But I guess there are languages within languages, and those can be foreign, too, even when you think you're understanding each other.

So my plan to make a friend proved to be an utter failure, and I was getting pretty desperate for something, for anything different from my family and Ami—like Tokyo, I thought one afternoon at school during a listening test in Japanese class. My dad made an hour commute to Tokyo every day without any problems. If Tokyo couldn't distract me, I thought, nothing could.

The nearest train station was in Ushiku, just fifteen minutes away. I had my mom drop me off at a nearby game center after school that day and told her I was meeting Colin and that his mom would bring me home later—but after she drove off, I ran across the street to the station. Then it was nearly an hour of nodding my head in time with the other passengers, swaying to the lilt of the train as it pulled us further away from the suburbs. The emptiness inside me felt like a bubble expanding, taking up the space where once my stomach, my lungs, my heart had all been. It sucked to want something so badly and not even know what it was I wanted.

Forty minutes later we arrived in Tokyo, and as I stepped down to the station platform, I found myself immersed in a sea of dark eyes, white-tiled floors, and harsh fluorescent lighting. There was no stopping the downward rush of passengers. Before I knew what was happening, they had picked me up and carried me away on their current. I kept bumping into shoulders, backs, and arms, saying, "I'm sorry, I'm sorry, I'm sorry." Someone spun me around in a circle as he ran past swinging a briefcase, and when I finally came to a stop I faced a stairwell leading up into the city.

It was late afternoon and the streets were busy. Teenagers and twenty-somethings wearing leather pants and Victorian corsets and Catholic schoolgirl skirts and those leg warmers dancers wear breezed by. A group of girls wearing these animal suits—tigers and chipmunks and skunks—stood in a huddle by a store on a corner, laughing and shouting through a bullhorn at passersby. They stared as I walked past them, as if *I* were the weird one. They had white paint streaked on their foreheads and noses and cheeks to look like whiskers and animal ears. The boys were skinny like girls, wore their hair like girls, even giggled like girls. And everyone seemed to be smoking. A forest of towering skyscrapers arced across the horizon. TV shows played in endless loops on the sides of buildings. I felt like I might fall over, but managed to not trip over my own feet as I wandered around looking at everything.

Tokyo was an origami city folded over and over until something was made of virtually nothing. Streets doubled back on each other, disappeared without warning, and later, after I got myself together, as I stepped into shopping centers, I found buildings hidden within buildings.

In Sunshine City, this mall that has something like seventy floors of stores, I went into what I thought was a game center called Namjatown. But the further in I went, the further in Namjatown went. It transformed from modern mall into ancient Tokyo alleyways, offering rides and games where the prizes were eels and goldfish, and the characters looked like Hello Kitty, only more nefarious.

In the Toyota building, an entire wall had been made to look like a waterfall cascading down the face of a cliff. Vines and flowers grew, or looked like they were growing, along the edges of the rocks. Escalators went from one building to another, and soon I wasn't even in the Toyota building but somewhere else altogether, where an advertisement for watches was being filmed. "*A-re*!?! *Kono heya ni haite wa dame da yo*!" a guy in a suit said as he made his way toward me, and the next thing I knew, I was hurried off the set and back out into the street.

Then it was night and neon outlined the city in pink, green, blue, and yellow. The streets were even more crowded than they'd been in the afternoon. Monks in robes strolled past. Retail workers stood on street corners, hawking the wares of their respective stores. Groups of men wearing blue robes that only covered them to their butts danced in the street while holding shrines aloft on their shoulders. The scent of burning incense drifted down the streets. Strange drumbeats filled the air, but no matter where I looked, I saw no drummers.

By nine o'clock, I was beginning to think I should be leaving, but no matter what entrance to the train station I ran down, I couldn't remember the name of the line home. I tried asking people, but no one spoke English, or no one who was able would take the time to help me. I ran into a white woman with blonde hair and almost hugged her. But when I said, "I'm sorry, can you help me find the train to Ushiku?" she opened her mouth and said something very not like English. "*Sumimasen!*" I yelled to no one in particular, out of sheer desperation, but I didn't have any words to help me ask for directions.

I always knew exactly where I was going back in the States. It was so unfair that my dad made us come here. But, no, that wasn't really true. He hadn't made us. Everyone had wanted to come except me. The majority rules, even though majorities can be wrongheaded. I slouched down on a bench in the station next to a bum who was out cold and smelled like stale beer. The only good things that had happened to me since we'd arrived were I'd found that shrine, and I'd seen that red fox. But even the red fox had disappeared on me.

Near midnight I got up to make one more stab at finding my train, and only a few minutes passed before I saw the strangest-looking Japanese girl I'd ever laid eyes on.

She stood on the platform, waiting for a train. She wore one of those animal outfits I'd seen earlier—a fox costume, red with a round white stomach. She had the hood down, so I could see her face clearly. And that, actually, was the strangest thing about her: not her costume or the one fuzzy paw daintily clutching her purse as she held her bushy tail in the other, but that she was Japanese and her eyes were green.

I blinked, thinking of my red fox in Ami, and cocked my head to the side like it had that day at the shrine. I must have stared for a while, too, because when I finally shook off my daze, I found her staring back and smiling. When she saw me snap back to reality, she put her hand to her mouth and giggled.

I was in love in one fast moment. Well, sort of. It was something like love, but conflicted. I mean, how do you fall in love with someone wearing a fox costume in a train station at midnight? I found myself involuntarily raising my hand like I was in class, and by the time I realized what I was doing, the girl was already walking over to me.

"You are lost," she said. "May I help you?"

"You speak English," I said.

She nodded. "A little. Many people do."

"No one I've asked."

"Then you ask the wrong people. Where are you going?"

"Ami," I said, and she raised her painted-on white eyebrows.

"*Honto ni*?" she said, like that talk show host Liz found so funny. "*Watashi mo Ami machi ni sunde imasu*," she said, pointing at her nose when she spoke. "Sorry," she said, registering my confusion. "You surprise me. I live in Ami, too. You follow."

"I can come with you?" I asked.

"Yes," she said. "Come. I show you the way."

The ironic thing is I'd been wandering around the line I needed. It's just that none of the signs in the station listed Ushiku as a destination. I didn't care. I was just happy to be finally getting home. Even this late, the train was pretty full, but we managed to find seats. When we settled in, I turned to her and said, "I'm Elijah."

"My name is Midori," she said. "*Hajimemashite. Yoroshiku onegai shimasu.*"

"*Hajimemashite,*" I said back, surprised and happy to hear the word come out of my mouth so smoothly. I was glad I could tell her I was happy to meet her. Not just because she was helping me, but because I knew her secret. I knew from the second I laid eyes on her that she was my red fox from the shrine in the forest. She'd followed me to make sure I got home safely.

She took a mirror out of her purse and checked to see if her makeup was still okay. Three lines of white face paint on each of her cheeks for whiskers, two upside-down V's above her eyebrows for ears. Her makeup was fine, of course. She was just trying to make everything look real for me. I wanted to tell her she didn't have to pretend. I wouldn't tell anyone. I leaned my elbows on my knees and looked up at her as the train pulled us away from the city. When she clicked her mirror shut and found me staring, she said, "You are very interesting."

"I'm not interesting," I said. "But you are."

"What do you mean?" she asked, which annoyed me. I was hoping she'd take the hint and know that behind my words I was saying I knew her. I thought that was very Japanese of me. But of course she was being Japanese, too, and wouldn't say if she understood my secret meaning.

So I said, "Your eyes are green. Japanese people don't have green eyes. That's very interesting, I'd say."

"These?" she said, pointing to her eyes and laughing. "These are contacts. Not real," she said. "Sorry."

"Not real?" I said. "Really?"

She popped one out and there it was, a brown eye next to a green one. Another illusion. She wasn't my fox woman after all, I realized. I felt stupid then. I should have known better.

"These are very expensive," she said. "But I like having green eyes. I feel different when I wear them."

"Different how?"

"Like I am someone else."

"Like you're a fox?" I chuckled.

"You don't like my costume?" she said, pouting.

"No, no," I said. "It's cute. Really."

"*Kawaii*!" she said. "Yes, very cute. I like it. My friends call me Kitsune when I wear it."

"What's Kitsune?"

"Fox woman."

"Oh," I said. "That's how I thought of you when I first saw you. Fox woman."

"See?" she said. "It fits me better than who I am when I am not Kitsune."

"Who are you when you're not Kitsune?"

"Just Midori," she said. "Daughter of a cabbage farmer. Waiting, wanting, waiting. My father won't let me move to Tokyo unless I get married. And my mother died when I was very young, so I don't have her to help me talk to him."

I was surprised by how open and honest she was about her life—how un-Japanese—but instead of drawing her out more, I was stupid and asked, "If your dad's like that, how did you get to Tokyo?"

She put a finger to her white lips and said, "Shh, it's secret."

What secret?

"A cabbage farmer, huh?" I said, and told her where I lived. She laughed and said we were practically neighbors. It was her father's farm I ran through on those days I didn't take the path to the shrine in the forest. She said we could take a taxi together from Ushiku since we lived nearby, and that's exactly what we did. She called a taxi on her cell phone, and when we came to the place where her father's farm and the road to my house intersected, I paid the driver and we stood in the middle of the road until the taillights of the taxi disappeared in the dark.

"You are safe going home now?" she asked.

I nodded. "Thanks for your help," I said.

"It is my pleasure," she said. "I am glad you give me the chance to welcome you to my country. I hope you will be happy here. I am. Now."

She bowed then, and I bowed with her. "*Oyasumi!*" I said, remembering what Liz told me every night before going to bed.

As she walked up the road to her father's house, she turned and waved at me with her tail. "*Oyasumi nasai!*" she called back, and I ran in the other direction, feeling like a nutcase.

It was nearly two in the morning when I got in, and my mom and dad were waiting up for me, their faces white and tense. "Where have you been?" they asked, well, practically shrieked at me. "You weren't at the game center when we went looking for you. And we called Colin. He said he never went to any game center with you."

Lousy Brit, I thought. *Doesn't he know you're supposed to cover for each other?*

I was too tired to lie, so I told the truth. And actually, though they were mad at me for lying, they didn't give me too hard a time. "You're grounded for two weeks, Elijah," my father declared, and though I thought about saying how living in Ami was going to be a yearlong grounding anyway, I held my tongue.

"I just wanted to do something fun," I said. "It's not that hard to use a train system." They couldn't argue with that, or at least they weren't going to argue with me about it. And by the time we went to bed, we'd settled on letting me take the train into Tokyo once a month if I wanted. Just no more lying about where I was going.

"If something happened to you," said my mother. Then she stopped and shook her head and looked like she might cry. "If something happened to you," she continued, "we wouldn't even know where to find you."

Americans have their own kinds of guilt trips, unfortunately.

The next morning when I got up to go running, I thought I'd stop by the farm and see if I could talk to Midori. I mean, we seemed to get along and I decided maybe it would be good to have a friend who could tell me what people were saying; maybe she could even teach me a little Japanese, I don't know. I couldn't tell how old she was, but she seemed around my age. Friends would be cool, I thought, but maybe we could develop something. She couldn't be that much older, could she?

I rounded the bend in the road a while later, and came up her father's gravel drive. When I knocked on the door, a little old man in baggy pants and a white T-shirt answered. But when I asked if Midori was home, he only frowned and crossed his arms in an X shape.

He said a lot of words I didn't understand, very angrily, then shouted, "No Midori!" and closed the door on my face.

I stood there for a minute, trying to figure out what had just happened, then turned around and ran back down the road. Instead of going home, though, I took the path to the shrine in the forest.

The shrine was still there with its coins and trinkets on its steps, the wood damp from a light rain earlier that morning. I shoved my hand in the pocket of my shorts and pulled out a hundred-yen coin. I knelt down and placed it on the steps that led up to the door and said "Thank you very much" in Japanese, "*Arigatou gozaimasu.*" And when I stood up again, a flash of something red behind the shrine caught my attention.

I leaned to look around the corner, hoping to find my red fox, but it wasn't there. Instead I found a pool of orangey-red cloth on the packed dirt. I went over and pinched it between my fingers, picked it up, and as it unfolded I saw that it was Midori's costume. I looked around the clearing, but she was nowhere to be seen. I imagined her without her costume on, her naked body, running through the bamboo thickets. I imagined her crouched behind a bush, staring with her green eyes while I stood a few feet away, holding her skin. Then it wasn't her, but the red fox with its real pelt of fur and its real green eyes staring out at me.

When I got home I called Mr. Fujita to ask if he could help me talk to the old man at the farm. He wanted to know why, so I told him I'd met a girl who lived there. "A girl-friend!" he said, and laughed like a crazy man for a second. "That's very important. Of course I will help you."

When Mr. Fujita and I went over later, the little old man answered the door again, and the two of them had a real long conversation on the front stoop. I kept looking back and forth as they traded what sounded like incredible insults and knowing grunts, and eventually it ended with the little old man bowing, then closing the door on us, less abruptly this time.

As we drove home I asked Mr. Fujita what they had talked about and he said, "He is very distressed by your question. He had a daughter once, yes. Her name was Midori, yes. But she killed herself many years ago. I'm not sure who you met, but it was certainly not his daughter. Perhaps a town girl playing a joke on you."

"She did *what*? Why?"

"He did not say," said Mr. Fujita. "We did not speak of such things, Elijah. Please."

I said nothing as Mr. Fujita pulled away from the farm. But the next day I ran back to the shrine again, looking for something, I don't know. Something to keep. When I got there, though, the fox costume was gone. And then, when it finally hit me, I felt so stupid.

It *was* her, I thought. I'd just allowed myself to be fooled by finding out the green eyes were contacts. I'd been too foolish to believe what I knew was the truth. I whispered, "I knew it was you," into the clearing, but nothing came back but a slight breeze. Not her. Not her voice. She'd made herself invisible to me.

I've never told anyone, but I have a picture of myself in my head that I sometimes think about. In this picture, I have no features, just a round face with curly brown hair and vague curves where my ears come out. It's not a picture, I guess, so much as an anti-picture. Whenever I think of my mom or dad or Liz, their faces form without hesitation. My mom's thick sweep of black hair, Liz's sharp little nose, my dad's big earlobes that Mrs. Fujita calls Buddha ears. "Buddha ears good luck," she once told him. Like the saying here goes, they're so big he can balance a grain of rice on them. But me? I can never really see what I look like.

I was thinking about this for a while after meeting Midori, about how she said she felt more like herself as Kitsune than she ever did as Midori. I think I understood something about her then. Maybe I even understood why she killed herself. I think what happened was that she shed one skin for another. One that felt more comfortable. One that fit her.

I won't say that everything changed for me after all that. I'm still here, I'm still lonely, and more than ever I'm aware I don't know myself that well. I'm looking into that. It was the reason why I didn't want to move here in the beginning, I think. I knew that if I took away the props of my America, I wouldn't know who I was any longer. I told Liz this a couple of weeks ago while she and I were in Asakusa, an old part of

Tokyo with this huge shrine she wanted to see, for a goddess called Kannon, so I took her for her birthday. Liz said not to worry. "It's okay to change who you are," she said. "That's natural." I think she's the smartest kid on the block, and I'm jealous of her, but I'm glad she's my sister and not someone else's.

I keep thinking about Kitsune, though, how in that last moment before she left me by the roadside she said she was happy now. In her new skin, I guess she meant.

I'm still not happy, but I'm calmer. Next year I'm going home to start college, and I suppose I'll be someone different then, too. I'll have to get used to it maybe, this shedding of one skin for another. Like Liz says, it's sometimes necessary.

I have to apologize for something, though. I said at the beginning of all this that I wouldn't try to make any sense out of sadness, but that was a lie. The truth is I do think there's a little sense to all the sadness. I think of Kitsune shedding her skin and realize there are ways of being in this world other than the one I didn't want to give up. And I don't have to take my life like she did to change the way I see it. The illusions of Japan don't even seem like illusions any longer. Or else the rest of the world feels just as made up. And that's a sort of freedom, really.

Nothing is more real than the masks we make to show each other who we are. Whether it's an animal girl or a salaryman, whether it's a Goth boy with his piercings and hair product or a Japanese housewife wearing an apron as she rides down the street on her moped, these are our masks. The best I can do is to love them.

The Suicide Club

①

Kazuko was the first member. She found Hitomi. Then Hitomi found Asami, who knew Tadashi would want in the circle as well. There were four altogether in the end. Frankly, not that inspiring. Clubs with as many as nine members had been found on deserted mountain roads outside Tokyo, van windows sealed tight with vinyl tape, charcoal burners smoking at their feet, while everyone slept a drug-induced sleep to make breathing the poisoned air easier. Four was comfortable, though. Four was enough to feel like a family.

Kazuko met Hitomi at a restaurant by accident. They were standing in the foyer—Kazuko waiting for her husband, Hitomi for her boyfriend—when Kazuko's cell rang. She flipped it open only to hear Yusuke's familiar voice with its familiar excuses. "Working late. The boss won't leave, so I won't be able to make it." Kazuko said it wasn't a problem, she wasn't hungry anyway. She'd see him later at home.

Kazuko was thirty. She'd been married for five years. She worked as a secretary for a company that hired North

Americans to teach English conversation to bored house-wives and children whose parents wanted them to grow up and go to Tokyo University. After a day of answering the phone and making tea for her boss, his customers and employees, she wanted something for herself. In this case, she had wanted to see Yusuke. Lately she never saw Yusuke but when they went to sleep at night and when they woke in the morning. Twelve-hour workdays helped keep them separate, but mostly it had been their own choice to live with this distance between them. It was a routine of silences and space. Wanting to see Yusuke was rare for Kazuko these days, and she had wanted to act on that feeling before it disappeared again.

When she turned to leave, Hitomi was standing in the doorway, head bent toward her shoulder, whispering into her own cell. "Of course," she said. "I understand, Nobuo. See you later maybe." Then she flipped her phone shut and stood very still for a moment, staring at the space in front of her.

Watching her, Kazuko felt something swell in her chest, as if a balloon were being inflated inside her. She couldn't breathe. She realized she, too, had been standing in doorways her whole life, waiting for something to happen. And just as suddenly, she decided to make something happen. Waiting got you nothing. And nothing was what Kazuko had gotten used to over the past few years.

"Excuse me," she said, and the girl looked up, startled and embarrassed. Already she was beginning to recite a litany of bows and apologies. "No, no, please don't," Kazuko told her. "I think we are both just a little hungry and a little alone. Would you still like to have dinner?"

Hitomi cocked her head to the side, her puzzled look slowly fading into a polite smile. Then she nodded and said that she would. Kazuko introduced herself and a waitress led them away to a low table where they slipped off their shoes and sat on red satin cushions across from each other. "It's not like me to be so impulsive," Hitomi said after they'd wiped their hands with wet, warm washcloths supplied by the server. "But you have a kind face. You remind me of my sister."

"Oh?" said Kazuko. "And how many brothers and sisters do you have?"

"Just one. It's me and Michiko. She's three years older, but she doesn't live at home anymore. She's married."

"And how old are you?"

"Twenty-six. I'll be twenty-seven in four months. In December."

"And on the phone? Your husband?"

"Boyfriend. He plays in a band. He's very busy."

"What sort of band?"

"Punk. They call themselves the Turtle Spoons."

"The Turtle Spoons?" Kazuko blinked. "What sort of name is that?"

"They think it sounds interesting," said Hitomi. "But really it's not any kind of name at all."

Kazuko smiled, and over the course of dinner, the women began to warm to each other. Soon they were laughing at how much they had in common despite their age difference. "It's so strange," said Kazuko as they rose to leave, slipping on her shoes again.

"What?" asked Hitomi.

"This. Us. Don't you think?"

Hitomi smiled without showing her teeth. "Yes," she said, nodding. "And yet I haven't had such a good time in a while."

"Me either," said Kazuko. "We must do it again."

Driving home, Kazuko was struck by the thought that meeting the girl had been a gift from the gods, a hand extended for the evening. She was almost embarrassed to find herself indulging in such fantasies, but the thought clung to her nonetheless.

Though she was later returning than she'd intended, Yusuke was not back yet either. Kazuko undressed and washed her face with warm water, puffing it dry with a towel. She stared in the mirror for a long moment, unsure of what she was looking for in there, before crawling under the blankets of her futon to escape the evening chill.

Outside her bedroom window, crickets were singing goodbye to summer. Their odd melody brought an old childhood memory to the surface, a song her mother used to sing. Kazuko hummed a bit of it as she stared from her bed at the window.

She hadn't thought of her mother for many months now. She had died from cancer two years ago, survived by her husband, Kazuko, and Kazuko's two older brothers. Survived by. Survived. As if someone's death can pull you into the dark with them. Kazuko had survived her mother's death, even if she rarely spoke to any of her family after the funeral. She visited her father, as was her duty, brought him gifts of cakes and cookies, and called on his birthday to hold an annual conversation with him about ordinary things. Without her mother between them, holding all their hands, they had come to realize the distance that lay between them without her. Kazuko shivered under her blankets, cold and growing colder.

According to the clock sitting on the floor beside her, it was midnight. Later, after too brief a flirtation with sleep, Kazuko opened her eyes to find it was three in the morning when Yusuke finally made his return. She heard him tug off his suit jacket, his shirt and necktie, she heard the drop of his pants and belt on the floor. She heard his ragged breathing. She smelled smoke before he even lay down, and when his body slumped next to hers and his hand found her hip, nudging like a blind animal, she pretended to be fast asleep—even when he reached for her left wrist and caressed the birthmark there, worrying the heart-shaped stain with the ball of his thumb. Kazuko once told him she thought it was ugly, this mark, but Yusuke, still in love with her then, had said it was not her birthmark but her charm point. "Really, Kazuko, you're lucky," he'd said. "You have two hearts. That's more than most of us get in this world."

Four hours later, when Kazuko woke to get ready for work again, she found Yusuke had left already. He was gone again, as if his late homecoming had been nothing but one of her dreams.

Hitomi was the sort of girl who wanted things without knowing she wanted them. She was constantly finding her-self in the middle of various transactions and exchanges, startled and bewildered, as if she'd been sleepwalking. She became adept at apologizing for the confusion this sometimes caused. And in moments when she regretted her need to apologize, she tried to make up for it by being more direct.

"I don't understand why you don't make time for us," she complained sullenly in a café in Shinjuku.

"If you're going to complain about being a rock star's girlfriend, maybe we shouldn't be in a relationship," Nobuo told her. He stared from across the table, batting his eyelashes as if he could not believe her audacity. His sculpted hair was wavy and dark, rippling out from his head like seaweed at the bottom of the ocean.

Hitomi lived in Tsukuba, a city an hour outside Tokyo, but she took the train in to visit Nobuo three or four times a week. Nobuo didn't really live anywhere. Mostly he crashed with friends in and around the city. When his friends needed a break from his body taking up space in their apartments, he'd stay with his parents in Tsukuba for a while. It was during one of these stays at his family home that he had met Hitomi at a gaijin bar one night, listening to an Australian rock band.

"You don't care about me," Hitomi said, but Nobuo laughed at her.

"You're trying to manipulate me. Stop trying to make me feel bad with your tears. It's histrionic. It's so . . . it's so damned Japanese."

Hitomi stood up to leave. Placing a hand over her mouth, she held in a sob. What had she been doing? She was twenty-six, beyond the age a young woman should be getting married, and had devoted the last three years of her life to a man—no, a boy—who was devoted to nothing but himself and his music. *So damned Japanese. What's that supposed to mean?* Hitomi click-clacked in her high heels through downtown Shinjuku, tears blurring the city lights as they reached her.

She looked back once before entering the train station, but Nobuo hadn't followed.

In the station, in the train that would take her home, she phoned her best friend, Asami. "*Moshi moshi,*" Asami said when she answered, and immediately Hitomi began crying. "*Doshita no?*" said Asami. What's the matter?

"I've broken up with Nobuo and I haven't even told him," said Hitomi.

"You poor thing, what happened?"

"He doesn't care, Asami. I don't understand how he could be in this relationship for three years and still not care."

"That's how men are," said Asami, all angry barbed wire curling in her voice. "They think they're still in junior high and all the world is a soccer field. Don't worry. Let's go have a drink."

Asami met Hitomi halfway home, in Kashiwa, on the outskirts of the greater metropolitan area of Tokyo. The city was made up of smaller cities, all clustered on top of each other, always changing, growing fatter and more crowded each day. To Hitomi, Tokyo seemed a sort of cancer, the way its shadow stretched further over the land each year.

"You shouldn't even tell him," Asami suggested once they'd got their drinks and sat down at a table. They were in the Hub, a foreigner's bar that Asami frequented. "Just don't go back. Don't call. Don't answer if he rings you or texts. Here. Let's order another round. Look at the guy at the end of the bar with the blue eyes and blond hair. He's so cute. He must be American, right? You should talk to him instead."

Asami carried the unfortunate burden of being over-weight in a country where women were adored for a sort of spun-glass fragility. She'd given up the prospects of a Japanese man taking interest in her and so prowled gaijin watering holes, foreigners' bars and hangouts, with the hope that a man from the West who was used to women with more flesh on them would marry her and take her away to his country, where she wouldn't look so different, she assumed, from anyone else. This hadn't happened yet, although she often attempted to strike up conversations with foreign men. The problem was, except for what she'd learned in junior high, Asami didn't know how to speak English. She remembered how to say, "I have a pen. I like English. I am twenty-six years old," but this didn't enable any exhaustive conversations. She wasn't sure if exhaustive conversations were necessary for love, though, so she didn't see any reason to learn more than what she already knew.

"I'm not looking for a foreigner," said Hitomi. "That's your specialty." She giggled, feeling awkward for a moment.

"Well, if you're not looking for a foreigner, we might as well go somewhere else."

"I'm not looking for anyone. I don't know what I'm look-ing for. I thought I knew what I had, but I don't have any-thing."

"You have me," said Asami.

"You know what I mean." Hitomi shook her head. "Sometimes I feel like I'm walking on the ledge of a very tall building, balancing like a gymnast, like I used to do in high school on the balance beam, and my arms are spread out like wings on both sides. There are pigeons on the ledge with me, pecking at my feet. I'm not even wearing slippers. I have to do backflips and front flips to avoid the pigeons, but it doesn't matter. No matter how many flips I do, there's always another pigeon waiting to peck at my feet when I land."

"That's a dream?" said Asami.

"No, that's how I feel."

"Sounds like a dream."

"An emotion," argued Hitomi.

"No difference," said Asami. "Emotion. Dream. Same thing, the only difference is that one happens while you're awake and the other while you're sleeping."

Hitomi was about to argue, but her cell chimed just as she opened her mouth. It was Kazuko. "Oh, this is the woman I was telling you about. One minute, I'll invite her out to meet us."

A half hour later, Kazuko arrived, waving and smiling as she approached Hitomi and Asami at their table. After introductions the three women toasted, clinking glasses together and cheering, "*Kampai!*" Hitomi sat in a daze with her glass in one hand and her head in the other, lost in thoughts of Nobuo as her friends talked around her, getting to know one another, until she heard Kazuko say the word *jisatsu*, suicide, and perked her head up to hear what was being said.

"Just like that," said Kazuko. "All six of them together. I read about it in the newspaper this morning."

"Amazing," said Asami. "I don't think I could be so brave."

"You mean foolish," said Hitomi, although another, silent part of her instinctively leaped to agree with Asami. Wasn't there a sort of bravery in it, too? To turn away from the world you've been given? Even shutting off the lights each night to give yourself over to darkness sometimes felt like a dangerous gesture, an act of faith that you'd wake the next morning. It was more difficult to do alone. It would be even harder, Hitomi thought, now that she'd lost Nobuo. "But I guess nothing is certain, is it?" she said to the others. Asami stared into her glass of absinthe, swirling the green liquid around the sugar cube at the bottom.

"No," Kazuko said, filling the silence quickly. "I don't think anything is certain except that we're all alone in the world. That's the only thing I've come to know."

"That's so dark," said Asami. "But I think you're probably right."

Everyone stopped speaking for a while, not knowing what to say now that the spell of social cheer had worn off.

"We could do that," Kazuko said suddenly.

"What?" asked Asami. She held her glass up and signaled a waitress to bring her another absinthe.

"Kill ourselves," said Kazuko. She looked from Asami to Hitomi, who felt compelled to nod. Said aloud, the idea already seemed familiar to her, as if she'd been considering it for some time. Kazuko looked back to Asami, who bent her head to one side as if she were trying to figure out a very difficult calculus problem.

"*Issho ni*?" asked Asami. Together?

"*Issho ni*," said Kazuko.

Kazuko lifted her glass of wine. "To the formation of a fellowship," she said, grinning. Asami and Hitomi lifted their glasses, too. "To the charter members of the Suicide Club," said Kazuko, and they clinked their glasses together once more.

They went home thinking the toast was nothing more than a joke. But as each crawled inside her separate covers, as each lay her head on her pillow and stared at the moonshine on the frosted glass of her window, the humor and flippancy of their joining became transparent, and soon they were caught in the embrace of the possibility of escaping the confines of their individual disappointments. This was the closest any of them had come to feeling like their lives were real in years.

Issho ni, thought Kazuko as Yusuke slid the bedroom door shut behind him.

Issho ni, thought Hitomi as her parents moved around the house, preparing to retire to their bedroom for the night.

Issho ni, thought Asami, pulling her covers up to her chin and shivering as the slim shadow of a bamboo tree swayed in the moonlight dripping through her window.

Issho ni.

❸

The next week, Asami met Tadashi at La La Gardens for a day of shopping. Being alone with her new secret made her itchy, and she needed to escape her own head.

Tadashi was small, thin, and beautiful. He was everything Asami wished she could be, except Tadashi was a man. He had long thin fingers, which he gestured with elegantly, and short-cropped, bleached blond hair with artfully unkept roots. He was twenty-eight years old, but he told people he was twenty-three. Tadashi was also gay, but he didn't tell anyone that except Asami and other gay men. Tossed back and forth from boy to boy until he couldn't recognize his former lovers in crowds, he had started dating foreign men in order to form a new category of boyfriends to aid in pattern recognition. The difference between Tadashi's affairs with foreign men and Asami's attempts at affairs with foreign men was that Tadashi spoke almost perfect English. He'd learned it in order to understand what his lovers were saying as they picked him up, made use of him, and left. He had known what each stage of their relationships was about before he spoke English, but felt it added something, being able to understand the words so often used during these maneuverings. Now when an American or Aussie or Canadian or, heaven forbid, a Brit with one of those unforgiving accents, picked him up in order to take him home for the evening and see him out before morning, Tadashi could understand when they said he had to leave and was able to say, "Fuck you, you fucking bastard," at the right moment. It was Asami's and Tadashi's interest in foreigners that had brought them together initially. It was their utter failure with the same that had bonded them in the end.

"So he says, 'I can't take this anymore, you've got to stop calling me,' and I say, 'What are you talking about? You call when you want to fuck and that's okay. But I can't call to ask if you want to have dinner?'"

"What did he say then?" asked Asami.

"He said, and you won't believe this, he said, 'Look, Tadashi, it was fun but it's over. If you keep hanging around and calling, I could get caught and that's not good. I'm in the Navy. They could throw me out, et cetera.'" Tadashi snorted. "He even said 'et cetera.'"

"No, he didn't!"

"Yes!" said Tadashi. "He did!"

"Bastard," said Asami. "What a bastard."

They were flipping through winter coats in a Takeo Kikuchi store, Tadashi flicking the hangers quickly, nothing apparently quite meeting his taste. Asami kept saying, "That looks nice," but Tadashi would just push it down the rod and move on to the next without acknowledging her. "And then," he said, "I get this call from my father. He tells me he and my mother have arranged for an *Omiai*, that they've found this girl for me to marry. Not even a year ago he asked me if I had gay friends and I told him I did, and that they were my best friends, so he could tell that I was gay. And now he's trying to set me up to get me married. So I had to tell him directly, and when I finally did, all he could do was sit there like a fat walrus and finally say, 'Unnh, I see.'"

"How strange," said Asami. She wasn't looking for clothes any longer. She was looking in a full-length mirror, only half listening to Tadashi rambling. Her hips were wider than most Japanese women's, her legs thicker than she liked. She had small breasts and a pouchy stomach. Her cheeks sagged like a bulldog's and her hair was long and black without any particular qualities besides the length and the blackness. "Sometimes I want to take a knife and cut off all the parts of myself I don't like," she mumbled to the mirror, and suddenly Tadashi snapped out of his monologue and craned his neck toward her.

"What did you say?"

"Sometimes I want to take a knife and cut off all the parts of myself I don't like," Asami said again, staring at her black eyes as if she were confessing a secret to a stranger.

"Asami," snapped Tadashi. But before he could scold her, she shot him a look. She knew Tadashi had that same thought himself. He'd confessed it to her one drunken night when she had accompanied him to a gay club in Shinjuku. Tadashi's problems were not about his body, but about himself, the him inside his body. He, too, had looked in the mirror in the middle of the night when life kept him awake with a heavy heart and had said, "I wish I wasn't me." This is not the same as saying "I wish I was him" or "I wish I were someone else." Tadashi had, in those dark hours, wished he did not exist. Asami knew her bluntness sometimes upset him, the brutal way she talked, but he would forgive her. They shared each other's secrets. Asami knew that if Tadashi were to make a list of the parts of himself he'd cut away if given the chance, the first thing to go would be his attraction to men. Then he'd begin cutting away at his neurotic relationship with his father. He would then cut out his feminine mannerisms and the part of himself that adored Celine Dion's and Christina Aguilera's music. *If we cut away all those parts,* Asami wondered, *what would be left? Would there be enough of us here to still be breathing?*

Tadashi stepped closer to Asami as she stared at him. She moved over to make room for him in the mirror, and they stared at each other in the glass. "I know what you mean," he said. "It's desperate, isn't it?"

"We could fix that," Asami whispered.

"How?"

"There's a way," said Asami, turning to him finally. "A way to cut out the things we don't like."

"*Honto ni?*" said Tadashi, a light shining in his dark eyes. Really?

"*Honto ni,*" said Asami. "Let me introduce you to my friends."

④

When Asami called, Hitomi was confused at first. "What do you mean? What club?"

"My friend Tadashi," said Asami. "He's really sweet. I told him about what we're planning and he wants in."

"You're crazy," said Hitomi. "Why did you tell him about that? It was a joke, Asami! What's the matter with you?"

"Oh," said Asami. Her voice weakened, backtracking.

Hitomi sighed. "I'm sorry," she said. "That's not true. I think we did mean it, didn't we?" She waited to hear Asami's reluctant grunt of agreement. In this way they understood each other, as a blind man will know his surroundings by a certain sound at a certain time of day.

Hitomi looked out the front window of her father's house at the spires of headstones rising from the ground in the cemetery across the street. An old woman was walking through the graves, bent so far over by age that, as she walked, she was forced to watch her feet shuffling her forward. "Well then," said Hitomi. "Let's get together later. Bring your friend."

Hitomi spent the rest of the day trying to gather courage. They'd had a joke that turned out to be the truth. That was how jokes always were, weren't they? People made fun of things they were too afraid to face in a sober light because it was easier to laugh at the truth, to pretend that truth was something easy to live through. *The Suicide Club,* thought Hitomi, remembering the clink of their glasses and their knowing smirks, the wit of the moment tinted by the shadows behind their faces, the things that had propelled them to speak of such things in the first place. There was nothing to laugh at now. They'd been acknowledged, those shadows, and now they wanted a life of their own. *In order to truly live,* Hitomi thought, *I'll have to die.*

Hitomi walked to the park where she sometimes went when she had to think something through. She realized that, as a matter of course, everyone—her family, friends, and coworkers—would all assume she'd killed herself because of the breakup with Nobuo. But Hitomi had reasons for dying even she didn't know about. She found herself standing beside a pond, staring at her reflection as the *magoi* and *koi* slipped in and out of the curves of her image, and for a moment it all made sense, as clear as the dark water. The fish circled as they swam, long and dark, orange and white, curling around each other like yin and yang beneath the rippled surface.

There is no difference, thought Hitomi. *There is no difference.* She repeated the words in her head like a riddle, the first half of a sentence awaiting completion. She glanced

from side to side, as if the rest of the sentence must lie outside her, as if the world around her could supply her with
meaning. *There is no difference,* she thought. What difference? Where? Between what?

Looking down into the glass of the pond again, she saw a
black fish hiding behind her face, and a moment later, as it
noticed her watching, it moved toward her at a terrible speed.
As it reached the surface, breaking the water, Hitomi's throat
filled with a sudden scream.

Kazuko was unable to make the club's next meeting. She
had to work late. Several new employees had joined the
teaching staff, a single girl and two bachelors, and her boss
wanted to take everyone to dinner. Kazuko would have to
speak English all night, except when the Americans wanted
to throw around their handful of Japanese phrases to seem
worldly. She didn't blame them. Most Japanese people did
the same with the small amount of English that had made
its way into the mainstream of their vocabulary. She could
remember when the word *okay* had been an English word
only, but now everyone in Japan used it as if it had always
been a part of the language. She knew a lot of her culture
was borrowed—the alphabet from China, pop music from
Western culture—but knowing that much of her world was
not her own didn't make it any easier to live in. It was an
explanation, not a consolation.

She remembered her English teacher in high school. He
had been from America. She remembered his red face, his

blue eyes, his skin so white it looked painful. One day in class he had told them that the Japanese were very good at imitating other cultures, and for some reason everyone had agreed. Kazuko had nodded and smiled along with everyone else, but she wasn't sure why she was doing so. Now she shook her head to rid herself of the memory. Fourteen years had passed and now that day somehow served to embarrass her.

The office dinner was at the same restaurant where she had met Hitomi a few weeks earlier. She was even at the same table. Once again, her dining companions were strangers, but they were not like Hitomi had been. They laughed loudly. They talked a bit too much maybe. They pronounced the accent in her name incorrectly, even though it wasn't difficult if they'd listen as she said it. Her boss was jocular and adept at being "Western"—at karaoke his running gag was to pretend he was going to take down his pants and dance on the table— which made the foreign employees love him. If they only knew how he could turn that on and off like a switch—on when they entered the room, off when they left. It was as if he had a split personality, thought Kazuko, but the Japanese half was in control. It pulled the strings of the Western puppet he dragged out whenever necessary. It made the decisions.

Her companions' conversation slid around her like rain streaking the pane of a window. She was behind that window. She could see their words, could understand, but was untouched by them. She sipped her wine and ate sushi, quietly smiling whenever the appropriate cues were given. Most of the night went by like this, Kazuko lost in a life outside her life, until one of the English teachers called her name once, twice, a third time, and she snapped out of her reverie.

"What do you think, Kazuko?" He was one of the Americans. A very serious fellow who didn't laugh as hard perhaps and asked quiet questions. She liked him but suspected his quietness was a formality, the way her boss's overly rambunctious attitude was an affectation to make the foreign teachers more comfortable. She didn't answer immediately, but apologized for not having heard. What had he said? "The suicides," he told her. "The suicide clubs here in Japan. The Internet websites where people can hook up and arrange to kill themselves with other people. Why do you think they do that?"

Kazuko blinked, startled. It was as if he was looking straight through her, his face against the glass of the window. Had he seen her thoughts in the same way his words had streamed down in front of her? She worried for a moment. Then another American, a tall farm boy from Wisconsin, interrupted, assuming Kazuko's hesitation meant she'd been offended.

"That's not a fair question," he said, trying to give her an escape route. "We have suicide in the United States, too."

"But not in this particular form," said the quiet one. He was not being so quiet now. Kazuko was certain now that his silence had been a ruse, a way to watch them all from behind his wall of quiet. She hated him for a moment. But she was angrier at the farm boy for assuming he understood who she was, how she felt. For leaping in to shield her. It was so American. Those stories about Boy Scouts helping grandmothers cross busy streets. She did not need that from anyone.

"No, I think he is right," she told the farm boy. "It is particular to Japan. I am not sure why it happens like that, though. Perhaps because people are afraid to kill themselves alone. But if they do it with others, they think it will make it easier."

"But don't you think it's also because Japanese culture is communal?" said the quiet one. He looked at her, waiting for an answer. She glared. How dare he ask these questions as if she were on trial? She cocked her head to the side, though, as if she were considering his question carefully.

"I think perhaps there is a bit of that," she told the quiet one. "We are, after all, taught to live for the group, to be in harmony. That is the way here."

"But it's not harmonious, is it?" he said. It felt as if he were trying to peel off her fingernails. But she couldn't retaliate. There was no script for her to do so. She wouldn't know what to say, how to say it. Instead she demurred and said that perhaps this was so for some people. Then she excused herself from the table, pretending that her cell was vibrating, and went to the bathroom.

In the bathroom she splashed her face with cold water and looked at herself in the mirror. Who was she anymore? Her marriage had failed. She knew within a year it would be over. She could see it coming. Yusuke would ask for a divorce. He would not take her sulking for much longer. Her reticence and resistance had begun at the conjunction of her mother's death and her discovery of an affair Yusuke had been having for over a year. She felt justified in withdrawing from him, and yet. And yet she didn't know what she would do if she didn't have their marriage either.

That American—she had already forgotten his name even though she had typed it several times that day on file folders—he had seen what she was planning, hadn't he? No.

She was only being paranoid. No one could tell if a person was planning to take her own life. Could they?

At least Kazuko hadn't been able to. The memory of Midori Nakajima rose to the surface so quickly, it seemed like the girl was suddenly there in the bathroom with her. Midori. The most beautiful girl in school, the most beautiful girl Kazuko had seen anywhere. Best friends since elementary school, for years they had shared everything with each other. Cleaning duties at school, crushes on boys, college entrance exams, the sudden death of Midori's mother—a heart attack that took her away in less than an instant—talks about what Midori politely referred to as her father's overprotectiveness, Kazuko's acceptance into a small women's college in Tokyo. Everything. They had shared everything with each other.

And then, three months after high school graduation, Midori Nakajima committed suicide. Kazuko had spoken with her shortly before it happened. *Happened.* Why did she still think of the event in these kinds of words? As if Midori had not done it to herself, as if suicide were something done *to* a person, not something a person decided? She had spoken with Midori just days before Midori killed herself, then. They had talked indirectly about Midori's father's demands that she not leave his home unless she married. Midori wanted to go to college to study with Kazuko, but even as respectable a plan as that her father would not allow. Mr. Nakajima was not an educated man, Kazuko's own father had said in explanation when she told her parents of Midori's troubles, and so he did not see the use of education. Midori could think of no way out. She had tried reasoning with him, then arguing with him, which had turned into a beating that

Midori told Kazuko about on the phone, several days before the girl took her own life.

Kazuko had called the police, and later Midori called to tell her they'd come to reprimand her father. They had told him his conduct had not been worthy of a gentleman and he had broken down weeping. His only daughter was going to leave him, and so soon after his wife's death. Who would take care of him? One of the policemen had come to Midori's room to speak to her in private, telling her she would do well to remain and care for her father, as any good daughter would. He had told her to think of her father's difficulties now, then turned and left.

After sharing the story, Midori had suddenly turned the conversation to Kazuko's upcoming freshman year of college. Was she excited? "That's not important," Kazuko had said, confused by her friend's detachment. "Midori, what will you do?"

Midori had ignored her question, though, and continued on with her concern about Kazuko's future. The last thing she said before disconnecting was, "I hope you will be happy, Kazuko."

Somehow, thirteen years later, she felt she finally understood why Midori Nakajima had taken her own life. *I'm happy for you,* Kazuko thought. *I am.*

Collecting herself, she pulled out her phone to call Hitomi, wiping the tears from her eyes. "Are you all still together?" she now asked Hitomi on her cell in the bathroom.

"We are," Hitomi answered. "We're at Jibun Katte."

Kazuko said, "Order a violet fizz for me. I'll be there soon."

Kazuko gathered herself and returned to the table, saying that, unfortunately, her husband was ill and needed her at home, she was so sorry. She was sure that everyone would see the lie on her face, but her boss apologized and sent his wishes with her for Yusuke's quick recovery. Her heart still fluttering, Kazuko thanked everyone for the evening and wished them all a smooth transition into their new lives in Japan. "I hope you will be happy here," she told them before leaving the table. "I am."

"Dogs, dogs, dogs," said Tadashi. "There really is no difference between them. Men, dogs. We should just have one word for them. I say we start calling men dogs and be done with it. That's what they do in English. A bastard is a dog in English, isn't it? It seems fitting."

"But you're a man," Asami pointed out as she lit her cigarette. "Wouldn't that make you a dog, too?"

Hitomi laughed, then came to Tadashi's defense as soon as she saw his blank look of surprise. "I'm sorry," said Hitomi, still laughing. "Tadashi wouldn't be a dog," she said. "He's better than that. He'd have special privileges to remain human. The new species of man. What every woman is looking for."

"Not me," said Asami. "I mean, I want sex, too, and I'm not going to get it if Tadashi is the model for the non-dog man."

"You shut up," said Tadashi. He pouted his lips and fake-kissed the air. Turning back to Hitomi, he put his hand over hers and said, "Go on with what you were saying, dear."

Kazuko arrived in the middle of their laughter and sat down smiling, shrugging off her coat. "What's so funny?" she asked. "I should have left earlier, I see."

"Don't worry," Asami said. "We were just discussing the new breed of man modeled off Tadashi here." Tadashi nodded sheepishly and introduced himself to Kazuko, and then the group settled into a serious mood now that the circle was complete, their backs turned to the world.

Kazuko briefly retold the highlights of her evening among the foreigners, about the discussion the quiet American had brought up about group suicides. A hush fell over the table as Kazuko spoke. "I wasn't sure what to say," she said. "He was so persistent, as if he were accusing me."

"Well, at least you had the sense to leave," Tadashi encouraged her. "It would have been worse if you'd stayed. Believe me. My last boyfriend was American. From Ohio. The Heart of It All. Ha! Heartless, is more like it. It's better to walk away than stay and fight."

"Of course," everyone agreed. It was better to turn your back than make a scene. There was a sort of honor in that.

There was a lull in the conversation as everyone sipped their drinks, waiting for the inevitable subject to be broached. Their suicide. It was brewing and they could feel it. Destiny was hurtling toward them like a *Shinkansen,* the wind pressing against their faces as it rushed past on the platform, easing to a sudden halt, the doors opening like a sigh for them to board and take off in a direction from which there would be no returning.

When they finally did begin to talk of their plans, they addressed where and how to do it, but no one mentioned why. It was understood. Whether it was Kazuko's loveless marriage or Asami's loveless life, Tadashi's loneliness as a man who fell for men who would always be leaving or the fact that Hitomi was Christmas cake—over twenty-five and still unmarried—their reasons were their own, and not to be disputed.

Their arrangement was unusual, as they'd met in person—Kazuko and Hitomi by chance, then Asami and Tadashi pulled into the circle as if they'd been attached to Hitomi without knowing it, like dolls in a paper chain. Most circles first connected on the Internet, and only met each other when the appointed day arrived. That their origins were different made them feel special, fated, more like a family than ghosts in machines arranging to meet in order to become ghosts in reality.

After a brief discussion, they agreed to rent a van the following weekend and drive into the countryside, where they would put into practice the things they'd read or heard about on TV or the radio, placing charcoal burners carefully at their feet, swallowing pills like a sacrament, waking up again in whatever place it was that death landed. They imagined the smoke filling the van, the windows sealed with vinyl tape. It would be slow but painless, and at some point later a farmer would find them, and by then they would be long gone, their lives abandoned. The world they had fallen out of love with left behind them.

When Tadashi arrived home, he changed out of his work uniform and into sweatpants, shivering in the frigid air.

Turning on his tiny kerosene heater, he was reminded of an American ex-boyfriend who used to endlessly complain about Japan's backwardness. Central heating had been point number one in his ex's argument. "Central heating isn't the watermark of civilization," Tadashi had said even while his ex shivered and said it might not be *the* watermark of civilization, but it had to be at least in the top ten.

That ex-boyfriend hadn't been as bad as some of the others. Mostly he'd been kind, just not at home in Japan. They had been forced to break up when his ex finally decided he needed to live in America again. He had asked Tadashi to come there with him, but how could he have done that? He would have had to go as a college student, and after college, how would he be able to stay? If Tadashi had been a woman, his boyfriend could have married him and they could have lived in either of their countries, but that was out of the question. Tadashi lay in bed and stared at the ceiling. Canada had made same-sex marriage legal. Sometimes he wished that boyfriend had been Canadian. He would call him now, if that were the case, and tell him he loved him and *please, yes, I'll come to you, let's get married. Let's be happy together. Somehow.*

Tadashi fell asleep sometime later, and soon after, the heater turned itself off on its timer, allowing winter to creep inside once more.

In the morning, Hitomi began to prepare for her inevitable conclusion. She watered the plants throughout the house. She gave her mother the code to her bank account in case something bad happened. "I saw it on the news," she said as her mother, a confused look on her face, examined the slip with the numbers Hitomi had written straight and clear on it. "They said it was good in case of emergencies," she told her. She resigned from her job, saying she would be getting married and would no longer be able to work. This was an excuse none of her coworkers would question, though they did wonder who she was marrying. They'd heard about her breakup. She told them she and Nobuo had gotten back together, and all the women smiled and congratulated her, happy for her good fortune. They'd been sure she was going to be Christmas cake. It was much better that Nobuo had come through in the end, that he had come to his senses and seen what a wonderful future it was he had almost rejected in Hitomi.

Hitomi walked the streets with her head down, her jacket collar up, watching her feet move one in front of the other, listening to the clack of her heels on the sidewalk until she reached home. There she began to fold her clothes and place them in suitcases, as if she were going on a trip. She would make it easy for her parents. When they discovered how far away she had actually gone, they would not have to pack her room up. They would only have to leave the suitcases out by the curb for the garbage collectors. She took some pleasure in the tidiness of it all. Hitomi had always been, if nothing else, a good daughter.

Asami, on the other hand, did not want to leave behind any comfortable illusions. When she talked to her mother on the phone that week, they spoke of usual things: Asami's dead-end work as a bank teller, her lack of marriage prospects, a new Italian restaurant that had opened nearby. She did not want her mother and father to look back and think, Our Asami was this or that or the other thing. She was good at math and a smart dresser. She wanted them to be unable to forget her details: that she was overweight, badly employed, unmarried, concerned with places to eat instead of dieting. It gave her a feeling of elation to be herself completely and have her mother chide her for it while knowing that, in a few days, she would not have a chance to be anyone other than who she had been. She imagined herself as a rock jutting up and out of the wild ocean, refusing to be eroded by the waves that battered against her over and over.

Unlike Hitomi, Asami decided to leave her apartment an utter mess, to allow her plants to yellow and wither. She wanted her parents to have to dig through her things, to be immersed in her presence, to be forced to handle her in the way that they had not since she was a child. There was nothing she regretted. Her suicide would not be an exit from misery but a reconnection, a way of finding a place in the world again by inhabiting her own absence.

Kazuko knew her absence would not count so heavily. She had been absent for many months and felt that taking her life was the next step in a logical progression. She was sure even Yusuke would not be surprised by her disappearance. She had forgotten his body beyond the weight of it next to her at night and the noises he made as he was leaving. She was certain he'd forgotten her body as well. Sometimes her body surprised her, too. Dinner with the foreign teachers, for example, at times when someone pulled her outside herself, she would be shocked back into flesh and feeling the blood course through her. It was always a bit startling to find everyone sitting before her, blinking, waiting for her to join them.

She was not sure how to say goodbye to Yusuke or even if she should. She felt they'd already said their goodbyes months ago, sometime after her mother's death, sometime after Yusuke failed to hide one of his affairs from her. That woman had called their home and asked for him. Kazuko could still feel the burn of the telephone against her ear as she realized what was happening, what she was being told. It was unforgivable. She knew these things happened, but she expected he would at least have the decency to shield her from the others, to allow her to maintain a modicum of self-respect in the midst of the simple humiliation of living in this world.

She had tried for years not to think in such a way. But it was increasingly hard to ignore as she left her childhood behind and the people who loved her—who had loved her completely—grew old, withered in their skin, grew sick and died. She thought of her mother and the song she sang at the coming of autumn, when the crickets, too, burst into song. Her mother's body had had a rebellion of sorts, hadn't it? Smothering its own life through excessive generation. There was a lesson in that, she thought.

Kazuko was unsure how she should proceed with her life before she ended it. Was there anything she wanted settled before she left? Had Midori settled everything before committing herself to her exit? Beautiful Midori Nakajima. At first Kazuko had been hurt that Midori had killed herself. Why hadn't she told Kazuko she no longer wanted life enough to live it? They had, after all, been best friends and confidantes since elementary school. And when Kazuko discovered in the newspaper how Midori had killed herself, as if she were just anyone, suddenly it felt as if they had been strangers to each other all along. They'd spoken on the phone four days, just four days, before Midori ended things.

Kazuko had tried to reach her in the days that followed, but no one—not Midori, not even her father—would answer the phone. She hadn't realized then that it had been their last conversation. Looking back now, she realized why she hadn't understood. She had been so young, still so unaware of the burdens the world could visit upon a person.

Kazuko decided not to live life differently before her leave-taking. That, she thought, was how death should happen. It was how people who do not know death is upon them die. It was the way people who were knowingly going into death should die, she decided. She would do her best by taking life for granted.

"It seems too easy," said Hitomi as they stacked the charcoal burners and bags of charcoal in the van Kazuko had rented. Tadashi twirled a roll of vinyl tape on two fingers and didn't look up.

"Buying everything was the hard part," said Asami. "Putting money down means you're really going through with it. After that, the rest is easy."

"Let's go," Kazuko said, starting the engine. "We have a long drive."

They pulled out of the store parking lot into the flow of headlights flooding the street. Kazuko turned on the radio and they sat quietly, not talking, listening to whatever music or talk-show babble came on for the next hour. Eventually the town was far behind them and yellow rice fields, reaped weeks ago, lay on either side of the van. Thickets of bamboo and groves of fir trees lined the roads. "I've never been this far out," Tadashi said from the backseat, but no one said anything in response.

Kazuko took several turns down bumpy, dusty back roads that spiraled and curved, going down then up a hill, down then up a hill once more, as if they were journeying to the center of the earth. At last she pulled the van off the road onto a dirt path that lay between two rice fields and killed the engine. Silence immediately rushed in to fill the empty space. No one spoke for a long time. Kazuko finally turned in her seat, the vinyl cover rumpling, and said, "Shall we get started?"

The charcoal burners were brought up from the back storage area. Tadashi and Asami placed one between them on the floor. Hitomi and Kazuko took the other. They filled the burners with chalky black briquettes while Hitomi sealed the inside of the van with the vinyl tape, breaking it with her teeth earnestly, placing it over the grooves of the windows. When she finished, she let out a long sigh and pulled a strand of hair away from her face. Kazuko pressed a button on the dash and the locks on the doors latched.

Kazuko distributed the pills she'd saved from her own store of sleeping pills and her mother's leftover stock of medicine. Each of them swallowed down a handful of tablets as they passed a bottle of water around.

"It will take only ten or fifteen minutes before we begin to feel something," Kazuko said. No one said anything to that. They just waited, trying not to meet each other's eyes. And when the world began to blur at its corners and their limbs began to feel heavy, Asami and Kazuko lit the burners.

Smoke began to slowly fill the van. As it circled around them, closing its embrace, Hitomi whispered, "I'm scared."

Kazuko grabbed her hand, then Tadashi and Asami linked hands as well. "Don't worry," Kazuko told Hitomi, squeezing gently. "In a few moments you won't feel a thing." She held her hand out to Asami then, who took it, and Tadashi held Hitomi's other hand in his.

"I don't think I've ever had better friends," Asami muttered. Her voice was beginning to slur under the effects of the pills. Kazuko had been right. Asami was beginning to feel something. She was beginning to not feel a thing.

"I love you all," said Tadashi, and everyone smiled at him. Their heads nodded as if they were still driving the van over a long bumpy road.

Hitomi, drowsy already, said, "There is no difference," and Kazuko pulled Hitomi's head down to rest on her lap as if she were her own child, her own little girl.

"Everyone's here," said Kazuko. She began to hum her mother's autumn melody. "Everyone's here now and we'll always be that way. Together," she said, as the van billowed with smoke, burning their eyes as they drifted through it.

"We're all together now," Hitomi repeated.

"*Issho ni*," said Asami.

"*Issho ni*," said Tadashi.

Sleeping Beauties

I remember walking down these streets with you, my love, when I was far away from home and alone. You found me standing outside that light-strung shop window one evening, staring at my reflection in the glass, pretending for one brief moment that I was not in your country but my own. The streets were full of people out shopping. It was winter in Japan, but if I squinted just right I could see America lurking around every corner. But as I looked at my reflection your face appeared beside mine, and the illusion of home dissipated like so much smoke, and I was forced back into the world around me. When I returned, though, I was no longer alone. You were there then, and that was the beginning of us, wasn't it?

These days, these cold winter days when the air is dry and bitter and the light grows weak early, I take comfort in the memories we made after we met and in the year that followed. It's by memory alone that I keep myself warm now. It's the memory of our love that keeps my heart still beating, beating still. It is a still life I lead, or a lively death, depending on your view of things. Perhaps I was always an object of mute meaning to you, though, and if that's so, then nothing has really changed.

As I roam this hall of memories, I can't help but remember who I was on my way to becoming after I arrived in your country, no longer a child, unable to feign innocence. And though my face wouldn't have betrayed me if I'd indulged in the lie, I no longer had the will to carry off that kind of charade. I had to focus on forgetting my origins. To sink successfully into oblivion is more difficult than one might at first imagine, but I was trying hard. Looking in that shop window, I could barely recognize my own face.

"What are you looking at?" you asked in English, assuming by my blue eyes and white skin that I couldn't speak your language.

"Nothing," I said. "Absolutely nothing." Then neither of us said anything for a while. Somehow this didn't make things awkward. I didn't care if strangers spoke to me for no apparent reason. I was a stranger to myself. Talking to another stranger was easy.

"Are you okay?" you finally asked, and I thought this was a signal for me to nod so you could continue on your way. When I nodded, though, you didn't leave. You touched my shoulder and asked if you could help in some way. I felt warmth through your glove and almost brushed my cheek against your knuckles right then and there, before we'd even said a proper hello.

We began there, on that street in Nagoya, with your hand upon my shoulder. I could say we began before that, with me staring at my reflection, or before that, while I was walking the streets alone. I could choose another beginning, but it's the moment your hand touches my shoulder that begins us, because it's then I understood what would happen. How I would come to live with you. How I would come to love you. But I admit I never imagined that you'd do what you have done.

As we walked the streets together, cups of bitter coffee warming our hands, the present told its story all around us. The present has no need for us to do anything except exactly what we're doing. It's the past and future that need our voices in order to live. So as we walked, as you spoke of yourself and your family, as you spoke of your past, I began to think of the future. I began to put us into a story. What happens after that first night is where I live sometimes, when I can gather enough of us together again, and this is how it goes.

I had no use for words until I met you, but afterwards I couldn't ever know enough ways to say the word *love*. Everything you said, everything you did, sent me reeling through the dark of myself as if I were no more than a cloudless stretch of midnight horizon. In every gesture, in the way you walked in long easy strides, in the way you spoke English like an eager poet, in the way you kissed me in the public domains of trains, taxis, boulevards, and shopping plazas, in the way you held me from behind as we lay in bed, your arms wrapped around me, in the way you straddled my legs to sit on my lap and kiss me while I sat watching incomprehensible television—in all this and more a note sounded, a piece of music I'd never listened to, played upon an instrument I'd never heard.

Like so many other foreigners living here, I'd been teaching English. You found me wandering your city during the winter holidays. You'd just returned from visiting your mother and father—a son's duty at the beginning of the new year, and you were a dutiful son. After walking and talking about your parents and older brother, about your brother's wife and their new child, you invited me back to your home. I could have thought you naive, as some Westerners view the kindness of the Japanese, but your people are not naive and neither were you. You were lonely.

You opened the door and moved out of the entrance to your apartment, long and narrow as a coffin, and I slipped past. "More coffee?" you said, but I didn't want any. "Beer?" you asked, but I shook my head. I turned in place, taking in your room. It was as unremarkable as my own apartment back in the unremarkable suburb of Tokyo where I lived.

When I came round full circle, my tour completed, you stood closer to me, only inches between us, and put your hand on my cheek. I hadn't been touched like that for months, since the last time I'd slept with someone, a girl I'd dated my last semester of college. *This should feel different,* I thought. I should have been frightened to be touched by a man. But when you pulled away from kissing me, I sighed, my eyes still closed, and leaned into you.

I cried that night in your narrow bed. I wept without making a sound, my face to the wall so you wouldn't see me. The winter holiday would end in just one week and I'd go back to my tiny apartment in a tiny town outside of Tokyo and already I wanted to be nowhere but in your arms.

"It's like that fairy tale," I said when later you turned my face to you and saw my eyes full of tears, "where you spend every night in the underworld dancing with beautiful strangers, but each morning you're forced to return to the world above."

You wiped away my tears and said not to worry. "This is only the beginning," you said. "You don't have to go home."

❋

In Japan, people have something called their charm point. A coy smile, a twinkle in the eye, a faultless sense of humor, or a laugh no one has heard in the history of laughs before. The thing that makes others love you. In your case, your stories were your charm point. Your stories made me fall for you. And like Alice tumbling down the rabbit hole, I fell fast and hard.

I floated through your childhood as if I rode a magic carpet, looking down as you and your older brother walked across a frozen pond during a winter twenty years ago. I watched as the ice cracked beneath your steps and you broke through to icy water. I watched as your brother slid his hands under your arms to haul you out, his breath turning into feathery plumes as he tugged and pulled, trying not to fall in after you. The way you looked into his eyes as you lay on the ice afterwards, his face peering down at you, the sky a sheet of blue veined with white clouds behind his shoulders, and said, "Brother, everything is blue. The whole world is ice now."

"More," I said. "Tell me more."

I watched your father bring home the American girl, who was studying abroad for the summer, to enjoy an evening of *hanabi* with your family. In your language the word *hanabi* means flower fire. I was charmed by words like that, too. I thought it a better word than *fireworks,* and grinned as your ten-year-old self pressed sparklers into the hands of the blonde American, saying "Please" each time you gave her a piece of flower fire, as your father had instructed you and your brother to do. He believed that word meant the same as *douzo* in your language, and indeed they're similar, but not quite the same. Nothing is quite the same when it comes to our languages, though, is it? It's not even a matter of meaning lost in translation, but of meaning found once you've given up trying to make words correspond.

"More," I said as we lay next to each other. "Tell me more."

I watched you go through the ranks of uniforms: the yellow caps of elementary, the black suit and brass buttons of junior high, the sports jackets and slacks of high school. I watched you grow into a teenager with ruffled hair and a mischievous smile. I watched you make love to a girl for the first time when you were sixteen. I watched you make love to a man for the first time seven years later. I watched as he built you a gilded cage, keeping you from others, afraid that some other lover might find you. That some other prince might be the keeper of your key.

"More," I said. And you gave them to me, as many as I asked for, your stories, until I knew yours better than I knew my own.

I came to you in stolen moments, on weekends when neither of us could bear to be alone. I lived far from you then, three hours away in another town. I rode the bullet train through the mountains, past Fuji-san and its snow-capped siblings, until I reached Nagoya where you lived in your one-room apartment. I came to you stripped of context. I'd thrown away almost all of who I'd been before coming to Japan. I couldn't remember that other me. Probably he had a life insurance policy, good job prospects, a family portrait hanging in a prominent position on his wall. But I had none of these. I was wandering. No self and no particular place to be. Neither of these conditions is suitable for love. Love craves the security of fixed positions out of fear that it will be lost. Love anchors wanderers from drifting. I realized quickly if we were going to fall in love, I would have to *be* someone again.

It was terrifying to give up being no one in particular, just another foreigner passing through the streets and rail-cars of Japan. I was a gaijin, and though people stared at me with my blue eyes and skin white as snow, I was something to be looked at, something out of the pages of a fairy tale, not someone to befriend.

I was afraid, but after the holiday ended and our stolen weekends became islands that broke up the distance between us, I grew to want more. I came to live with you six months later, giving up the life I'd made here, the way I'd given up my life in America. I didn't have much to leave behind this time. A job teaching in an English conversation school. An apartment. A company car. My anonymity. Nothing more.

There were other foreigners who worked at my school—almost all of us Americans, that's how the boss liked things—but I hadn't tried making friends. The one person

I occasionally talked to was the company secretary, a Japanese woman who arranged our schedules and cut our checks. She had heated conversations on the phone in Japanese with her husband, but after she hung up she'd look over and offer me a cup of tea as if nothing had happened. I sensed in her a certain kind of disappointment. But sitting at our desks, saying nothing, made me feel as if I wasn't all that alone. The only thing we ever did manage to kindle between us, though, was a conversation about group suicides in Japan at a company dinner to welcome new teachers. I hadn't spoken to anyone but students in so long that I didn't realize suicide wasn't polite dinner conversation. So when she excused herself and left early, saying her husband was sick and needed her at home, I knew I'd overstepped.

Several weeks later, when I came to work, she was no longer there. She'd been part of a suicide club herself. Apparently even then, when I'd been asking her about them. During our next morning meeting, our boss said, "Ms. Mizuno will no longer be with us," and we never spoke of her again.

Sometimes I think people like me and her, who live at the center of ourselves but at the edge of the world, don't like to get close to others like us. People who show us back to ourselves are a danger to our sense of isolation.

We had no room in your room once I moved in, but we didn't need it. We crawled on top of and over each other, as if we were ants tumbling through a tunneled hillside. On Mondays, Wednesdays, and Fridays, we spoke your language. On Tuesdays, Thursdays, and Saturdays, we spoke mine. On Sundays we rarely spoke, but lay in bed and made love without words coming between the strokes of our lips and fingers.

The terrible thing about love is that it takes away your safety net, your balancing pole. Even the tightrope you walk upon will disappear beneath you, yet love expects you to keep walking anyway, arms outstretched, one foot after the other, on nothing more than air.

It was magic, walking on air like that, managing a miracle, falling in love in a country that called itself loveless. It felt as if we'd trumped the so-called natural world. If I could have, I would have had us embalmed holding on to one another, together, so that our love would remain that way forever.

You said, "I think I've been living all my life waiting for you to come to me." We were stretched out on your futon, the blankets peeled back, our bodies damp from making love in your bitterly cold apartment under piles of blankets. You never did like to use the heater. I nodded. "It's difficult to say what I mean," you said. "I don't know how to describe where we are now."

"Uncharted territory," I said. "The parts on the maps of our lives that we don't understand. In cartographer's language they call these places sleeping beauties." But as I spoke, you began to squint and I could see that you didn't understand.

So I told you the story of the sleeping beauty, of the princess who pricks her finger upon the cursed spinning wheel, how she and her kingdom fall into a deep sleep and a wilderness grows up around them. How they are lost to the world until a prince stumbles upon the ruins and kisses her, reviving her and her world. By kissing her, she's been recognized. And through her, her kingdom is known again as well. Once a sleeping beauty is known, she and her land have been mapped. Understood.

"We have a story like that in Japan," you said. "Only it's not a prince. Here it's old men who pay a madam to drug young girls so they can sleep with them and feed off the essence of their youth in the night."

"You mean prostitutes?"

You shook your head. "They don't have sex with the girls. The old men just sleep with them."

"Nothing else? Just sleep?"

You nodded. "They are a sort of vampire. They feed on the dreams of the young."

We talked about our own sleeping arrangements. At that time we'd been living together for only a week. "Have you heard me laugh in the night?" you asked. But I hadn't. "Don't worry if you do," you said. "It doesn't mean I'm awake. I laugh in my sleep, but I never remember why."

"I talk in my sleep sometimes," I said. But you hadn't heard me do that either.

"Does what you say in your sleep make sense?"

"Complete sentences," I said, "since I was little." I'd outgrown sleepwalking by age thirteen, but I'd never stopped talking. "My father used to tell me I'd got that from my mother."

"The talking in your sleep?" you asked.

"No," I said. "The nonstop talking."

I smiled and slowly a smile crept up your face as you

realized I'd made a joke. You laughed and I laughed at you laughing. When you were done, your smile faded and you looked at me, your mouth pinched, your eyes narrow, as if you were about to pronounce judgment on me.

"Don't speak to those who talk in their sleep," you said. "If you do, you will trap them in the other world. The world we enter in our dreams."

"What's that?" I asked.

"A superstition," you said. "A Japanese curse."

You leaned over and kissed me then, your tongue search- ing my mouth for something. I sometimes still find it a complete surprise even to me that I'd never kissed a man before you, but when you kissed me it felt as if I'd known your mouth for years. There was an urgency in your kisses, always. What was it you thought you'd find in my kiss? I still wonder about this sometimes. Usually when I've grown so tired of my own voice, when I wish you'd place your lips over mine and silence me again.

You were worried, you said. "One day you'll wake up and want to go home. It's how it always happens," you said, "with foreigners."

"Why do you love foreigners," I asked, "if you know they'll only eventually leave?"

"Japanese are boring," you said. "I can't see anything in them."

I wanted to say that you were Japanese, as if you didn't al- ready know that, but I said nothing. I looked at you and held my tongue. What made you different from those men in whom you saw nothing? What was it you thought you saw in me? My blue eyes? My white skin? Were you still a boy fascinated by the surface of someone different, pressing your life into my hands like *hanabi*, saying "Please" as you closed your hands over mine?

"I will listen for you at night," you whispered, looking away from me, "and I will answer you when you speak in your dreams. That way I can have you forever."

I turned you back to face me, kissed you to keep you quiet. To be wanted like that repulsed and attracted me at the same time. I grabbed your forearms, rolled you onto your back and leaned over you. "Listen," I said, and pulled your hand up to my heart to feel it beat beneath my skin. "This is who I am."

I came to Japan with a letter to America repeating in my head. *Dear America*, the letter went. *Dear America, I don't know how to say this.*

I came with what I could carry in one suitcase and a backpack I'd used to carry my books around campus for the past four years. I wasn't doing the just-out-of-college thing where a young guy goes to another country to find himself. I was trying to lose myself. I was pretending I didn't exist.

It was after the attacks on September 11th that I started to not understand people, really, the things they said and did. One of my housemates came to my room that morning and said, "Get up, quick. I think we're being attacked."

It sounded like a movie.

All of us came downstairs to sit around the television together. We didn't say anything for a while, just watched the news replay the planes going into the towers over and over, as if we needed to keep seeing it in order to believe it. Then one of my roommates said, "Looks like we're going to have to turn another country nuclear."

It didn't take long before everyone was talking about what happened and what would happen, as if we knew what was going on. We watched the news and read the papers. We listened to radio shows. We skimmed through blogs. We were informed. We knew what we were doing. We bought gas masks, electric generators, three-month stores of food. People were gearing up, getting ready for something, but I couldn't understand when my mother said, "They're going to kill us Christians," or when my father went out to buy another gun.

Months passed and we waited. The president came on TV and told us the evildoers would be brought to justice. Carefully coiffed politicians sat across polished tables and agreed. People I'd never heard of came on TV and told us there were bombs in Iraq with our names on it. We were waiting through it all. Waiting for it. And finally, in my last semester, the war began.

Maybe my heart was defective, I thought. It had to have been. I sat on the edge of my bed after school and stared at the floor, feeling somehow like I'd lost something. My heart was defective. It was defecting a little more each day. And by the end of spring I had exchanged e-mails and spoken on the phone with that secretary at the English school outside Tokyo. There was work for me there, she said.

I wasn't worried that I didn't know Japanese. By then when I spoke to my parents or brother and sister, when I spoke to my roommates and friends, it was as if a glass wall slid down between us. I could see them and they could see me, but we couldn't hear what each other was saying. Living in another country would be easier, I thought. I'd no longer expect to feel I was a part of things. That was the plan.

Dear America, the letter began. *Dear America, I don't know how to say this, but I'm leaving you and I don't know if I'll be back again.*

❈

"Listen," I had said, and put your hand on my chest. But when I tried telling you about my family, my friends, that girl who'd been the last person to touch me before you, when I tried telling you about the letter in my head, the life I once lived, you only nodded, smiled, and interrupted to say once again how blue my eyes were.

"Like a husky's," you said, and pressed your lips to mine before I could finish. I didn't stop you. I thought there'd be time. But now I think if I'd spread out the years of my life like a tapestry for you to look at and consider, if I'd made you listen, really listen, we would not be who we are today.

❈

I dreamed a flood came through a valley, sweeping everyone out to sea. I clung to a tree on the side of a cliff while the water raged below, and shouted into the open sky, "Tell my father his son is still alive." Like a shocked traveler, I woke that morning wondering how I'd gotten to a country on the other side of the world, how I'd get home again, and if I could convince you to come with me.

"Impossible," you said. "What are you going to do?

Marry me? I'm Japanese. You're American. We're men. We're not allowed. Remember?"

You laughed about America calling itself the Land of the Free. At least, you said, Japan didn't pride itself on promises it wouldn't deliver.

I didn't come home after work that evening. Not right away. I walked the streets of Nagoya the way we'd walked them together the evening we met the year before. I didn't know where I was going. I didn't know why I was wandering again. It'd been months since I'd felt that. And when I remembered that feeling and everything that went along with it, I realized our future—that story I'd been putting together the first night we met—would never come to be. I walked deep into the night, to the other side of town, ignoring your text messages and phone calls, until I'd made a circle and found my way home at so late an hour you'd already fallen asleep.

I didn't come home right away the next night either. Or the night after that. I was disappointed in something. Being with you made me feel that disappointment more than I wanted, as if I'd been given a travel brochure for a future I'd never be able to visit. This is where you can't go, the brochure said. This is what you can't have, sweet prince, without giving up your kingdom.

I sat in cafés and sipped coffee because I couldn't bear to see you any longer. Because I couldn't bear to feel you hold tighter as I walked away. When I'd get up in the middle of the night, slouching toward the kitchen for water, you'd roll over and say, "Come to bed," as if I'd been up all night, withholding the nearness of my body. I'd drink slowly, considering you over the rim of the glass. Your face was a word I could no longer fathom; your eyes blinked in the dark like a cat's. Once, a long time ago, you had given me a word— *abunai*—and said to use it whenever danger was present, the way I'd say, "Watch out!" I'd begun to use that word lately. I'd begun to use it when I thought of you and me.

One night when I came home, you didn't pretend to be asleep. You opened your eyes when I got in bed beside you and said, "Where have you been?"

"Out," I said, "with coworkers. Having a beer."

"That's different. Are you feeling well?"

I nodded, but didn't say anything.

"Who are they?"

"Who?"

"Your coworkers," you said.

"No one," I said, and rolled over, turning my back to you, saying good night and yawning.

"Sweet dreams," you said.

My dreams weren't sweet though. In them, Japan had sent me a letter. It had been sending me letters for a while, actually, but I hadn't received them. There'd been a delay in delivery after I moved to your city, a mix-up at the post of-fice. So I didn't receive it until months after we'd moved in.

Dear American, the letter went. *You've come here for the wrong reasons. But we expected that. It's nothing new. You thought a country like ours, so devoted to the group, would produce a population of nothing but kind, loving people, and that your own country has got everything wrong. Surely by now you've noticed a few things. The high school girls selling sex and conversation to salarymen after classes; the strangers who meet in Omiai bars hoping to make a match for the*

evening or for life if the right deal can be struck; the quite pop-
ular group suicides, and of course the work ethic that sepa-
rates men and women from their families. Also, here we do
not speak of the kind of person you are. Please don't take it
personally. We know that, like so many of your countrymen,
you thought we'd be the cure for your sorrow, but it is our
great regret to inform you that we have our own problems.
Anyway, welcome. We hope you have a nice stay.

I once heard my mother tell my sister love only comes at
a price, there's no way around it. You give up parts of yourself for love, she said. If that's true, I thought, the cost of our
love had risen. And despite wanting to be as real to you as
you were to me, I couldn't afford us any longer. We were beyond my means.

It was when I came home one evening several weeks
later, shaking the spring rain off my umbrella, slipping off
my shoes before stepping up into the kitchen, that you
asked in a voice like an undertaker, "Where have you been?
Why do you never come home anymore?" I looked up, not
answering, leaned the umbrella in the corner, and finally
spoke.

"I'm here," I said. "What's the matter?"

"You know what I mean," you said. "Tell me. Where were
you?"

"A travel agency," I said, "buying a ticket home." I'd done no such thing in truth, and yet I found the words spilling from my mouth.

"*This* is your home," you said. You were both plaintive and scolding. I was angry. I wanted to shake you until you could see me. Why had you waited so long to ask me questions?

"This isn't my home," I said. "It's where I live. There's a difference."

"And me?" you said. "I suppose there's no question of what I'll do after you leave. No consideration for my feelings. What makes you think you can just take love away when it's no longer convenient?" You stared at me, trembling. And when I told you that I'd do what I want when I wanted, you shouted and stormed, said how you knew I'd say that, how I was so damned American, how you should have known better, how you knew in the end I would be like the others, the most selfish people on earth.

"Stop this," I said. "You have no idea what you're saying. Of course I'm American. But, no, I won't stay just to keep you happy. You haven't been happy for a long time anyway, and no matter what I do, that won't change."

"What do you mean?" you protested. "I'm happy! I'm so damned happy!" you said, following me as I pushed past you into our room and began taking off my clothes.

"You've stopped loving me in order to worry about whether or not I'm leaving," I said, tugging my shirt up over my head. "When you look at me, all you see are the ways I may leave." I unbuttoned my pants and stepped out of them. "You don't talk. You don't ask me anything. You just assume I'm doing something on your list of possible fears."

I slipped under the covers of the futon and then you began to undress, too, throwing your clothes on top of mine. You got in bed and put your arms around me. I didn't want you touching me, but it was so cold, I welcomed the heat of your body. "I'm sorry," you said. "You're right. Please don't go. I couldn't bear it."

I held you back and kissed your forehead and told you to go to sleep. "We'll talk in the morning," I said. But that was the last time we'd speak like that, that was the last time I'd be in the same world with you.

Later I heard your voice, faraway and tinny, like music playing in another room. I'd been dreaming about my childhood. A small farm in western Pennsylvania, the sun rising over the tree line on the horizon, mist in a pasture where cows huddled under a tree together, chewing their cud while dreaming with their eyes half closed. My father rising from bed to begin his morning chores. My brother and sister sitting down to eat the breakfast my mother had cooked us. The dinner table where I used to say absurd things just to make everyone laugh, before I left for university and came home after my first semester to find everyone wondering what I knew now that they didn't, worried they'd say something stupid in front of the first of us to go to college, and so they said nothing at all.

I'd been trying to explain how difficult it was being so far away from the person I'd been. I was trying to tell you things I hadn't said in our waking hours, when they might have calmed your fears. I wanted to tell you I'd amputated my past and wanted it back, even if it meant I'd limp around on the replacement like an invalid hobbling on a crutch. My desire for my past didn't mean I'd abandon our future—there might have been another way—but I'd made it seem that way to spite you. So when I spoke in my sleep about things I hadn't said while awake, you began to answer.

"It's okay," you said. "I understand. Everything will be all right now. Sleep tight," you said, as if I were a little boy you'd take care of. You told me you loved me, that you'd love me forever, that I was your lover, the only one worth loving. That from the first time you saw me you knew this was how we would come to be. You'd resigned yourself to it. That you wouldn't see my eyes alive and peering at you any longer was your great regret. You would lose one of the most sought-after gifts love gives. You would no longer have someone to witness you living.

I was happy to hear your voice in my ear until I realized too late what it was you were doing. That you'd cast that spell, locked me away from the rest of the world, hidden me away in a dream.

The thing about dreaming is that once you do it long enough, you realize nothing about them is real. When I left home, I realized this about the waking world, too. Everything—our myths and cultures and religions, our borders and boundaries and rhythms, all of us—are things we've made up. Nothing about our lives was there before we made them. It's the same with dreams. We create them. But after you know this, you seek out old memories to live in, now that it's harder to believe in the things you see when you close your eyes to the day-lit life you lead.

I had few memories of my life in America to live in, though. I hadn't been able to tell you that story, to tell it to myself by telling you. I hadn't been able to take back what I'd abandoned. So I lived in the memories we made over our year together. It was enough at first to feel your hand on my shoulder again, the way you touched me the night we first met. It was enough for a while to hear the loudspeaker announce the bullet train to Tokyo, the way you kissed me on the *Shinkansen* platform when I left to return home after the winter holidays, before I'd come to live with you. You hadn't cared if anyone saw, and everyone did. Of course, this being Japan, no one said anything, but we were certainly looked at, weren't we? Suddenly it was a movie, you kissing me in that place where everyone could see our love. But when I realized the theatricality, I made myself stop. I didn't want those few memories of a year in love to be changed, tinged with a kind of unreality in the very moment I recalled them.

I allowed myself the pleasure of remembering those first few months of ordinary sweetness, but the decline into your fear of my departure would always drive me back to the beginning, our beginning, starting again, starting over, returning to when it was good. And each time I arrived at the beginning again, at the moment your hand touched my shoulder in front of that shop window, those memories would grow a little colder. I've had a chill creep deeper into my bones and blood with each diminishing return.

At night I feel you pull the blanket over my body and wrap your arms around me like always, but I can't feel the warmth of your hands anymore. Nothing you do will ever be enough to chase this chill from my body. I am on ice. You have seen to it that I have been preserved. My way would have had us both frozen; it would have been the both of us together. That, I think, would have at least been fair.

You come and go. I hear the sound of your footsteps, the

intake of your breath in the night as you sleep beside me. I still talk in my sleep, now more than ever, but you no longer reply with anything but a word, a vague apology, an order to sleep. I wonder why you now ignore me when you used to cling to me so tightly. Where have you gone? Where are your stories? If you gave me more memories to dream, it might at least make this more bearable.

It's been a long time now that I've been sleeping. I no longer know just how long. I lie with my arms at my sides, my eyelids fluttering, waiting for you to see me again. To really see me. Because when that happens, when you realize what you have done, when the day comes that you return from work and see me—the man you loved and gave up for a corpse who speaks of nothing but dreams and old memories—you will come to me and kiss me, deeply, the way we used to kiss when I could kiss you in return. You will awaken me by knowing me, and in my waking I will return to my kingdom across the sea. And there, my love, I will be more real to you than I ever was in your world. In your world of dreams.

Kiss me. I beg you. It doesn't cost me anything to beg anymore. Kiss me until you feel my lips warm beneath you. Kiss me until you know that I'm yours.

If You Can Read This You're Too Close

This is the truth. A blind man saw me on the train. I don't know how he did it, but it happened while I was riding the Yamanote line from Shinjuku last week, and this is how it goes.

I'm standing next to seats by the exit doors where two old ladies with hunchbacks sit curled in on themselves like question marks. They sway together in commuter rhythm, but never lift their heads. I hold tight to the strap above and think about my own grandmother. I haven't seen her since my grandfather died three years ago from stomach cancer, but Grandma is still alive and kicking. I learned that phrase from an American at a club in Shibuya. I think his name was Steve. Anyway, my *obaachan* is still alive and kicking three years after *Ojiisan* kicked the bucket, but I haven't seen her since his funeral.

The trains of Tokyo are mostly quiet. The slight hum of voices, the roar of metal on the tracks below, the whoosh of wind in the tunnels, the crisp station announcements as we slide to a stop at platforms, the recording of the Englishwoman's voice letting foreigners know where they are and where they're going. There's not much else beyond these noises. On trains we're as silent as possible, switch our cells to manner mode so they'll vibrate. We won't answer even if they vibrate, though. It'd be rude to break the silence. Instead we close our eyes and nod off until instinct wakes us right before we reach our destinations. Every now and then that inner voice fails and we end up in another part of the city, or far out in the suburbs, wondering how we got there, wondering how to get home.

I think a lot while I ride the train, and people-watch, so I'm prone to getting lost. Usually when I get lost like that, I'm out looking for a song. Sometimes I'll find a song on the train. Sometimes a song arrives on its own, offering itself up like a sacrifice to the Turtle Spoons. That's the name of my band. We do a little of everything. Punk/hip-hop/trance. We play at a bar in Shinjuku once a month, and also in the sticks of Ibaraki where I know some people. It's a side thing for everyone in the band but me. I don't work. I don't do anything really. But my parents keep me in yen rather than let me shame them with my shiftlessness. It's for their own sakes, though, so don't pity them. It's their own faces they're saving, not mine.

It's a lazy weekend, and the train is full of people out looking for something. We're all looking for something, I think, we're all trying to get to the next thing—whatever that is—that will make our lives meaningful. Maybe there's a song in that. Maybe.

I'm thinking about this when I notice a girl sitting on the bench across from me. She was staring with a sly smile at first, but when I smile back she opens her cell phone and starts pressing buttons, pretending to type a text message. The train stops at another platform, releases a horde of passengers, but she doesn't leave. She looks up from her phone for a moment to watch the others depart, glances over at me with that smile of hers, then turns back to her phone. Before any of the boarding passengers can take the empty seat beside her, I cross the space between us, sit next to her, and look down at her phone.

It's not a text message she's writing after all. It's a mobile game she's playing. Winnie the Pooh with his jar of honey, various fruits falling from the sky above. She maneuvers him back and forth across the square of her cell phone screen, catching fruits and avoiding the spiders that sometimes drop down on threads. "Ah, Pooh san," I say. "All he wants is honey."

She doesn't look up, but I notice her cheek rising as her grin widens. She misses a fruit, catches a spider instead, and I know I've successfully distracted her. She flips the phone shut and looks at me, shaking her head. "What a weirdo you are," she says.

"No kidding," I say, and she grins. I can tell by the way she's looking at me, blushing, that she'll be my ticket for the evening, my way out of remembering the things I want to forget. Dinner, drinks at a club, a love hotel afterwards. *That's it,* I think. And the rest of my night is planned.

❋

The girl's name is Ai. I've always liked that name. It means love. Ai has long hair with springy curls and dyed blonde streaks in it. Her skin is so dark from tanning that she looks black. She's a *kokujin*, a black person. One of those kids who hang out in Tokyo, wearing hip-hop clothes, tanning their skin, doing their hair like American black women, calling themselves black. I have a Canadian friend who says he can't understand why Japanese kids dress like people from other cultures. He can't understand why we adopt another culture's identity so breezily, and I can't explain it well. I tried to tell him. I told him once, "It's a way of separating ourselves from others. Like Goth kids in America and Canada dress in black and wear white makeup to be different."

"But why other cultures?" he persisted. "Goth is one thing, Nobuo, but trying to look like hip-hop stars is another."

It isn't so different to us really. We don't see many black people here except bouncers at clubs and on TV. Black people are about being strong and not backing down from others, they're about getting angry, so if your life is being walked on, maybe you'll become a black person and find out how to be strong and get angry, too. It's a way of figuring out how to feel and do things you don't know how to feel or do if you're Japanese.

My ex-girlfriend, for example. She was so fragile. She'd cry at the drop of a hat and expect to be coddled. She wore tiny fur jackets in winter and her favorite word was "*kawaii!*" How cute! She'd say it in a shrill, babyish tone that I came to hate. She was a typical Japanese girl, Hitomi. I dated her after we met at a club in Tsukuba, back in Ibaraki prefecture where we grew up. I dated Hitomi for three years, as well as a few girls in Tokyo. Hitomi didn't know about the other girls, but she rarely came to Tokyo, so the chances of getting caught were next to nothing. Thinking about Hitomi gives me a headache, though, so I chase her out of my mind.

I look at Ai instead, my black woman. She's chewing the straw in her drink at Club Code in Shinjuku, the only club left in this part of town that isn't gay. I look at the lipstick staining her straw and get excited about getting a blowjob from her later, and my headache begins to fade. *That's the ticket*, I think. *That's the ticket.*

Ai and I drink whiskey. She can knock back the strong stuff. Not really feminine, but what can you expect from a *kokujin*? She gets drunk in an hour and soon we're pressed up against each other, surrounded by a swarm of gaijin and Japanese hipsters on the dance floor. You can barely breathe, you can barely see anything but the disco ball scattering light across our upturned faces. The DJ plays a song by Jennifer Lopez and all the girls hold their hands in front of their faces and open and close their legs, back and forth, like butterfly wings. Some wear those hats J-Lo made famous, with big hoop earrings and lots of skin showing around their midriffs. A perfect place for men to put their hands to sample how the women will feel beneath them later. I put my hands on Ai and she backs up against me. "Let's get out of here," I say.

Outside, after we collect our jackets from the lockers in the lobby, I ask Ai if she'd like to have coffee with me in the morning. It's a good way of asking if a woman wants to spend the night with you. She smiles and nods, so instead of finding a place to crash for myself tonight, we walk a few blocks to Hotel Chez Moi, my favorite love hotel in Shinjuku.

At this time of night, love hotels all over Tokyo are crowded, but we manage to find some selection. Looking up at the picture chart of vacant rooms on the wall above us,

I see the usual rooms without any personality are already taken. But several of the tacky theme rooms that got old in the nineties are open: the leather room, the aquarium, the lover's abode, and so on. Ai wants the lover's abode but I think it looks like a Valentine's Day bomb blew up inside it. Instead we settle on the aquarium—I like watching the electric fish swim across the ceiling while a girl rides me. Then I don't have to look in her eyes. Girls will try to trap your emotions. I know their tricks. Hitomi made me an expert. Even the last thing she did was an act of manipulation. I'll never forgive her for that.

But Ai. Ai is who I'm with tonight. As we ride the elevator to the fish tank room, I nibble the back of her neck. As soon as we get out of the elevator and into the room, we hear water gurgling. Blue watery lights fill the room. Electronic fish swim overhead. Ai turns around and pulls me to her lips and we start kissing, wet and sloppy. She's a French kiss aficionada. I don't like French kissing—it's messy like the language—but I indulge her anyway.

We move toward the bed, Ai stepping backwards, her hands pulling my jacket off my shoulders. When she reaches the bed, she sits down, unbuckles my belt, and takes my dick out. It's what I've been waiting for, a slow burn that leads to the sex that will short-circuit my brain for an hour or five minutes; as long as it happens, I'll be satisfied. I can hear the crack and fizzle, I can smell the smoke curling inside. I can't think at all. I can only inhabit my body; during sex it moves with a life of its own and I'm outside at the same time as being inside it.

I tilt my head back and watch the fish float across the ceiling while Ai moves over me, and before she makes me come I start taking off her clothes. Then I climb on top of her, slip my dick inside, and it's a catapult to the future, a flash of time travel where everything is on fast-forward. The fish blur around me, yellow and pink electric lights burning trails across the walls of my vision. Ai's moans speed to a squeal and my breath is a train chugging. At the last minute, I pull out so I don't have to worry about getting her pregnant. I can pull out of a woman the same way I can wake up before it's time to get off a train. By instinct. Even though I may have blanked out because feeling took over, and the me—whatever it is inside my body—disappeared momentarily.

Afterwards we lie in bed, exhausted, grinning. Ai traces a finger around my nipple, then gets out of bed. "I got thirsty, how about you?" she says, and opens the fridge to pull out a beer. The fish have slowed and are floating peacefully. I tell Ai to give me a beer, too, and she brings one over and puts it on my chest.

"*Tsumetai!*" I shout, and jump up howling. Damn, that's cold! I think about pulling her onto the bed to tickle her in retaliation. Then I think better. I lay back, say nothing, and pop the beer.

Ai wanders around, examining everything. She kneels near the bedside table and pages through the room's diary. There are books like this in most love hotel rooms. People leave messages in them. Some are sweet, some are odd. Mostly you find things like *I lost my virginity here on such and such a date*, or *I love Taka*, or *Natsuko and I made love for six hours.* Ai giggles as she reads them, but after a while I don't hear anything, so I sit up and look at her. Her face is serious and a tear is running down her cheek, slow at first, then it gathers speed and curves around her chin and falls to the blue shag carpeting. "What's the matter?" I ask, even though I'd rather not know.

Ai looks up and wipes her face. "It's so sad," she says. "There is this entry by a man who comes and stays here alone."

"So what?" I say. "Lots of people come to love hotels to be alone. To get away from their families. I know a guy who comes with his wife because they can't get away from their kids to have sex at home. That's what love hotels are for."

"I know," says Ai, "but this man comes alone. He doesn't live with anyone, has no children or lovers. He has no reason to come here. He says he comes to this room and thinks about the lovers who have been here before him, imagines himself as one of them, imagines himself having someone to hold. Being in this room helps him imagine what it is like to be loved. He stays for an hour, sometimes two; once he spent the night when he was terribly lonely. He tells whoever is reading this that he's grateful for the love we share without knowing."

Ai is beginning to annoy me. I get up and pull my underwear on, my jeans, my shirt. Ai looks bewildered when I grab my jacket. "What are you doing?" She puts the diary down and comes over, puts her hand on my jacket and takes it away. "What's this?" she says, trying to distract me. "You've written something on this jacket, haven't you? It's in English. What does it say?"

"Adolf Hitler," I tell her. She looks up, her mouth parted slightly, her eyes round as saucers. Or is it dishes? I hate when my memory fails.

"Adolf Hitler?" she says. She says this name as if she's

never heard it. Probably she never has. I read *Mein Kampf* my first semester of university and was in awe of his charisma. People did what he told them. He loved his country above all else. That's a gift. I admire people who can lead others to follow a vision. "But didn't he kill a lot of people?" Ai says. "Isn't this that guy from *Schindler's List*?"

I take the jacket and pull it on. It's from my high school days, my beginning-of-university days. Made of black leather, it has a bunch of buttons on the collar with English sayings on them: *Fuck Off, Eat Me, If You Can Read This You're Too Close.* I like that one especially. On the back there's a picture of a blue guitar, and on the guitar in black marker is where I've written Hitler's name. I'm surprised Ai even noticed, as it's written in cursive. I learned cursive because I wanted to know everything I could about English, even this second style of handwriting. Not as many people read cursive, so I feel like I know a secret. Like there's something no one can understand but me.

Ai is still staring at me, and I start to hate her just a little. I pull some yen out of my wallet to pay for the room, and feed it to the machine to unlock the door. Then I leave that girl standing in that blue fish tank with the blankest face I've ever seen.

⬤

It's a February night and the lights of Shinjuku are bleeding together in the freezing mist. It's colder out than I expected, and I decide not to waste any time wandering, though that's what I'd like to do more than anything right now. I'd been hoping for a night of abandon, but Ai was more trouble than I thought she'd be. She reminds me of Hitomi, that blank look, the way she couldn't understand anything I told her. Crying over someone she doesn't even know. That kind of sentimentality is so Japanese. You won't find it anywhere else in the world.

I'll go to my Canadian friend Peter's apartment in Ikebukuro. Peter and I exchanged language when I first met him a year ago, but he eventually gave up on Japanese. We stayed friends, though, and I always get him free tickets for the Turtle Spoons when we play Shinjuku. It's good to keep up friendships. You never know when they'll come in handy.

I catch a train in Shinjuku. The cars are full even this late at night, full of drunks, bums, salarymen, and women who look down into their purses the entire ride as if they're afraid to meet anyone's eyes. The seats are all taken, so I grab the strap near the doors. The conductor announces we'll be leaving in a moment, and that's when this blind man gets on, swinging his stick wide so he'll know if there's something in his way. The stick hits my leg and he says, "*Gomen nasai*," I'm sorry, but I don't bother answering. He smiles and grabs hold of a rail as the doors close. Then the blind man and I turn our faces away from each other to sink back down into our separate worlds.

A few minutes later I'm thinking about a song I want to write—a song about Ai and her love hotel diary, the sham of love and sentiment—when I notice the blind man looking at me. He's not looking at me face to face, though. I see his reflection in the glass of the doors and I swear this guy is looking at me like he can see me. The eyes that were cloudy and dead when he got on seem alive in his reflection. A few seconds pass before I notice him looking surprised, too. His eyes widen, his mouth drops open. He sees me and realizes I see him seeing me and it's freaking him out as much as it freaks me. "Oh my," he mutters. "Oh my oh my oh my."

"You can say that again," I say in English.

"*Nansu te*?" he says. Say what?

"*Nan demo nai*," I tell him. It's nothing. "But how can you see me?" I ask.

Until that point he hasn't been able to tear himself away from our reflection. Then he turns, ready to speak, but in one fast moment his face falls. "No!" he cries. "Just a little longer!" His eyes fill and tears streak down his cheeks, leaving trails in the canyons of his wrinkles.

Gone. All gone. His eyes have returned to what they were. It's as if a veil has been replaced. He looks at the window again, but can't see his reflection. I want to tell him it's okay, that it was all a bad dream. I want it to be a dream so that he doesn't feel so bad and because I don't want to feel bad either. Those eyes. That recognition. Something inside me woke up when the blind man saw me, and I knew right then bad things would happen unless I put it back to sleep.

When the train arrives in Ikebukuro, I go to leave and the blind man grabs my shoulder. People press against us, trying to push out. "Please," I say, "you're holding everyone up."

"You saw," he says, tightening his grip. "You're the only one who knows. You saw!"

"I don't understand what you're saying," I tell him. "Now I must be going. The train's about to leave."

"Not yet," he says, fumbling in his pants to fish out a business card dirty with thumbprints. "Contact me at this address or phone number. Do it soon or else—"

"Thanks a lot!" I say and pull away, stepping down to the platform. The doors begin to slide shut behind me and the blind man continues staring out the windows at me as the train pulls away, even though he can't see a thing.

* * *

The streets in Peter's neighborhood aren't crowded at this time of night. Couples stroll the sidewalks together, holding hands, their breath steaming in clouds before their faces as I pass them. I keep my head down, my chin tucked into my collar, trying not to look up if I don't have to, watching my feet go one in front of the other on the concrete, steady as the click of a metronome.

I run into someone in this way, a salaryman who's had too much to drink, I can tell by the fumes on his breath as we catch hold of each other instead of falling over, and right ourselves, apologizing profusely before bowing and continuing on our way. The road seems blurry when I look at it. I'm not drunk anymore, but it makes me wish I was, to warm me up on this cold evening.

The neon lights of a karaoke parlor hit me full on in the face. I squint for a moment, blinking and blinking, as if I'm watching a star explode in front of me. Then the lights blink off on a timer and I can see again. I need to stop and have a coffee, I think, before showing up on Peter's doorstep. That'll give me pep, that'll make me *genki*. But before I can find a vending machine, something else happens. The world starts dimming.

At first I think it's just my eyes still adjusting to the flash of the karaoke and game center signs surrounding me, but after a few minutes I realize it's not stopping. The sky grows darker than it already was and the street shadows stretch and lengthen, spread until they cover buildings, roads, the street corner I'm standing on, as my eyes fill with a liquid dark and I can no longer see. Am I dying? Is this how death comes, like a stranger who's always been behind you, following? Then suddenly it reaches out to stroke your cheek, to wake you like a lover?

I'm not sure what to do, so I turn in place, my hands grasping at air, as if I might fall off the edge of the earth if I can't find something to hold on to. I find a tree in a cement potter and move backwards slowly until I'm pressed up against a building. I place my palms on the cold surface and listen for a while to the sound of my breath going in and out.

I want to crouch down in a ball, but I force myself to stand. I'm afraid to move to the right or left, though, and at this point I'm not sure where I am. I know that I'm only a few blocks from Peter's, but I've lost my sense of direction and I'm ready to shout for help after a few minutes of sniveling. Then I hear someone approaching. "Are you okay?" they ask.

"I'm afraid," I say, breathing hard, pausing to catch my breath, as if I've just run a race. "I'm afraid I can't see very well at the moment."

"Can I help somehow?"

"Please, will you call a friend for me?"

The stranger taps out the numbers I give him, and puts his phone into my hands. I nod stupidly, thanking him. And right away, when Peter answers and I ask if he can come get me, I can tell he's been drinking. "What's your story this time, Nobuo?" he slurs. Then: "Oh, forget it. Where are you?"

It's good to be friends with gaijin like Peter. You can drop in on them or call at odd times and not worry as much about imposing like you do with Japanese people. Foreigners mind, but they mind differently. They won't hold it against you.

I thank the stranger for lending me his cell phone, give him a courteous bow, and tell him I'll be fine now, that my friend is coming for me. He asks if I'm sure and I nod, bowing again, thanking him, excusing myself for being an imposition before sending him on his way.

"Sorry for dragging you out of bed," I tell Peter when he arrives fifteen minutes later, smelling like the salaryman I ran into earlier. "It's just that, well, it seems I've gone blind."

"What are you talking about, Nobuo?" he says, his voice betraying his doubt.

I'm not sure what to say, so I look down and say nothing and eventually I feel his hand on my shoulder. "Peter," I say. "I mean it. I don't know how to explain it. I think I've gone blind."

"Let's get you to a hospital," he says, finally believing me. "Here, take my hand." I feel his skin on my skin, warm and soft and slightly sweaty. I imagine its comforting pink color. I don't know why white people think their skin is white. It's more like pink and even red sometimes.

"Thanks," I say as Peter puts his arm around my shoulders. I'm only twenty-eight years old. I'm too young to go blind. I have so much left to do. Then I think, *What do I have left to do? What was it I'd been doing anyway?*

❖

What does the world of a blind man look like? It doesn't look like anything at all. It's black and full of emptiness and the sounds of the world crowd you until you feel like you might go deaf as well. You feel movement nearby. But when you reach out, the only thing you touch is air. Something brushes you and it's like you're swimming in the ocean and something scaly rubs your leg for a moment. Your first reaction is panic. What you can't see, what is unknown, you fear. A blind man is defined by his inability to know the world.

In the hospital they take blood and X-rays and slide my body into and out of various caverns. They explain everything they're doing, but I can't contain their words in this darkness. I find myself thinking about Ai, then Hitomi. Did Hitomi go into a deep darkness like this, the world moving unknown around her like some strange animal?

I'd let her run after her story—love, marriage, a family—alone. But the ending wasn't what either of us expected. I imagined she'd find someone to play those roles with her. I didn't want to. I'm not sure what I wanted, but I didn't want to be like that. Like anyone. Not even like myself. I wanted to be no one. No one at all.

The thing is there's not much to me. I'm a simple guy. I'm simple that way on purpose. There was a time when I thought there was more to the world, that it was good to dream and want things. I wasn't always who I am now. I went to college for a year. I used to be a good student. I used to honor my parents. I had intentions. I'd made a plan for my life. But that first year away from home, I found out the world isn't as eager to provide for us as we're told.

There was a guy living in the room next to mine who was in some of my classes. We became friends early our first semester, studying together, going out on the town for breaks every now and then. His name was Momotaro, but everyone called him Taro. I used to call him Peach Boy jokingly, like Momotaro from the folktale we all hear when we're little kids. He was good like the storybook Momotaro, did everything the best he could, for others more than for himself. He was what every Japanese boy should aspire to: good grades, friendly, clean cut, good at sports, ambitious. He had the most beautiful girlfriend at school, Ayaka Sato, and had already mentioned his wish to marry her. He hadn't mentioned it to her, but he told me he planned to ask her after graduation. I felt lucky he thought of me as his close friend. Close enough to tell me these things we normally keep inside, protected.

Ayaka, too, soon became my friend. The three of us spent every day together. Studying, sharing meals, going drinking and dancing together, discussing books, politics, philosophies our professors introduced in class. It was the most exhilarating time in my life. I was in love with learning. I was in love with living.

Then one day Taro didn't show for one of our classes. Taro never missed class. He got straight A's and didn't earn those by slacking. I thought he must be sick. After class, instead of going for lunch, I went back to our dorm and knocked on his door. "Taro?" I said, but he didn't answer. I could hear music playing on the other side of the door, though, so I knew he was in there. I knocked once more, called his name again, then finally I jiggled the knob and the door swung open.

Taro was sitting on his bed, elbows on his knees, his head propped up in his hands. He didn't act surprised or even look up when I entered. He just sat there and when I said his name, he said, "She's gone, Nobuo. She's left me. She has someone else."

I couldn't believe what I was hearing. No sane girl would leave Taro. He had everything anyone could possibly want in the palms of his hands. All the ingredients necessary for the perfect future. A high-salaried job on the horizon, a family with a sterling reputation among the wealthy circles of Tokyo. And this girl wanted to leave him? To leave Taro, the Peach Boy, who could have offered her the sky and everything beneath it?

I didn't know what to say to Taro that could make him feel better. Instead I just sat down beside him and arranged my elbows and hands and head like his, as if that could tell him how I hurt with him, for him, as if I'd been left as well. Eventually Taro stood and turned his stereo off. He turned back to face me, but wouldn't lift his head. His red-tinted hair framed the fine curves of his cheekbones. "Thanks for trying to help, Nobuo," he said, "but I'd like to be alone."

Outside I leaned against his door, wondering what else I could have done. I should have touched him, I thought. I should have said something, not just sat there trying to look like him as he grieved. But what could I have done? I felt helpless.

Then I got the idea to find Ayaka, and ten minutes later, after I ran over to her dorm, I was pounding on her door, too, shouting, "Open up, Ayaka!" as if I were the jilted boyfriend. Not Taro.

The door opened a moment later and Ayaka stood before me with a confused look on her face. "Nobuo?" she said, as if she hadn't registered it was me, even though she saw me and even though I'd shouted my name through the door.

"Why did you do it?" I said. "How could you?" Ayaka backed up and pushed the door halfway closed, as if she thought I might burst in and hurt her. I wanted to hurt her, to make her feel what Taro felt, to make her feel what I felt right then, but I could never do that. I still loved her.

"I think you should go, Nobuo."

"What sort of answer is that?" I said, my voice climbing higher with each syllable.

"I don't owe you answers," said Ayaka. "You aren't my boyfriend. But if you want to know why, ask Taro. He knows why. I told him."

She closed the door on me then and I stood outside for a moment, thinking. I wondered why I cared as much as I did. What angered me so much?

I walked around the city for hours, looking into shop windows at people—lovers and mothers and daughters, fathers and sons—doing simple things together. Buying clothes, eating, choosing a new computer or cell phone. It reminded me of all the times Taro and Ayaka and I hung out and how good it all was, that time spent together. And then I realized why I was so angry. I had fallen in love. Not with one or the other, but with all of us. I had fallen in love with the three of us together. I'd never felt that before, not even with my own family. That Ayaka had gone and thrown it all away, that Taro had asked me to leave, that Ayaka treated me as if I were a stranger—those were the cruelest moments of my life. I had lied to myself. I'd allowed myself to think they loved me as I loved them without allowing myself to know that I loved them at all. How is something like this even possible?

Love isn't what we think. It's a living, changing creature that takes as many shapes as the fox women in the old tales my mother used to tell me. Love comes in and sometimes she's a woman who woos you with soft words and promises. Love comes in and sometimes he's a man with a strong smile and a sure grip on your shoulder. Love comes in and sometimes it's something beyond the usual circumstances of two people becoming one. It can slip through our hands before we even realize what it is we're holding.

I'm kept overnight and my parents are phoned to let them know what's happened. They'll be coming to Tokyo tomorrow, a nurse tells me. Wonderful. Just what I need. My mother and father getting into my business.

I lie in bed through the night, surrounded by darkness, hearing how the world sounds for the first time. The squeak of sneakers, the bleep and grind of machines, the air circulating. The hum of breathing. Then voices. First nurses down the hall at their station, then the night doctors gravely discussing the evening's emergency cases. Then, further still, I think I can hear the late night radio shows playing in taxis and in the cars of night shift workers. The call of a man to a woman who he believes to be a prostitute. Her harsh rebuttal. The laughter of teenagers on street corners out past curfew.

I fade into sleep for a while, and know when I wake ten minutes or two hours later that someone is in the room with me. I hear breathing. "It's me," says Peter, and I am relieved. I thought it might be my parents, even though the trains to Tokyo are down for the rest of the night by now. "How did this happen?" Peter asks, as if I know anything.

"A blind man saw me on the train," I say. "I don't know how he did it. I'm not sure he knew either, but he did and he tried to tell me something, but I didn't listen."

"Are you on drugs, Nobuo?"

"No," I say. "I wish I were. That would make things easier. You'll find the old man's card in my pants. He gave it to me before I got off the train. He insisted I contact him."

"Here it is," says Peter. "But it's in kanji. I can't read it."

"Bring a nurse," I say. "I'll have her read it out loud, then I'll translate his address and phone number for you."

Fifteen minutes later, when the blind man picks up his phone, I don't even have a chance to tell him who's calling. He just says, "I've been expecting you," and rattles off a set of directions. I'm forced to interrupt to tell him I can't come myself. A friend will bring him to me. "Of course," he says. "A friend. Of course."

An hour and a half later Peter returns with a Mr. Ishii of Jimbocho. Poor Peter. By now he's probably sorry he knows me. He shouldn't have to be doing this, running around Tokyo in the middle of the night to pick up blind Japanese men, young and old alike, bringing us to hospitals. He knows my parents will be coming in the morning. He could have left me to the wolves.

I hear them open and close the door, settle in beside me. "Nobuo?" Peter says. "Mr. Ishii's here to see you."

"You're probably wondering what's happening to you," says Mr. Ishii. I hear him shuffle his feet a little. I nod and say that indeed I'm wondering what's happened, and what does he have to do with it. "You must brace yourself," he tells me. "What I'm going to tell you isn't something you want to hear."

"Go on," I say, and Mr. Ishii begins.

❋

Ten years ago there was a man who lived in Kobe with his wife and two children. He was a businessman for a company that dealt in the manufacture of electronics. He was a success in his company, and because of this he was also very wealthy. His bosses gave him large bonuses each Christmas. They sent him on business trips that doubled as vacations without any of the other employees knowing. The man's family didn't know either. When he visited America or any number of Asian countries, he told them he was on business, which he was, but he would also spend several days or a week after finishing his job there in the company of beautiful women. Sometimes he paid for these women; sometimes they were given to him by the company he was there to do business with. They were always young creatures without much education but who knew how to do exactly what he wanted.

At home his wife and children continued their regular

lives of school and social commitments without seeing their husband and father often. It was as if he didn't exist. Even when he was in Japan, he was only home to sleep a few hours before returning to his office. He saw his kids on Sundays. Sometimes he went to the park with them and drank beer while they kicked a soccer ball around. This life was not an unusual one really; it was the life of any salaryman, and he thought nothing of it.

Then something happened, as it always happens. While the man was traveling, having a cocktail with a blonde woman whose hair sparkled like sunlight and whose eyes were like blue fire, an earthquake happened back in Kobe. You know the one. It was in January of that year, 1995. He heard word of this first on American television, then from a phone call from his sister, who said she and her family were all right, but that his own family was missing and he needed to come home.

The man flew back to Japan immediately, but it was two days before he could even enter Kobe. The city was a disaster area. When he finally made it home, he found nothing but a pile of rubble. His children and wife hadn't survived. He had lost everything and he had been sipping whiskey beside a pool when it happened.

In his grief and shame, the man wandered away from Kobe and began walking through the countryside, through forest and fields and mountains. He ate the food given to dogs in their bowls in the evening. His hair grew long and his muscles thickened. He walked forward without knowing where he was or where he was going. And then one day he reached Tokyo, where he sat down on a bench in a park and wept. He cried until he wept tears of blood and fell asleep with his face and hands and arms smeared with the stains of his grieving.

The next morning, when the man opened his eyes, he couldn't see a thing. Overnight he had gone blind. A police officer found him there, took him to the station, and over the course of several days the man became a ward of the city.

The man thought at first that his sight would return, as the doctors could find no cause for it. According to all of their tests he was normal. There was no explanation for the blood he wept, there was no explanation for his blindness.

At night he lay in his bed and the ghosts of his family would visit him. He could not see them, but they spoke to him, and he could feel their cold hands on his arms and face as they wept and begged for him to come home. "Home?" the man shouted. "What do you mean?"

The man's life continued like this for many years, until one day he realized what they had been trying to tell him. And on that day, the man's vision returned, and the first thing he saw when he opened his eyes . . .

❋

". . . was me," I say, finishing Mr. Ishii's fairy tale.

"Unh," he says, and in my mind I can see him give a quick nod of his head, the way everyone does when we say "uhn." It reminds me of everything I hate about this world. The easy way everyone does the same things over and over. The comfort taken in sameness and similarity. The same gestures, the same jokes told over and over. Congratulating each other on sharing the same sports club in high school

or for having the same birthday. As if these things are indi-
cations of who you are. As if they are nothing more than
things we do or like or, in some cases, have no control over.
My head hurts thinking about it.

Mr. Ishii says, "I see your problem. It's here." His fingers
touch my forehead, driving down the center of my skull until his whole hand sits on my head like a cap. "You've got my
dark in there," says Mr. Ishii. "When you saw me in the train
earlier, it was like looking into a mirror for a moment. But
when my vision left again, I thought I had perhaps imagined the entire thing. A short while later, though, when it
became clear that my sight was truly returning, my first
thought was of you. I wondered where you were when the
dark finally claimed you. It has no concerns for us, you see.
Once it's found a place to live comfortably, it's a difficult
guest to be rid of. It's been so long since I've seen anything.
But I'm seeing you now. I'm seeing you not see me."

He stops talking then, and I wait for him to go on. After
a long silence, though, I say, "Is that all you have to tell me?
A fairy tale about the darkness in my head? Thanks. Thanks
very much, Mr. Ishii. Now, really, you must be going."

"I'm sorry," he says, shuffling away from my bed a few
steps before pausing again. "I can't do anything to help you
other than tell you that story. That's the only medicine I
have. It took me over ten years to understand the cure. I'm
giving it to you because fate led you to be the first person I
saw with clear eyes, and I feel I should help you in some
way. This is the only thing I can do. I know it isn't much, but
it may be worth something if you listen."

"I listened," I say. "Thank you. But unless you have anything else to tell me, I should probably rest as the doctors say."

After Mr. Ishii leaves, Peter puts his hand on my arm and we stay that way for a long time as I lie in a hospital room in Tokyo, not seeing anything, not saying anything, sharing this long silence through the remainder of the night.

Then morning comes. Then the footsteps and bustle of what sounds like several people entering my room. Then my mother's familiar voice, small and particular, as if each syllable is an object she's taken off the mantel to dust before saying it: "Nobuo?" Her question mark lingers in the air. Peter removes his hand. Surely she and Father must be wondering who this gaijin standing beside me is, but they can't bear to ask the question.

"It seems I've got a problem with my eyes," I say, trying to laugh it off a little.

But *Okaasan* is not having any of this humor. "Come now," she says, and her hand lands on my wrist as if I'm a child, as if I've disappointed her in the supermarket once more, pleading for candy after she's told me three times that I can't have any. "Come now," she says. "We're taking you home."

Home. I'm not sure what she means by this. But I have nowhere else to go but to this place with them.

Outlanders

There were four of them living in the same town. Four Americans. For some reason they had all expected there would be more Canadians. But to meet a Canadian, you had to drive nearly two hours away, to a village called Shimotsuma that no one but Laurie had ever heard of. Laurie had come from Boston three years ago, and had been in country the longest out of any of them. His first year, he'd been assigned to teach in the junior high of that little hamlet where nothing but 7-Elevens and pachinko and karaoke parlors existed amid the rice fields. Now the town of Ami, he told the others, was a step up the ladder. At least here he had a view. Every day on his way to and from his school in the neighboring town of Ryugasaki, he could see the Great Buddha of Ushiku's knobbed head and stone-shrouded shoulders over the treetops. Each morning Laurie would nod at the world's tallest statue of the Buddha from his tiny death-trap of a car as he sped by on the narrow, labyrinthine back roads, acknowledging the statue just as he and his Japanese coworkers nodded politely at each other throughout the day.

Hannah came to Japan a year after Laurie. She came from New York City without a story for why she was there in the first place, and she came with no plans for when she'd be leaving. She carried herself tall and straight, like the Great Buddha of Ushiku, but sometimes her shoulders would drop, her smile would deflate, and she'd turn from the conversation in progress and look away from the others. No one could ever tell what she was looking at, and only Laurie had ever asked her, just once, to which Hannah replied, "Sorry. I thought I saw someone I know." Laurie asked if it had been one of her coworkers, but Hannah shook her head. "No. A friend. But it wasn't him."

Ted came from Wisconsin. He came with a girlfriend, Veronica, but six months into their stay Veronica had had enough and went back to Oshkosh without him. Ted had started dating Japanese girls soon after. Usually they lasted a few weeks before he'd lose interest, and eventually they'd stop calling and showing up on his doorstep. His latest was Miyuki, who liked to sit in his lap with her arms around his neck while they watched movies on his laptop. Miyuki had short spiky hair, wore large hoop earrings, and spoke enough English that Ted had kept her around for slightly over a month. The others had bets going. How long would Miyuki last before she was out? Laurie said week five, Jules thought week six, Hannah said she didn't understand why she was still here to begin with, but maybe Ted had virtues he didn't share with everyone. Along with exes, Ted collected gaijin trivia, jokes, and foreigner-related stories. Whenever Ted heard something amusing about gaijin, he'd wait until their weekend get-together to share it. There was an unspoken competition between him and Laurie to see who could find the funniest gaijin story possible. The tricky part was how to bring the story back without being the butt of the joke, as so often was the case.

Jules came from California, straight out of college. She came with a mountain of luggage containing a wardrobe big enough to wear a different outfit every day for three weeks straight, and a ready smile spread across her face when Laurie and Hannah and Ted picked her up from the airport, as if she'd known them her entire life. Laurie, sure that she was an old pro at this, asked if she had ever lived abroad, but Jules hadn't. Except for one wild two-week vacation in Mexico, she'd never even left the country. Hannah asked what her major in school had been, and Jules just kept smiling. "A little of this, a little of that," she said.

But Canadians. They were suspiciously absent. As were Australians, British, Irish, and New Zealanders. There was a logical explanation for the missing Ozzies, Brits, Micks, and Kiwis—many schools in Japan preferred North American English—but there was absolutely no excuse why there were no Canadians nearby. This bothered Jules to no end. She'd arrived ready to enjoy her single status. She'd heard Canadian men were built like lumberjacks and liked women who were hard to handle, which would have made her prime girlfriend material. Alas, there were no lumberjacks within two hours by car, and even then no one knew if the Canadians in Shimotsuma were men, women, or worse: married.

"You'd think there'd be at least one around here," Jules complained several months after settling into her teaching position. "If I'd known Japanese men didn't go for big, blonde, and beautiful before I came, I'd have gotten married and brought someone along!"

"You know, I'm single, too, and I don't mind," said Laurie, typing away at an e-mail on Ted's laptop. They had congregated for their weekly gathering at Ted's apartment, where beer and wine and sake were plentiful.

Laurie's full name was Laurence, but everyone called him Laurie. One night, on one of the rare occasions when Hannah drank with them and seemed like she was paying attention to what was going on around her, she had said his name reminded her of Laurie from *Little Women*. And even Jules, who thought the nickname weird at first, had come around to liking it.

"I can relate," said Hannah. "To Laurie, I mean. Sometimes alone is better."

But she's thirty-something, Jules reminded herself. She made a silent vow then and there to get married before she turned thirty. She had six years to get it done. Surely that would be enough time to fall in love with someone who loved you back and was good-looking and had a good job on top of that, wasn't it?

"There!" Laurie said, and hit the Return key. "All done."

"Who were you writing?" asked Jules.

"My ex."

"From back home?" Hannah asked, taking another sip from her glass of merlot.

"No," said Laurie. "A girl I dated my first year here. But now she's living in Sydney."

"She is Australian?" asked Miyuki from her perch on Ted's lap.

"No," said Laurie. "Japanese."

"Are you trying to get her back?" asked Jules. She turned to Hannah and feigned a romantic sigh. "What I wouldn't give to be in love in Japan," she said. Then, "Oh, hell. What I wouldn't give to be in lust in Japan either."

Hannah smiled but furrowed her brow.

By thirty, thought Jules. *By thirty.*

"Actually, I can't reach her," said Laurie. "I send her an e-mail every week or so, but she doesn't write back."

"Wow," said Ted. "That's harsh. You should come out to the clubs with me sometime. There are other girls, you know."

Miyuki turned from the conversation to give Ted a look. Ted grinned, shrugging helplessly. "For Laurie!" he assured her.

"Don't even think about it, Laurie," said Hannah, waving the conversation away like a bad odor. She took a long drink of wine and said, "Give her time. She'll come around again."

"Okay, movie time," Ted said, and Miyuki hopped off so he could get up to take the laptop from Laurie. Ted had spent the past day illegally downloading movies released the year before back in the States. "Who's up for *The Incredibles*?" he said to a collective groan. "What? Doesn't anyone like superheroes?"

Laurie, Jules, and even Hannah said they'd rather karaoke. They could watch movies anytime. They could sing karaoke anytime, too, but karaoke was heaven, said Jules.

Ted didn't agree, but he liked the *nomihodai* special at karaoke parlors. All you could drink for three hours straight, and nonstop songs from the eighties onward, songs from their childhoods, college days, and the now they found themselves making up as they went along together.

"If Japan didn't have karaoke," Jules said as they left Ted's apartment, "I think I'd commit *seppuku*."

"If Japan didn't have *nomihodai*," said Ted, "I'd go broke buying regular-priced drinks."

"If Japan didn't have you two," Laurie said, "I think it would be more foreigner-friendly."

"Oh, shut up, Laurie," Jules said as they walked through the misty spring night to the nearest karaoke club, lit up like a casino at the far end of the street.

For gaijin like them, karaoke was one of the few places they could use English without being a disturbance to the locals. Even if they were the one gaijin in a group of Japanese, at karaoke their English was not only enjoyed but respected. "It's ironic," Ted told the others three hours later, as they exited from a fairly high-energy session in a private neon-lit booth at Party-Party, their parlor of choice. "If I speak English out in public—for example, if I ask a grocery store clerk or a train attendant something in English—they freak out. But if I go to karaoke with those same people, they request Beatles songs and do nothing but clap and shout."

Miyuki giggled. Was she confirming Ted's observations, or simply laughing at his view of her world? No one could tell. And since Ted's start-to-finish record with girlfriends was setting land speed records at this point, there was no point in finding out. There'd just be another Miyuki in a few more weeks to replace this one.

"Don't think too much about it," Hannah suggested.

"Is that what you do?" Ted asked, laughing.

"You mean, don't do," Jules corrected.

"I'm just saying it doesn't help trying to figure out every inconsistency in Japanese culture. I mean, there are lots, sure, but there are lots in ours, too."

"I'm not bothered by the inconsistencies," said Ted. "I just find them amusing."

"Why?" asked Hannah.

"Why not?" said Jules.

Ted pointed at his nose and said, "*Pin pon, pin pon,*" the chime of "You are correct!" from a thousand Japanese game shows. "But I guess you're right," Ted added. "I didn't mean to make it sound like only Japanese culture is screwed up. Our own is even weirder sometimes."

"How?" Jules asked. She was weaving a little as she walked ahead of them, as if she were trying to catch her shadow on the sidewalk under the streetlamps. Three hours of karaoke and *nomihodai* had made them all a bit drunk.

"Cowboys," Miyuki offered. "Cowboys are weird, aren't they?"

Hannah and Laurie pursed their lips in knowing smirks. Maybe Miyuki knew what she was dealing with after all.

"*You're* weird, Laurie," said Jules. She looked over her shoulder and rolled her eyes. "But so are cowboys, Miyuki, you're right. Now I'm going to stop at this convenience store and get another drink or else everything you just said is going to make sense."

Hannah chuckled and Laurie laughed with her. At the next corner, they stopped at the 7-Eleven. "My oasis," Jules said, sighing. She pulled two cans of *Chu-Hai*—peach for her, pear for Ted—from the cooler. Hannah and Miyuki opted for bottles of water, Laurie a curry-filled bun. On the way out, they moved into single file on the edge of the side-walk to allow a group of Japanese college students—also in the middle of laughing at something one of them had done or said—to pass by.

At Ted's place, Miyuki said she was tired and left to go home. Then Ted and Jules smoked a bowl of hash. Laurie and Hannah passed, but agreed to stay and watch *The Incredibles.* Ted had bought the hash from an American col-lege student he'd met in a bar in Tokyo a few months after arriving in Japan. During breaks in the school year, the kid would fly to Amsterdam and return with the stuff in zipped-up plastic bags stuffed inside shampoo bottles. He said it was the perfect hiding place. Even the dogs, the kid said, didn't smell it under the shampoo. Ted wasn't sure that was a fail-safe method—weren't the dogs trained to smell drugs beneath other scents?—but it wasn't his own incar-ceration or deportation at risk, so he didn't worry about it.

On the laptop screen, Mr. Incredible was sneaking out of his house late at night with an old superhero friend to save the lives of citizens who had made it a criminal act for superheroes to save people. Ted smiled. "Superheroes are awesome." It was true, the world needed saving. It needed saving a little more as each year passed and weirder, scarier things happened. At the beginning of the movie, there was a moment when they each felt this exact feeling, and might have talked about it, might have made individual lists of the weird, scary things that had been happening in recent years, and might have discovered they had more in common than the fact that they were all Americans. Or perhaps they might have discovered the things on their lists were weird and scary *because* they were all Americans. But the moment passed, and they continued watching the movie together in a companionable silence, until it was over, and each returned to their own, individual apartments to fall into their own, individual dreams.

Jules nearly cried with gratitude when she got her period the following week. She'd been chucking coins into a box at a nearby temple and folding her hands together before going to bed at night for the past two weeks, waiting, and had thought for a while now that she wouldn't be getting out of it this time. Luckily she'd come to Japan with a small supply of morning-after pills and had taken one an hour after he pulled out, finished, after she had sobered up enough to realize what they'd done.

She'd met him at a party for foreigners in Tokyo. He was from France, and she had a thing for men who spoke French. He was a little shorter and just a little chubbier than she usually liked, but what was a tall blonde American goddess exiled in Japan to do but take what Frenchmen the little island country had to offer? His name was Jean Michel, which even at the time she'd thought he'd been making up, and most likely he had been because the number for his mobile he'd given her was made up, too. When she tried calling a couple of days afterwards, a Japanese woman had answered and Jules had quickly said "Sorry!" into the phone before snapping it shut like Pandora's box. A moment later she thought perhaps she should have said she was sorry in Japanese. Whatever. Just because she was living overseas didn't mean everything in her life had to be about international relations.

She sat on the tatami mat floor of her bedroom now and breathed a sigh of relief. Jean Michel, whoever the fuck he was, was no longer inside her. She couldn't help but want to go out and get drunk and celebrate, but it was the middle of the week and she still had to teach two more days at her elementary school. It would have to wait till the weekend, this party for one. She hadn't told anyone she might be pregnant or how she'd gotten that way. Everyone would have yelled at her, she knew, so she kept it to herself. She had little kids tugging on her dress and shirtsleeves day after day, talking to her in Japanese when they knew she didn't understand a word of what they were saying. Every trip to the grocery store was an exercise in humiliation. She wouldn't alienate herself from the only other English speakers around by telling them how stupid she'd been. And with a Frenchman who didn't even have the decency to make up a more believable name. "I mean, come on, Jules," she could hear Laurie, that do-gooder, chastising, "he might as well have called himself Jacques Cousteau!"

She thought about going down a few doors and pushing Hannah's buzzer. One glass of wine couldn't hurt, and though she was in the clear now, with nothing to hold the moment to her but a number in her cell phone and a bad memory, she still wanted to confess it to someone. Ted was a total impossibility. He was probably out at some bar picking up another Japanese girl to bring back to his lair anyway, never mind if it was midweek or week's end. But maybe Hannah could keep a secret. She seemed to have enough of her own. Out of all the gaijin in the area, Hannah was the one they knew the least about. She'd spent two or three years here but didn't seem to have gone all weird like Laurie. What did Laurie say to give Jules this impression? Months ago now, after their boss had asked him to mentor Jules with a few English conversation classes at the main office, to help her find her feet, Laurie had been showing her how to play *karuta*, a card game younger students would love playing to learn vocabulary, and somehow Jules had begun complaining about Japan, how hard it was adjusting to life here. "You have to let go of yourself, Jules," he said, "or else the world is always going to be hurting you."

That was it. *Let go of yourself.* Those words had lodged in her mind for days after he'd said them, for months now, she thought as she considered who to talk to. It sounded simple but in the end Jules wasn't sure what it all meant. That was Laurie, though. He'd been in Japan longer than any of them, had gone native, is how Ted put it, had nearly mastered the language, had even studied Buddhism and Shinto, which was probably why he said things that sounded vaguely mystical and disconcertingly hippieish. *Let go of yourself.* What would that even look like? She tried to imagine herself letting herself go, as if there were two Juleses, one struggling to hold on to the other, the other struggling to cast her off like an unwanted shadow. Get out of here! Go! *Why do we always act like Laurie's the one we don't understand,* Jules thought. So it was Hannah she called. Hannah was safer. She was a girl, and even if Jules didn't know much about her, she seemed normal. Well, normal enough for someone in her thirties and still unmarried.

She grabbed a bottle of wine and padded down the outside hall in her slippers to Hannah's door. "One moment!"

Hannah's voice came buzzing through the speaker after Jules pressed her doorbell. The speaker stayed on for a few seconds longer and Jules could hear Hannah whispering to herself, and the clatter of things being picked up or thrown away. A minute later she opened the door and Jules held up the bottle. "I have something to celebrate and didn't want to celebrate alone."

"Oh, really?" said Hannah, grinning. "What is it?"

"Let me come in and tell you."

"But my apartment's a mess."

"Please. As if my life isn't?" Jules said, and pushed her way past Hannah into what must have been the best-kept apartment she had ever been in.

Two hours later a second bottle of cabernet had been opened, and Jules had taken her time warming up, telling Hannah about more than she'd intended before she could tell her what she had actually come to confess. How spring vacation had been a relief, but she was already suffocating after three days back at her elementary school. All day long she sat at her desk in the long rows of desks in the teachers' office, prepping to face classrooms full of small Japanese schoolchildren and teachers who could barely speak a word of English. She smiled throughout the day, waiting anxiously for the moment she could leave. The students were sometimes interested in her, but they seemed to always be laughing and she couldn't help but wonder sometimes if they were laughing at her. It made her feel like she was in junior high again. It made her want to cry, recognizing this set of neuroses she thought she'd been done with years ago. Do junior high all over again. Only now with the added bonus of having absolutely no clue why the other kids are

laughing at you. "I thought these Japanese kids were supposed to be more polite and respectful than Americans,"
she told Hannah.

"Well," said Hannah, "some of them are and some of
them aren't. Kids are kids anywhere, I guess."

She lay spread out on Hannah's extra futon, glad she'd
come over to share her problems instead of staying home
alone. She couldn't stand being alone. It was the hardest thing
about life here. No, it was the hardest thing about *living*. She
needed people like the vine needs the rain, like the moon
needs the sun if it's to be seen by anyone. It didn't really matter that she wouldn't necessarily have been friends with all of
these people back in the States. What mattered was that they
spoke her language and were decent enough company to
keep her sane.

When Jules finally got around to Jean Michel and what
had happened, Hannah took the confession well. She didn't
lecture like Jules had expected. She just nodded and made
sad faces at all the appropriate moments and patted Jules on
the knee after she finished her story and said, "It's over now.
You don't have to think about it anymore." Jules nodded and
looked down into her empty glass and shrugged.

"I just—"

"What?" Hannah prompted.

"I just, I don't know," said Jules. "I guess for a moment,
even though I was scared to death, there was this odd happiness I had about the whole thing. Because I might have
been able to, you know, do it. Make a baby. I think I've always worried I'd never have a chance to do that or couldn't,
but I found out maybe I could."

"Well, that's a good thing!" said Hannah.

"Yeah, but I still took the pill."

"So? You were just being careful. And with good reason."

"I don't want to think about it anymore," Jules said.

"You don't have to," said Hannah, and then she brought out a third bottle of wine and poured Jules another glass. "You don't ever have to think about it again," Hannah told her.

"Fuck," Jules said, and shook her arms and hands out wildly in front of her, feeling as if ants were suddenly crawling all over her. "Fuck fuck fuck."

"You can say that again," said Hannah.

"Fuck," said Jules.

She couldn't say it enough.

❸

Laurie was at home drawing pictures of people he'd gotten to know since coming to Japan three years ago. Scratching carefully, he finished the lines in Noriko's hair.

Noriko had been his neighbor when he moved to Japan. At first she was the girl upstairs who attended classes at the local university and threw wild parties on the weekends. Later she was his best friend and then a little later his girlfriend, the best person he'd ever known anywhere. She was the first person to make him feel welcome in her country. When Laurie moved into his apartment, she'd brought down cream puffs from a local bakery. He could tell she was curious about how a gaijin must live, sneaking looks past his shoulder through the door.

His room wasn't anything special. Just a drawing table

and the futon he never folded and put away like Japanese people did daily, his television and laptop, a small bookshelf filled with novels in English and stuffed characters from Miyazaki anime: Totoro and Cat Bus, Howl and Calcifer. Noriko had knelt by his bookshelf to look at them. "*Kawaii!*" she said, exclaiming how adorable they were. She reminded him of the junior high girls he taught. He picked up the Totoro doll and held it out to her. "For you," he said, "a present. I'm glad we're neighbors."

Noriko said she couldn't take it, but when she left his apartment, she went out hugging the little gray and white doll in one arm, waving back at him with the other. "*Watashi no hey, ni itsudemo asobi ni kite ni!*" she said. Come over to my place sometime and play!

By now this invitation didn't make Laurie laugh as much as it once did. It turned into such an odd phrase in English when you got to the part about playing. But the concept of play in Japan was different from play in America: it was a sweet, innocent utterance, and a scripted thing to say to someone you wanted to become friends with in Japan. He no longer took it literally.

After that, Noriko often came down to invite him up to her weekend parties. None of Noriko's friends spoke English, but when Laurie came to the parties they all acted as if they wanted to learn. He gave them his *meishi*, his business card, one side of which was printed in English, the other in Japanese, and told them to call if they wanted lessons. Noriko was the only one who took him up on the offer. She began to take lessons from him, taught him more Japanese in exchange, and soon she had switched her major at college to English. With English, she had once told Laurie, she could go anywhere in the world.

Her hair needed to be a little longer, he decided, and so he sketched more in past her shoulders. Large hoop earrings. A wider smile. Hair covering one eye. He paused and tapped his pencil against his chin. Usually he didn't draw in such a cartoonish style. Perhaps being surrounded by anime and manga was having an effect on him, making people into caricatures instead of fully realized human figures.

Finished, he put the drawing aside and took out the portrait he'd recently drawn of Hannah. When he'd first met Hannah, he'd found himself a little attracted, but it didn't take long for him to see that, while Hannah had a certain appeal, she was hiding from something. He wasn't sure what. The world maybe. There were several types of gaijin in Japan, besides tourists, and Laurie had gotten good at spotting them quickly over the years. Hannah at first seemed like the Cosmopolitan American—which she of course was, the categories weren't always mutually exclusive—but once you scratched the surface he saw that she was more of a Hider. People who came from afar on the run from something or someone, from the life they'd been leading. Hiders sometimes had drug dependencies or the beginnings of minor criminal records; they had family issues or exes they'd never escape if they stayed behind and tried to remake their lives in their countries of origin. Hannah had lost a boyfriend, Laurie learned one drunken evening soon after her arrival more than two years ago, but before he could discover how or why or who, she had closed herself up, snip-snap, and returned to her carefully composed Hannah-ness. He wouldn't be surprised if, later, he discovered she'd left a string of odd jobs behind her. Nude modeling. Gutting fish at a factory in Alaska. Cocktail waitressing in Las Vegas. He pegged Hannah as the kind of girl who abandoned every life she lived, like a hermit crab shucking off one shell for another.

He'd finished his drawing of her last week. Hannah probably wouldn't like it, however. It was a scene at an art school with a nude but non-racy Hannah sitting in the center of three student easels, and on each canvas the viewer could see a smaller, naked Hannah a student had drawn, though the students themselves were absent. Each had a slightly different style. Laurie liked how the scene implied the presence of an invisible gaze. When Laurie thought of Hannah, he thought of invisible presences. Past lives. Ghosts. That sort of thing.

His mobile rang with a number he didn't recognize and he answered in Japanese, just in case. But when no reply came and he heard seabirds and waves crashing in the background, he knew it was Noriko. "Say something," he whispered. But she didn't say a thing. "Say anything," he said. But he only heard a choked sob as she disconnected.

This was the third time in two weeks Noriko had called and hung up without speaking. The first time, Laurie had been in a movie at the Tsukuba U World Cineplex. The second time, he'd been at karaoke with Jules. Six months ago, Noriko had left in the middle of the day while Laurie was at work, leaving only a note apologizing for not being able to say goodbye properly. If she tried, she said, she wouldn't ever have been able to leave. She thanked him for their time together, but she was going to Australia. She was done with college, the world was waiting for her, and Laurie loved Japan, while she wanted to leave it, to see who she was outside of the only place she'd known since she was born. She was sorry, but she didn't know what else to do, how else to explain. Two weeks ago, the calls began coming. Always the ocean crashed in the background, always the seabirds cried in the distance. Laurie imagined her on a beach in Sydney, crying without making a sound, digging her toes into the wet sand beneath her.

It was still light outside, and Laurie slipped out for a jog, trying to run away from Noriko's face, lit up in his mind as it used to be when he'd come to meet her at her favorite *izakaya* after his workday ended, making his way to the table where she and her friends sat drinking beer and laughing over soba and sushi. She'd stand as soon as she saw him and cross the room to greet him, taking his hand, leading him to the table to make a space for him to sit by her side.

Now he ran faster, harder, until his lungs began to hurt and he found himself farther away than he'd intended. Looking over his shoulder, he saw the head of the Great Buddha of Ushiku rising above the treetops, red lights blinking in the dark like a giant robot standing guard, ready to lift off on rocket-powered boots to defend Japan in times of dire need. A comic-book hero, watching over the lives of those who lived in the towns that lay beneath his shadow.

On Friday evening, after she finished teaching at school, Hannah drove to Tsukuba with the address of the Minamis'

house written on a scrap of paper. She referred to it occasionally as she drove, looking up to find the street, and after she located it, the house. When she found it, her breath caught in her throat for a moment. It was a large, traditional Japanese-style home with a sloping blue-tiled roof, walled off from the other buildings and homes around it. She could see the branches of trees, sculpted like statues, reaching over the wall. She knew the family within must have money if they were hiring her to have conversations in English with their twenty-eight-year-old son, but she hadn't imagined they'd have a home of this size in a city like Tsukuba.

Mr. and Mrs. Minami had contacted Hannah through an ad she'd placed months ago on a Japanese website for people looking for English tutors. She was always looking for work outside of her regular school day, anything to keep busy. The Minamis had apparently asked a friend who understood English, at least somewhat, to respond to the ad for them, and the friend had sent a brief and mysterious message.

Our son already knows English, but cannot see to go out into the world any longer. We kindly request your services. Please come to our home on Fridays and speak with our son. You'll find he makes a worthy conversation partner, so it will not be difficult. We will pay you twice the amount you advertise.

Mrs. Minami answered the door with the immediate, friendly smile of a Japanese shopkeeper. She greeted her in Japanese, and Hannah provided the appropriate polite response. Despite having addressed her in Japanese, Mrs. Minami seemed surprised to hear Hannah speak it. Her smile grew wider and she motioned Hannah up into the foyer, where Hannah removed her shoes and stepped into the slippers Mrs. Minami had set out.

The house was immaculate, clean and sterile as a museum. One room they passed was furnished in a Western style, while another was filled with traditional Japanese furniture. Hannah had been in only two other Japanese families' homes before, and those had been modest and ramshackle, the homes of working-class families, nothing like her own family home back in New York. People had lived in those houses, died in them. This house, however, this museum, made her shiver.

Mrs. Minami led Hannah up a staircase and down a long second-floor hall. At the end, they came to stop in front of a closed door. Mrs. Minami knocked lightly, opened it, and stood aside. "*Osaki ni,*" she said, and gestured with her hands for Hannah to enter, as if she were nudging a child along.

When Hannah crossed the threshold, Mrs. Minami closed the door behind her. Sitting in a chair in front of the room's only window was the son. He did not look at Hannah. Late afternoon shadows fell across his face and dark hair. He was thin and wore a black robe. His hair was long but Hannah could tell it was trimmed to frame his face. Before she could even speak, he turned to her and said, "So you are their next attempt at a cure for me?"

"I'm sorry?" said Hannah.

"They've brought you here to cure me," he said. "Haven't you been informed of my condition?"

"You're blind, right?"

"Oh yes, blind is what I am, but the interesting thing about my blindness is that, according to tests, I'm not blind.

A series of doctors have concurred. They have placed colored mats before me on a desk and asked me to choose the
color they call out, and I have chosen correctly every time.
They have put cards with various shapes printed on them
before me and asked me to select the diamond or the
square, for example, and each time I have selected correctly.
Their scans of my brain show no damage. And yet I cannot
see."

"That's horrible."

"Yes. Horrible. But forgive my rudeness. Please," he said,
gesturing to a chair in a nearby corner, "sit down."

"If I may, do you mind if I ask how you came to be
blind?" Hannah was not so unnerved by his presence now
as by his degree of English ability. He spoke better than
some people back home. It reminded her of Daisuke. Heat
rushed to her cheeks when she thought of him, though, and
very carefully, very quietly, she put his memory away again.

"The origin of my blindness," he said, looking back out
the window. "I'm afraid that's a long story."

"I'm being paid," Hannah said. "Unless you don't want to
talk about it, there's no reason to hesitate."

"Of course," he said, grinning. "Well then, how I went
blind. It happened when I was riding a train in Shinjuku last
winter. A blind man saw me. I mean, he regained his sight
on the train. I was the first person he saw. And the next
morning, I lost mine."

"Are you making this up?" said Hannah. "I don't mean to
be rude. It's just hard to believe."

"That is one theory advanced by several doctors," he
replied. "They say I am either lying or suffering an odd
form of *hikikomori*. Social withdrawal, in your language."

"I've heard of it," said Hannah. Actually, she had seen something like it in several students at her school, children who seemed crammed into their own bodies, who trembled or lashed out if anyone spoke to them or touched them. "So you've become a shut-in?" she said.

"Not because I am blind," he said. "Because of why I can't see."

"So you know why?"

"Yes."

"Is it treatable?"

"Only with time and meditation on the path I took in life."

"What path led you to blindness?"

"A simple path. I was rejected by love once, and afterwards, out of spite, I rejected love at every turn. In fact, on the same night the blind man saw me, I had walked out on a girl because she cried over an entry in a love hotel diary. Do you know what that girl's name was?"

Hannah shook her head.

"Ai," he said. "Do you know what that name means?"

"Love," said Hannah.

"You know Japanese then?"

"*Sukoshi dake*," Hannah said, unconsciously putting her thumb and forefinger together to illustrate. Just a little. "But this isn't about me. So this girl, Ai, is why you went blind?"

"Love is why I went blind. Because I refused to see love every time it presented itself to me."

"And the cure," said Hannah, "is meditation?"

"It seems that's what it took the old man to regain his."

"And me?" said Hannah. "How do I fit into your story?"

"You don't. You are what my parents hope will be my

cure. My specialty has been English since I was a little boy. Since they brought me home from Tokyo, though, I haven't left this room. I think they must hope someone who speaks the language I love will be able to talk me out of this predicament."

"And what do you think?"

"I think it's not likely."

"Why?"

"Because we've been talking for the past twenty minutes and neither of us have enough social grace to have introduced ourselves properly."

Embarrassed, Hannah said, "*Watashi wa* Hannah *desu*," and grinned despite his inability to see her.

"Call me Nobuo," he said, grinning too. "So, Hannah, tell me. How long have you lived in Japan?"

⑤

Jules was singing "O Canada" into the mic while they waited for the next song to load. Laurie laughed. It was just the two of them. They'd texted Hannah to see if she wanted to do something, but she had a private lesson that evening. "Again? At night?" Jules had said to Laurie, eyebrows raised. Ted was going to the gym that afternoon and was going to meet Miyuki afterwards to do some bar hopping. "He means bed hopping," said Jules, and laughed. "Looks like it's just you and me, kid. What should we do?" Laurie smiled and Jules smiled and then at the same time they said, "Karaoke!"

Four hours later they were drunk, had gone through

most of the good English songs in the karaoke machine, and had racked up an enormous bill in drinks and room hours. They didn't know how much the bill was, but they'd gone to karaoke enough to know four hours in a booth with drinks arriving two or three times an hour was expensive. They had credit cards, Laurie said when they were two hours in and he had already sung "Careless Whisper" by George Michael for Jules twice. The second time she insisted he dance with her while he sang the lyrics on the television screen over her shoulder. "We make really pathetic drunks," Laurie said afterwards.

"Oh, Laurie, we're only pathetic if you call attention to it. Shut up and sing!"

"My Funny Valentine" scrolled up on the screen, one of Jules's karaoke standards. If she were a jazz club singer, she would sing it every night.

Laurie stood up and grabbed the phone from the wall to order two more Moscow Mules. They were bleeding money at this point, but neither of them wanted to leave. What attracted them to this idle, superficial distraction? It wasn't just boredom. They both knew plenty of other ways to distract themselves. It was the coziness of a karaoke room, the sound of their own voices and the voices of their friends contained in a tiny space, it was the nurturing care of the hostesses, who, with one call, would bring you anything from alcohol to ice cream. And the booths were soft enough to lie down on and go to sleep if you wanted. They could pretend this was the only place in the world, that Japan wasn't outside the frosted-glass door, and that your songs were never sung by anyone better.

Eventually, they stumbled out into the wet, early spring

evening and started the walk back to their apartments. When they came to the intersection where Jules and Hannah usually split off from Laurie to go back to their place, he told Jules he'd walk her the rest of the way. "Don't worry, honey," said Jules. "I practically live in the woods. No one should have to endure that walk but me."

"No, no," said Laurie. "We're drunk and if something happened to you I'd feel like it was my fault."

"Laurie, I get drunk at least twice a week. It's Japan. Guns are outlawed here. Japanese people shrink in fear when they see this giantess coming toward them on the street. Sweetie, don't sweat it."

But Laurie insisted, and they turned together, walking the dark, bamboo-lined lane, then turned down a narrow side street that led out of the forest and into the center of a suburban development. "You and Hannah really *do* live in the boonies, don't you?"

"Naturally," said Jules. "It's where they place the trouble-makers." When they reached the apartment building's outer stairwell, Jules stopped and stared, gazing beyond Laurie into the rolling fields and forest that lay behind the apartment complex.

"What are you looking at?" Laurie turned to look where she was looking.

"I'm not sure," Jules said, shaking her head. "I just—I sometimes see Hannah come out here, just standing and staring out that way. When I first came here, I was out on my balcony one morning—this was before I even knew another American lived in this building with me—and I saw her standing where we are now, staring back there for a while, and then finally she walked down that little path in the field until she disappeared into those woods. I thought I'd seen a ghost."

"In a way, she kind of is," said Laurie. "I remember when she moved to town. As soon as she got her assignment, I hardly ever saw her unless the boss called her into the office."

"What do you think is back there?" said Jules. She looked serious now, afraid and undeniably curious.

Laurie shrugged. "I don't know. Want to find out?"

They walked across the parking lot toward the woods, but before they even reached the field the sky opened up above and rain burst through in big fat drops, soaking them immediately. They ran back to the stairs to hide beneath the awning for a few minutes, but it seemed it wasn't going to be just a short spring shower. "Want to come up and dry off?" Jules offered.

"No, let's keep going," said Laurie. He bent over and un-laced his shoes, took them off, removed his socks and set them down on the stairs.

"Are you serious?" said Jules as he rolled his pants up to his calves. "Christ, Laurie, it's still too cold out."

"Come on," said Laurie, looking up and smiling as he rolled his other pant leg. "It'll be fun."

"You've had far too much to drink, young man," said Jules. She sighed, exhausted, but told him to wait while she put her purse in her room. A minute later she was back, barefoot and wearing a jacket. She smiled. "Let's go."

The fields were turning to mud already. It squished be-tween their toes, cold beneath their feet. Jules claimed she'd seen a snake and if she was bitten and died she was going to blame all of this on Laurie. Laurie laughed. "You can't pin this all on me," he said. "The rain's washed all the alcohol out of us. You're making your own decisions."

"Counts," said Jules, and Laurie smiled over at her as their bare feet sucked into and out of the mud as they walked.

When they reached the back of the field, they found a cemetery, the graves littered with wet incense, bottles of tea and beer. "Offerings," said Laurie. "I didn't know there was a cemetery back here."

"There's a gravel road, too," said Jules. From what they could see, it led deeper into the woods, where it was so dark the road seemed to disappear not too far from where it entered the tree line. Laurie started following it into the woods. "Hey," said Jules, "I really don't think that's a good idea." Laurie pulled his mobile phone from his pocket. Using its glow as a makeshift torch, he waved her forward into the dark. Jules sighed. "Fine," she said, taking out her own mobile, and the two of them wandered down the gravel road, their feet smarting from the occasional pinch of a stone, with only the faint light of their cell phones lighting the path before them.

It took no more than ten minutes of walking the path before the forest opened up to reveal a temple, hidden inside it like a secret. It was surrounded by a high wooden fence, and the sculpted pear trees and stone statues of gods in its gardens were bathed in the bluish-white light of the moon hanging above them. Neither of them spoke, and after a moment, Laurie noticed that at some point silence had surrounded them, covering them and everything in the night in a deep quiet. "It's stopped raining," he whispered.

They crept up to the entrance of the temple, trying to

match the quiet of the night, skulking like thieves. A small gate had been put up at the entrance, but it seemed to delineate more of a symbolic boundary than an actual one. They had only to lift their legs a little higher to cross into the temple grounds if they wanted. They stayed outside, though, not sure if it would be an offense to go in. Rain dripped from the fronds of ferns and off the petals of flowers, a soft pat-pat of water falling from the tiled roof of the temple and from the statues along the garden's central path. Jules tugged at Laurie's hand, and when he looked down, she slipped her hand into his. When he looked up, she was still looking in at the garden. Tears were streaming down her face. "Where are we?" she whispered. "Why does this place make me feel so alone?"

Laurie squeezed Jules's hand and turned back to look into the garden with her. It was as if they were children in a fairy tale, entering another world for the first time. But they had forgotten to leave crumbs behind them to find their way home.

6

Ted clicked his laptop closed and sat back in his chair. *What the hell am I doing?* He stood up straight, stretching his arms as high as he could, then went into the kitchen to find Miyuki making lunch. He'd called her yesterday to meet up for some drinks, some dancing, and some affection. He'd expected that she'd already have let herself out by now.

"Hey, sweetie," she said, as if they'd known each other for months now. "All done with lesson plans?"

"Mm-hmm," Ted said. Why was she still here? He watched as she shaped a rice ball filled with salmon in her tiny hands.

"You seem tired."

"I am."

"Why don't we eat, then you rest for a while? I'll wake you later and we can go to the movies. Sunday is movie day for foreigners, did you know?"

Ted nodded. He often went with Jules or Laurie. American humor didn't always translate well, though, and their laughter in the silent theater often earned them stares and whispers. Ted hated movie day. It reminded him too much that the world around him wasn't like the one on the screen, the one he hadn't seen for over a year now, except for a brief visit home last Christmas. He realized a while ago that he didn't want to be in Japan anymore, but he'd already signed a contract for another year. He could probably get out of it, but didn't want to cause trouble for anyone. He'd already done that with Veronica. They'd only been dating for three months when he convinced her to come with him to Japan. He guessed he was what some people would call impetuous. Or an asshole, as Veronica had called him as she closed the door and left nine months ago. He'd wait to leave. He'd be responsible for *something*.

Coming here had only served to reveal what he really wanted: a life back in his own country, a life back in his own language, which had surprised even him in the moment he realized it several weeks ago, after he'd taken his driver's test for the third time. It's too hard to live outside of everything you know, he decided after having finally learned enough Japanese to understand the examiner beside him and pass the test. Despite its flaws, he realized he really did love America. And to love something despite the things you dislike about it was nothing more than true love. He'd listened to Laurie and some of the others complain about America over the months they'd known each other here. Lots of people were upset, with good reason. The war, the president's surreal disconnection to his people, the way life itself had taken a curve into a bad dream seemingly overnight—it wasn't what anyone liked to associate themselves with. Ted felt it, too, but he couldn't get angry about any of it like he used to. Now, his impetus for leaving home having left him, he wanted to return. How Laurie never managed to tire of constantly being the foreigner, he didn't know.

"I think I'll sit this movie day out," he told Miyuki. She looked over her shoulder and frowned. Even when she frowned she was cute. He wasn't sure if he wanted her to leave or stay a little longer. He was supposed to enjoy being a young twenty-something and single—especially here, where being American seemed to be the only condition necessary to attract beautiful women—wasn't he?

"What's the matter?" Miyuki said, turning away from the rice cooker to face him full on.

I want to go home.

"Just a little sick, that's all," he said, then turned and went to the bedroom and lay on his futon thinking about the smell of his mother's house, a cinnamon and coffee scent, the way his father used to wake him up on Sundays by singing Johnny Cash songs in the bathroom as he shaved, the student union back in Madison where he'd hung out with a big circle of friends he actually liked; he thought of his cat, which he'd left with his parents when he moved to Japan, the feel of its gray fur against his face when things were at their worst. He lay lost in his thoughts for a long time, until he heard Miyuki let herself out a little while later, and when he could feel that she was actually gone—when he recognized her absence—he sat up, suddenly afraid. He tried to wait the feeling out, but after another minute passed it only grew stronger. His lungs hurt, and the room seemed to close in around him. He rubbed his chest and breathed deeply. *What's the matter with you? Calm down!* He counted only a few more beats before he couldn't bear it anymore, then got up to run out the door before he even knew what he was doing.

Outside his apartment complex, the air was crisp but the pavement was wet and dark from last night's rain. He looked up and down the sidewalk, scanning the faces of people out walking their dogs or out for a stroll of their own, until he spotted Miyuki's little skirt as she clicked away on the heels she'd danced in at the club last night. "Miyuki!" he called after her. She was too far away to hear, but an elderly man walking with what must have been his grandson turned to stare. "*Gomen,*" said Ted, and nodded. Sorry.

He took off then, chasing after her in his socks. Laurie was always getting drunk and talking about his old girlfriend Noriko, always drawing pictures of her, which were plastered all over his apartment like wallpaper. Ted worried now that someday he might understand something like that all too well, and ran harder.

At the end of the street, near Party-Party Karaoke, he caught up with Miyuki, put his hand on her shoulder, and she spun around with a shocked look on her face. "*Gomen,*" he said again, and though she looked confused at first, a moment passed and she gave him a hesitant smile.

"*Daijyobu*?" she asked. Are you all right?

"Maybe," said Ted. "Can we still go see that movie?"

Miyuki snorted, then looked away, covering her mouth with her hand. When she eventually took her hand away, she looked serious again. "Ted san," she said, "we can still go. But only if you really want to. I want to. Do you want to?"

"I want to," said Ted. He didn't know what else to say but that, and looked into her open eyes and nodded. He said it once more, "I want to," just to make sure they both knew what he was saying.

⑦

"I don't feel understood here. It's like no matter what I do, no matter how hard I try to fit in, it's not good enough. I speak Japanese pretty well, but inevitably I say something wrong or my pronunciation isn't as good as it should be by now and the kids laugh and adults cock their heads and act like I'm an alien who's beamed down right in front of them. Sometimes, when I'm driving home from a lesson, I want to keep on driving to Narita Airport and buy a ticket to America.

"Actually, I drove all the way there once. I stood in line at the counter and it wasn't until I got to the front and the woman behind the counter waved me forward that I realized what I was doing. I walked back to my car and drove home, and even then I felt like I'd failed at something. Failed to even get on a plane, to do something, anything, to leave this world behind."

"It's the same world, Hannah," said Nobuo.

"Same planet," said Hannah, "but not the same world."

He laughed. "You got me there," he said.

"Did you ever live overseas?"

He shook his head.

"How did your English get this way?"

"What way is that?"

"Natural. I've only met a few Japanese people around here who can speak that way. Usually they've lived in an English-speaking country. You speak very well."

"Thank you," he said, smiling and bowing his head a little, embarrassed. So there was a Japanese man in there after all. "Many of my acquaintances are native English speakers. Most of my Japanese friends speak English together, too. *Spoke,*" he corrected. He looked down again. This time it was not due to embarrassment.

"I'm sorry," said Hannah.

"No, no, don't be. Anyway, your difficulties here, I think maybe that is a common feeling for foreigners anywhere."

"I think so, too. I never realized how hard it is for foreigners in America to get used to things until I became a foreigner, too. And, really, how helpful is the average person? Probably not very. I remember friends complaining about foreigners who didn't speak perfect English. 'Learn the language!' they'd shout. So self-righteous. They have no clue how hard it is. They should be forced to go to a non-English-speaking country for a year and see how easy it is to learn the language. When I go home, I'll never let another lost-looking foreigner pass by without trying to help if I can. We gaijin have to stick together."

"Do you know what that word means, Hannah?"

"Foreigner, right?"

"Well, yes and no. There are two words people use for foreigners here. *Gaijin* and *gaikokujin*. A lot of foreigners don't like the word *gaijin* though."

"I hear it's not as polite," said Hannah.

"Actually, within Japanese culture, they mean the same thing. The kanji characters in *gaijin* mean 'outside' and 'person.' So to foreigners this sounds like *outsider*, and in your culture this would be offensive."

"True," said Hannah.

"But *gaikokujin*'s characters mean 'outside country person.' Or a person from a country outside of Japan. There is a word in English I like even better than that commonly used definition of the kanji characters. It is an old word, I think. 'Outlander'?"

"That *is* outdated," said Hannah. "Either of the longer definitions do seem more polite to me, but I don't know why."

"To a Japanese person, they mean the same. We shorten words because it's easier to say shorter words, don't you think? But in English I notice when people shorten words it's often to show annoyance or dislike. So when a Japanese person shortens *gaikokujin* to *gaijin*, maybe it sounds rude to you. For example, isn't there a word in English for us that's similar? 'Jap'?"

"Unfortunately, that's true," said Hannah. "It's not a nice word."

"Think about this now. A husband is trying to sleep and his wife has the television set on in the next room. It's very loud and he can't fall asleep, so he shouts, 'Either turn that thing off or turn it down!' and then the wife gets up and turns the volume down."

"What about it?" said Hannah.

"He didn't use the word 'television.' It becomes 'that thing,' which, wouldn't you agree, is more an irritated way of speaking?"

"I never thought of it that way," said Hannah.

"Because it's your first language. People don't usually understand how their own language works. If you ask a Japanese person to explain Japanese, most won't be able to do it. It's like asking the ocean why it makes waves."

"It's such a paradox," said Hannah. "To speak a language and not understand it."

"It is. That's the condition of living as well, though, don't you think? We live, but we don't truly understand how or why."

"You're extremely smart," said Hannah. "But I imagine you know that."

He grinned, but it melted into a frown almost immediately. "If I have any intelligence at all, I've wasted it for the past five or six years."

"I wish I'd met you earlier."

"Why?"

"Because maybe my time here wouldn't have been so lonely."

"You have foreign friends, though. You've mentioned them."

Hannah looked into his dark eyes, and somehow she felt seen. "I don't spend a lot of time with them, actually. Sometimes I feel loneliest when I'm with them, to be honest." It was her turn to look down now. "Sometimes I feel like they're more foreign than anyone else I know."

She waited, unaware at first that she was waiting for him

to say something consoling, waiting for him to lean over the space between them and place his hands in her lap, to find her palms and hold them gently in his own and sit like that, his dark, unseeing eyes staring into hers in silence.

But he did none of these things, and she found herself crying silently, wondering why she expected this from him, a near stranger. "Do you know what I mean?" she asked finally. But Nobuo looked away, toward the window.

"You want something from me, Hannah," he said quietly. "But I do not have it to give."

They sat in silence after that for a while, retreating from each other.

When his mother knocked on the door a half hour later, to hand Hannah an envelope full of money before showing her the way out, Hannah turned to look at him as she left his room. "Do you ever think you'll see again?" she asked. "I mean, do you *believe* you will?"

He shrugged, then nodded, then shrugged again. "Let us hope," he said.

She nodded curtly, like a serious schoolgirl, then turned and followed his tiny mother down the hall and down the stairs to the front entrance, where she changed out of her slippers and back into her shoes, and went out into the cool March evening with the tears she'd been holding back pricking at her eyes.

8

Laurie arrived in Mito, the capital of Ibaraki prefecture. The train was nearly empty during the afternoon, so there was no press and rush to get off, no hurrying through gates to make it to work on time or to an appointment. He had traveled an hour from Ami to visit the Ibaraki Immigration Office.' Mito was a mundane city, lacking the bustle of Tokyo and the mysteries of Japanese small towns and villages.

Laurie only ever visited Mito on official government business, and the thing he always liked best about the trip was the walk across the bridge to the business district, where the Immigration Office was located. Beneath the bridge, the river flowed cool and calm, and on the opposite bank, a cluster of downtown offices stretched along the riverside. He'd made this walk twice before, when, like today, he'd come to renew his work visa so he could continue living in Japan for another year.

As he walked across the marbled bridge, watching a group of ducks float on the slow-moving river, watching the Japanese men and women crossing the streets ahead of him and the mountainous mass of clouds soaring in the watercolor blue sky above him reflected on the surface of the black river below, he suddenly came to a halt, stopped by an odd feeling.

He was nostalgic. He was already missing everything that surrounded him. It would all disappear one day. He wouldn't always be here. It was the first time that thought had occurred to him, and it was then, too, he realized that he wouldn't go any further than he'd come at that moment, that he wouldn't continue walking across the bridge to the downtown or wandering along the river to the Immigration Office as he'd planned. He put his hands in his pockets instead, and turned back to the station, where he caught the next train back to Ami.

The ride back felt longer, and Laurie was so lost in his thoughts that he didn't notice the passing suburbs and villages and farmland as the train coursed through the countryside. It seemed that one moment everyone's lives are spread flat as a map on a table, and the next they've folded it up and put it away. The roads change, the places where construction had been are open. New landmarks appear. Maps become so useless so quickly. How did humanity manage to even make them in the first place? Maybe people have to feel as if they know where they are going, even if the destination is a mystery.

Or maybe it's because I'm American. The train pulled into Arakawaoki station, and Laurie walked down the steps in a daze to the parking lot, his head full of confusion and wonder and sadness. He had to admit it to himself that one day he would no longer live here, the place he had come to call home. *Maybe it's because I grew up being told there's no place better.* He realized now that they'd all come to Japan thinking it would be whatever they wanted, that they'd continue being who they were before they came, or if they did change, it would be a change they selected and welcomed, not a path unknown, stretching before them into darkness.

He pulled into the traffic and drove slowly, carefully back to his apartment, trying to hold all of his questions in his head so that he wouldn't forget what he was learning. Buddha had said to make a light of yourself, and if Laurie had anything to say about it, one day he would glow.

He was startled when his mobile rang, and worried for a moment that he'd flip it open to nothing but seabirds crying and the sound of the ocean. But when he had it in his hands, he saw that it was only Jules. *"Moshi moshi."*

"Hey, darlin', *moshi moshi* back at ya. I'm thinking tonight is going to be another karaoke night. But let's drive over to Shimotsuma instead. I'm hungry for Canadians. Hey, what's up? Why so quiet? Where are you?"

The head of the Great Buddha of Ushiku appeared over the crest of trees on the horizon at that moment, its face turned slightly away from Laurie, the remnant of a grin lingering on its chiseled cheeks. "Nothing's up," said Laurie, smiling even though no one but the Buddha was there to see. "I'm on my way home."

What They Don't Tell You

Spring in Japan is the true turn of the New Year. The cherry trees begin to bloom, casting everything in the shades of their pink-white blossoms, turning the world into a frothy, frosted confection. For two weeks the only thing anyone talks about is the coming of the *sakura*, the cherry blossoms. People gather in parks throughout the city and countryside, bringing blankets and baskets full of sushi and *onigiri*, rice flavored with pickled plums, and bottles of wine and sake.

For Hannah it's the time of year she feels most foreign. Even though the teachers at her middle school shower her with compliments, comparing her to the blossoms, as her name means "flower" in Japanese, she can't help but feel a tug deep inside, as if someone is pulling her away from the world she's lived in for the past three years. Where this tug comes from, who does the pulling, she has her suspicions. But she doesn't indulge in supernatural fantasies any more than she has to. And she does have to sometimes. After all, if she didn't believe in ghosts, she'd never have come to Japan.

Three years ago Hannah took the floral comparisons as compliments, but she's thirty now and has lived in Japan long enough to know it isn't just the bloom of the *sakura* that holds meaning here, but their fall as well. She's also come to know that meaning here is often communicated by what's not said, so she can't help but think that a second, secret message has been embedded in their comparisons between her and the blossoms whose brief lives represent the circumference of a life in this world. If she hadn't been an English major in college, she occasionally wonders, would she still be searching the world for symbols? For a secret, hidden meaning beneath the life she sees?

"Tell me, Hannah," Aoki sensei says. "In New York, is it spring now? Does New York have flowers like our *sakura*?"

Hannah nods. "Yes, of course New York has flowers, but not as beautiful as the *sakura*, I'm afraid."

Aoki sensei smiles, suspicions confirmed. Her black hair curves around her jaw like a scythe. Hannah thinks of Aoki as a best-girlfriend type, someone who dispenses advice along with a general banter about nothing important. At least this was the kind of best girlfriend Hannah had back home. She speaks to Aoki more than the other English teachers because Aoki's English is so natural Hannah sometimes forgets the language barrier and can pretend everything she says is completely understood.

"Your family," Aoki sensei says, flipping through student files, looking up to make well-trained eye contact. "Are they well?"

"As far as I know," says Hannah. "I spoke with my mother last night actually. She said to tell you *yoroshiku*."

"Oh, she is so nice," Aoki says, grinning sharply. "When will she come back to visit? I want to see her again."

"She won't be coming," Hannah says.

"But why?" Aoki looks shocked. "Didn't she like Japan?"

"She loved Japan. But she wants me to come home, so she won't visit anymore, hoping it'll make me come back sooner."

"Clever woman," Aoki sensei says. "But we will be unhappy when that day comes."

"So will I," says Hannah. Then quickly, silently, she revises Aoki's remark. *If* that day comes, thinks Hannah. She turns to her desk, lifting her teacup to her lips, and stares out the office windows at the white buds opening, at the blooms cupping sunlight in their petals.

It's been a year since Hannah has seen anyone she loves. Parents and friends have traveled to Japan, but after a second year, the novelty wore off for everyone. If Hannah wants to see someone from home now, she has to go to them. It's punishment of a sort, she thinks, for leaving to live in a different world. When everyone had been afraid to fly for months after September 11th, Hannah had booked a flight and flown across the world. She told only her mother and her best friend, Alice, the real reason why she was going. "To find him," she had said. Alice thought Hannah needed to see a doctor, but Hannah's mother said, "Life is easier when you're a martyr." This is something she used to say after she and Hannah's father divorced fifteen years ago. Hannah's mother is full of platitudes like this. Hannah sometimes thinks she understands why her mother and father divorced.

This was something her mother said, too, while they were speaking on the phone the other night:

"Won't you come home, darling?"

"I am home," Hannah told her.

"Come on, now. You know what I mean."

"I still have things to do here."

"You're still thinking about him then, you mean."

"Don't. Please."

"You have to come home sometime, dear. You're not going to find what you're looking for there."

"I don't want to talk about it."

"But sweetheart," said her mother, "the things you don't speak of are the loudest things you say."

There are six new teachers at the junior high this year. Hannah's first morning back after her two-week vacation will be spent meeting them. They'll ask how she likes Japan, how long she's been here, how long she plans to stay. They'll ask where she lives and whether she lives alone. When Hannah says she lives alone, almost everyone asks if she's scared. Hannah is used to this. In Japan, in the countryside at least, if you're not married, you usually live with your family, even if you're past thirty. They forget she has no family here. If they thought about that, they might not say anything to remind her.

Hannah is relieved to find that there is only one new English teacher this year. She'll have to teach alongside the new sensei, and it's always a bit of a hassle at first to learn how to teach with someone, to find out what they want from her.

He arrives midmorning, sliding the door to the teachers' office open, ducking his head in as if he's afraid to disturb someone's sleep. When the head teacher acknowledges him, he slips in, tall and lanky, twisting back as quickly as he entered to slide the door closed. After a moment he's ushered into the principal's office, where mysterious conversations are held with each new teacher as they arrive. A half hour later the door slides open and he's shown to his desk. Hannah doesn't know what they talk about behind those doors. Even though she was once a new teacher, she was never taken aside to have that chat.

While the teachers prepare for the new school year, Hannah cleans her desk, throwing away last year's unnecessary refuse, organizing materials she wants to keep. By the end of the month it'll be a mess again, but she likes to try. As she's leaning over the side of her desk to throw a worn-out deck of ABC cards away, a pair of long, thin legs appears beside her. She feels as if she's in a beauty salon, where the legs and waists of hairdressers meet your eyes.

"*Sumimasen,*" the new sensei says as Hannah follows his legs to his belt buckle and then up to his face. "I'm Koichi Yamamoto. Nice to meet you."

He does a little bow and his hair flops over his brows. Hannah stands to meet him. "*Hajimemashite. Yoroshiku onegai shimasu. Watashi wa* Hannah *desu,*" she says. She doesn't like to start relationships with Japanese people in English. She prefers they know she can understand them for the most part, that she's taken the time to care about their language, too.

"You speak Japanese!" Yamamoto sensei says, blinking in surprise. Most people are as shocked when they realize Hannah can speak the language. She nods and he smiles as if he's been given an early birthday present. He looks as if he's going to say something but hesitates. Hannah's seen this hesitation before. It happens when someone here wants to say something but feels it may be too personal or offensive. Hannah hates those pained looks as they scramble to find another conversation, so she's developed a method to deal with these moments. A method that works at least with English speakers.

"So," she says, switching back to English, "what's your favorite music?"

This is a question that she is unable to ask with a straight face. It's a construction taught to all first-year students, so she's always being asked what her favorite thing is in a variety of categories. Movies, books, food, places. At first Hannah thought this line of questioning was so prevalent because the students didn't know enough English to initiate other kinds of conversation, but as she learned more Japanese it became evident that both kids and adults still often asked her this sort of question in Japanese as well. She smirks then, and waits for Koichi Yamamoto to answer.

"I like British punk and American rock," he says without any sarcasm, and her smirk falters. She repeats his answer and Yamamoto sensei looks worried. "You don't like that kind of music?" he asks.

"No, no, I *do*," says Hannah. "I just expected you'd say jazz or J-pop. Orange Range, Crystal Kay, Utada Hikaru. The usual answers."

"Oh, I can't listen to Utada Hikaru," says Yamamoto. "I prefer music that's about something."

"When I first got here, I listened to Utada," says Hannah.

"Oh, that's terrible," says Yamamoto. "Why on earth would you do a thing like that?"

"She was the only singer who sang slowly enough for me to understand the words. I used to practice Japanese listening to her."

"Oh, you mustn't," says Yamamoto with great serious-ness. "I will introduce you to good Japanese music. Utada Hikaru—" he says, offering a shiver of his lean shoulders.

"Great," says Hannah. "I need something new to listen to. You can help me find my next CD."

"With pleasure," says Yamamoto. Then he leans in con-spiratorially and says, "I have to start being busy now, but it was great to meet you."

"*Kochira koso*," says Hannah, likewise, and Yamamoto sensei walks back to his desk on his long, reedlike legs like an elegant crane.

Hannah isn't often included in classes at the beginning of the year, so her day passes slowly. The Japanese teachers must set a standard of conduct with the students, and they do this better without including Hannah. Hannah wishes she could set a standard with the students as well, but since she's the foreign teacher she's never alone with the students anyway. A Japanese teacher must always be with her if she's teaching, as if she's a liability that must constantly be kept in check.

So she spends the morning at her desk, preparing lessons for later, and at lunch she grabs her chopstick case and goes to the second floor to sit at an island of desks that have been pushed together in an eighth-grade classroom. Every day Hannah eats with a different class. Usually when she ar-rives, the students are as startled as they were the first time she ate with them. Their eyes widen, they shift nervously, some smile, others fight over where she will sit. Some want her next to them, others want her far away to reduce the chances of having to speak English.

Today's lunch is with a class that's always excited to see her. The eighth graders are good students in general, happy to study and do their best. It makes time go by easier for their teachers and for themselves. In some ninth-grade classes, though, the students sit at their desks and stare angrily, or else put their heads down and go to sleep. They were the first group of students she met, when they were in the seventh grade. Back then they'd been cheerful and happy during class. Now they're only cheerful and happy in the hallways. She's not sure what changed them. Maybe puberty. She'd like to use that as an excuse for the spite that steams off their heads during class, but she's not sure it's really an explanation.

The students at her table take turns asking questions in a mix of English and Japanese. Since Hannah has become proficient in Japanese over the years, the children speak it when they don't know how to make themselves understood in English. Before she learned enough Japanese, she'd listen to them as patiently as possible, but had always felt helpless in the end. Now that she can communicate, she and the kids are more real to each other.

Mostly the students ask her the same questions over and over. Does she have a boyfriend? Will she get married? Which are cuter, Japanese or Americans? Which have bigger penises? Does she miss America? When will she go home? At first she'd been startled by the sex and penis questions, but when she told her coworkers about this they only laughed and said, "They're adolescents, they're curious."

Now Hannah does her best to break down the stereotypes the kids have received about Americans. She tells them the size of a penis doesn't depend on race, that both Japanese and Americans are cute, that people of every race are attractive, that she may or may not get married ("Why," she asks, "is it necessary for people to marry anyway?"), that she does not have a boyfriend, but that once she had been very much in love. When she talks about America, she says, "I miss it, but I don't know when I'll go back."

At the end of lunch, the children shout, "*Gochiso sama deshita!*" giving thanks for the food, and begin cleaning up the classroom, slopping leftovers into a bucket, pushing desks back into place. Two girls hold out their hands and smile as they ask for Hannah's tray. She thanks the teacher for having her. Then she slips out of the clatter of cleanup and returns to her desk.

The teachers' office is always empty for a while after lunch. Hannah enjoys being alone for this sliver of the day, when no one is speaking around her, when she can hear her voice—*my soul,* she thinks—surfacing from deep inside, speaking itself back into being, into the shape it held before she came here, before she began to reshape herself so that she couldn't recognize what she had once been.

It is a particular thing, a soul. What is it even made of? Is it smooth and solid, she wonders, like glass? Or is it soft, giving under pressure like flesh? Can we even touch it? Or would our hands pass through if we tried? Hannah tries to imagine her soul while sitting in the quiet of the teachers' office. Sometimes it is round like a ball, spinning in the center of her chest, and sometimes it is long and wormy with tendrils wavering around its perimeter like the many legs of a centipede. It's made of light, it's made of stone, it's made of blue air and a stroke of cloud, it's made of rose petals. It has a slip, a shine, it has a wandering eye. It never sees what she wants to look at. In this way Hannah always sees something other than what she's experiencing. It is both gift and curse. It's what brought her so far from everything she knew when she had to find a way to leave without faltering. It's what keeps her from knowing what bothers her most. She would like to—

"Are you okay?"

She gasps and jumps out of her seat, throwing her hands to her heart like her mother in moments of surprise or terror. "Oh, I'm sorry," says Yamamoto sensei, and she sighs heavily.

"You had me there for a moment," she says, and she moves her hand from her heart to rest on the desk in a gesture of composure.

"You were very far away," he says, blinking his long, girlish eyelashes. "Are you sure you're okay?"

"I'm fine," says Hannah. "And yes, I was just in outer space."

He smiles and nods at her metaphor, and at that moment she can see the origin of his love for her language surface on his face, how he obviously enjoys the playful poetry and silly comparisons that confound so many.

"Next time," he says, "don't forget to take a radio with you. That way, if you get lost, you can send a message back to earth. 'S.O.S. This is Hannah Foster. I need someone to help me find my way home.'"

He pretends to talk into a button on his shirt, as if he were a *Star Trek* character. Hannah laughs. His silliness is surprising, welcome. She feels lighter than usual. When her laughter finally subsides, Yamamoto sensei pushes his hair out of his face and smiles. "Must be going now. There's class. Talk later."

As the bell chimes, Hannah stands beside her desk and wonders how long it's been since she laughed without hesitation. Then, as the other teachers filter in, she wonders how he knew her last name. She doesn't remember telling him this morning.

❋

At five o'clock, Hannah leaves, stopping as usual to exchange her in-school slip-ons for her outdoor shoes, which she stores in a locker at the entrance of the building. She leaves before the other teachers every day. They don't enjoy a workday that ends when classes end, as Hannah's foreign status affords her. They're expected to stay until the principal leaves. Often he putters around doing nothing much until seven or eight at night. Hannah has heard stories from colleagues who have been kept at school until ten or eleven or, in rare cases, even midnight. It makes her feel guilty, this gap between what's expected of them and what's expected of her. She tries not to think about it, just as they try not to think about things that might trouble her.

The driveway of the school slopes down a steep hill into the heart of a ramshackle village where housewives on mopeds, wearing aprons and tiny white helmets, can be seen throughout the day, carrying shopping bags in the baskets of their motorbikes. Dogs roam unleashed. Butcher shops roll up their metal night grates and sell chops from behind a glass case on the side of the street. A river flows through the center of town, and when Hannah drives over the bridge she often sees old men, straw hats balanced on their heads, fishing on the riverbank. It's a remnant of old Japan nestled among the hills like a secret. On her way out of town, she drives through neatly cut rice fields. In the coming months, those fields will be flooded with summer rain. For now, though, it's the moment of the *sakura*, of roads limned with a pink aura that will continue to blossom over the next week until the air shimmers with a kind of magic.

She stops for groceries at a local market. Rice, *tonkatsu* and shredded cabbage, sesame dressing, beer. At home she makes dinner and sets a place at her tiny table. The kitchen and bathroom share the same space: sink on one side, shower on the other; hand basin in one corner, washer and dryer opposite. It used to confuse her, bathroom and kitchen melded into one room, but she's come to like this fusion of disparate elements. It makes sense to her now, this blurring of what used to be so easily categorized. *That's life,* thinks Hannah. *Normal is a setting on a washing machine.*

She's lifting a tuft of shredded cabbage to her mouth when she realizes she's broken one of the rules without thinking. *That's something he used to say,* she thinks. That's something he heard once, in college, and said from time to time afterwards. All at once her appetite disappears. She looks around, as if he must be here if she's said something of his. In the past she'd made a game out of it: how long could she go without thinking his name, without thinking of his body, the way it was hairless and smooth as her own. How long could she resist recalling their last evening together, drinking red wine at a bar in Manhattan, taking a taxi home, him kissing her neck in the back as if they were new lovers, him newly returned from Japan after being away for almost a year, slipping his hand between her thighs without any care of the driver glancing in the mirror.

But the room is quiet and he is not here. Again. She thinks of the fire, the floors collapsing, smoke and ash pouring over the city, the screams. She'd never heard him make a noise like a scream, not once, but when the towers fell she's sure his voice was there among the others.

"Daisuke," she says, allowing it to slip out like a badly kept secret.

He doesn't respond.

"Do you believe those things?"

"What things?"

"You know. The *kami*? That we're all spirit stuff, that the body dies but we'll still be around, our spirits? Do you believe even the rocks and trees have spirits?"

"Sure, I guess. But that's more Shinto. My family is Buddhist. Frankly, I don't really hold too much stock in any of it. Does it matter?"

"No. It doesn't. I'm just curious. Because I think I might believe something like that."

"But your family is Catholic, aren't they?"

"But your family is Buddhist, aren't they?"

That bright smile that broke like the sun on the harbor whenever he realized she'd won a round.

"When will you return?"

"I don't know. My parents sent me here to study. I've managed to do that for six years. After my degree is over, my internship at the bank will finish. Then there's nothing else that can keep me here."

She swallowed that bitter pill in silence.

"I don't mean you."

Better, better.

"I meant, after my graduate work is finished they'll expect me to return. And my visa is for schooling. That's all."

"I could go there, couldn't I?"

A nod. "But I don't think you'd like it."

"Why?"

"It's hard to live there if you're American. People will be polite, but even when you make friends, it won't be how you are with friends here."

"How's that?"

"It's hard to explain. They'll want to be friends with you, but our ideas of friendship are different."

"How?"

"I don't know how to tell you."

"You mean you *won't* tell me."

"That's not what I mean." Silence and snow drifting around his frustrated face. He stops and takes her hand, warms it with his breath. "I think you would miss America." Steam rolls from his mouth in a billow.

"I don't even really like America."

"That just means you'll miss it all the more."

"Con-cen-tra-tion, let's-get-rea-dy!"

Slap, clap.

"One, five."

Slap, clap.

"Five, ten."

Slap, clap.

"Ten, two."

Slap, clap.

"Two—"

"Out! Out, Hannah sensei!" the eighth graders shout. She has broken the rhythm and must suffer the consequences: removal from the circle for the rest of the game.

"Oh no!" Hannah hams, and the children laugh and mimic her "Oh no!" as if it is the funniest thing they've ever heard.

"Oh my God!" a boy cries out, slapping his hands to his cheeks, making his eyes go wide, and the laughter grows even louder.

Hannah moves out of the circle and the kids begin to chant again. It's a game she plays to help them get used to using numbers in English. Usually she stays in until the end so she can battle one of the kids for the championship, but her mind isn't on her job today, her thoughts go anywhere other than on what's in front of her, and instead of forcing herself back to what's at hand, she falls out. They'll continue on their own for the rest of the class, leaving her a blessed fifteen minutes of freedom.

It's her first day of the new school year working in the classroom, a week since the kids returned. The teachers have been racing through the building all week, bowing and excusing themselves each time it seems they're getting in someone's way. "We have much to do these first weeks," Aoki sensei explained over hot green tea that morning, and Hannah said she remembers from last year how hectic it was. The teachers often review things that were explained to Hannah three years ago. How to sign out a key to use a free classroom, where to put your coffee cup once you've finished with it, what time to come to class (even though the schedules change infrequently). Things to make the workday go smoother. The basics. But she already knows these things, and sometimes she has to remind Aoki and some of the others that she's been here at least as long as they have.

The bell chimes and she says goodbye to the eighth graders, who gather up their materials and head back to their classroom. Other than this particular English class, optional and centered around music, and P.E., most subjects are held in the children's homerooms. The teachers move from room to room, bringing their knowledge to the group instead of the kids going to a room that belongs to a teacher.

Through the maze of halls and students, Hannah finds her way back to the first floor, where Aoki sensei stops her outside the office. "Could you do me a favor?" Aoki asks. "It's James, the boy from the Philippines who moved here a few months ago. He's having trouble because he can't understand Japanese. He understands English, though. They teach many classes in English in his country. Could you tutor him a few days a week? You know enough Japanese to help."

"Of course," Hannah says.

"Mr. Yamamoto can help you at first," says Aoki. "James is already waiting in a free classroom on the second floor."

When Hannah arrives, Yamamoto sensei and James are talking about movies. James likes science fiction and movies about superheroes. *The Matrix* and *Spider-Man*. He's not sure if he likes Spider-Man better than Neo, though. Both are pretty cool. Yamamoto sensei is teaching him how to say what he likes in Japanese. Simple stuff. Hannah can remember when she was learning the basic grammar as well, only able to utter simple statements like "This is a pen. I like Japanese food, but I don't like octopus. I want to eat. I want to go, too." At the time, she rarely used what she was learning because it made her feel like an infant. Now she sometimes wishes she could go back to that darkness, that unknowing. The more she learns, the more she wants to forget.

When they realize she's in the room with them, Yamamoto sensei exclaims in surprise and quickly stands to pull a chair out for her next to him. "Please sit down!" Hannah thanks him and folds her skirt under her legs as she sits. "Now we can really get started," he says, and James beams a smile at Hannah.

They sit around the table, practicing numbers, basic vocabulary, introducing several new verbs to James. He's quick, which Hannah says will serve him well now more than ever. "If you can make friends with the kids," she advises, "you'll learn Japanese faster."

"They won't talk to me," James says. "I don't think they like me."

"They're just shy," says Yamamoto. "It's not that they don't like you. It's that they don't know how to speak to you."

"But they're learning English," James says, blinking back and forth from Yamamoto to Hannah. Hannah wants to hug him. He's right. They've been learning English since elementary school, but they're still not quick to use it. She can't blame the kids, though. Who else can they use English with except her? Then again, here's a perfect chance for them to speak it, to help James, and they don't. Who knows? She can't remember what kind of a person she was in junior high. Probably she wouldn't have gone out of her way either.

As they're wrapping up, sliding the door closed and locking it behind them, Yamamoto turns to Hannah and says, "Are you free this evening?"

"I am," says Hannah. "Why?"

"I'd like to come to your place and talk with you. We could go have dinner. If that's all right."

Hannah is shocked—none of her coworkers has ever been to her apartment before, nor have they asked to spend time with her outside of school hours beyond the faculty parties everyone goes to—but she manages to make a face devoid of perplexity. "Of course," she says. "What time should I expect you?"

"How about eight?" says Yamamoto.

"That'll be great," she says. Yamamoto smiles and turns to stride down the hall, his walk almost the same as the bounce of the happy schoolgirls.

***

The last time a Japanese person saw Hannah's apartment was several months after she arrived and needed help figuring out how to work a kerosene heater. It was winter and at the time she hadn't realized many Japanese homes didn't have central heating. She pulled out the kerosene heater that the previous tenant had left in the closet, but she couldn't read the kanji characters on the buttons. Her boss sent his secretary over. She had helped Hannah settle in the first few weeks after she arrived, but Hannah hadn't seen her since.

Kazuko pointed to buttons on the heater, explaining which turned it on, which off, which set the machine to turn on automatically each morning. "Like a coffeemaker," she said, offering Hannah a smile, and afterwards they walked through the apartment's tiny rooms together, Kazuko complimenting Hannah on her choice of picture frames, the color of her futon cover, the kitchen table she'd purchased. She thought Hannah's view of the cemetery in the wooded hills behind the complex was somehow romantic. "There's a temple back there, too," Hannah had said, and Kazuko had grinned as if they were sharing a secret. She'd been lovely. *We might even become friends,* Hannah thought after Kazuko left. But Kazuko never called, nor did she return to the apartment. It had only been a business call after all.

This was the first in a series of people Hannah met and hoped to become friends with, only to find that as often as she met new people, they just as frequently disappeared into the background of her life. After Kazuko, the teachers; after the teachers, the woman who taught her Japanese on weekends. In the case of Kazuko, Hannah thinks it was personal problems that kept her so distant. Last fall the woman had killed herself with a small group of strangers. They had driven a rented van into the countryside and taken pills, lighting charcoal burners at their feet before settling into a

long, dark sleep. Hannah never heard about this from the
teachers. It was the students who first told her the day after
the bodies were discovered, and then later her boss had
called all of his teachers from their respective schools in for
a morning meeting to let them know Kazuko would not be
returning. Hannah thought saying someone had "passed
away" was a kind enough euphemism. "Not returning"
seemed to be a phrase that approached the point of escaping talk of the subject completely. Her students, on the
other hand, did not restrain themselves so much. "Did you
hear?" several girls asked, wanting to also know if there was
suicide in America, and Hannah had said there was, but not
in this way. In America, people usually killed themselves
alone, she told them. They asked if doing it in groups wasn't
normal. "No," she said. "Not where I come from."

Not normal. Like Yamamoto sensei knocking on her
door at this moment, saying, "*Gomen kudasai,*" and when
she opens the door and says to come in, "*Ojama shimasu.*"
I'm sorry but I'm going to get in your way. He makes her
laugh, a British punk fan using formal Japanese sayings
when visiting someone. He's like her kitchen/bathroom,
Hannah thinks. A fusion of disparate elements.

She gives him the quick tour of her place: the bedroom,
the living room and balcony. Back in those woods is a local
temple and up on that hill is a cemetery. "And then here's
the kitchen," she says. Bringing him back to the starting
point, they sit at her table with cups of green tea.

Yamamoto compliments her apartment. "It's so neat and
clean. I'm surprised you have tatami mats in your bedroom.
I don't care for them myself." Hannah asks why and he says,
"Frankly, they tend to stink."

"Not if you keep them clean," Hannah says, laughing, and Yamamoto agrees that's true, which is also why he can't have tatami mats.

"I'm a bachelor. You can't expect me to be cleaning tatami mats, now can you?"

She is delighted by his easy humor and the way he makes eye contact without any apparent effort. In Japan it's more polite to avoid eye contact with people you don't know well, but Yamamoto sensei looks at her straight on. His eyes are almond shaped, and for once Hannah agrees with the Japanese when they say that their eyes are black. She's often thought they're brown, but in Yamamoto's case she can't help but think they're truly black, an absence of light.

"By the way," he says, "call me Koichi. I don't like all this 'Yamamoto sensei' business. It makes me feel old."

"All right then," Hannah says. "How old are you anyway?"

"How old do I look?"

"Oh no," she says. "I don't play that game."

"You aren't any fun," he says with a grin. "Twenty-eight. Do I look younger or older?"

"You look twenty-eight," Hannah says, laughing as his eyes go wide and his mouth drops open in mock horror.

"No one told me you're so mean!"

Hannah says perhaps it's because no one has had a conversation with her outside of the school building.

"You must be kidding," says Yamamoto.

"*Uso ja nai*," says Hannah. No lie.

"Well then," he says. "It's their loss, isn't it?"

They spend the evening talking, never leaving for dinner as he'd suggested. Hannah gets up at one point to make a quick meal of chicken and green beans cooked in Thai spices, and they continue to talk as she cooks and as they eat. At ten he says he should be leaving. They have school in the morning.

"It's been lovely," Hannah tells him at the door, and he bows his head slightly, his long locks falling over his brows.

"We'll do it again then?"

"*Mochiron*," says Hannah. Of course.

Then he waggles his fingers at her, playing the fool, and turns on his heels to go down her steps.

"Let me get this right. You go to the cemetery, all of you together, and bring home the dead person's soul?"

"Yes." He nods vigorously, happy that she understands.

"And the spirit stays with the family for a few days and then the family takes the spirit back to its grave."

"That's it!" he says brightly, taking her hand and swinging it as they walk through the Central Park zoo. On her right a polar bear stares at her, pawing at the exhibit glass, its white fur fanning in the water. It opens its maw and seems to roar silently before shooting up to the surface. She squeezes his hand as it ascends.

"I think it's interesting," she says, "bringing a spirit home. If I ever die, will you do that for me?"

"Well, you're only supposed to do it for family," he says.

"But will you do it for me?"

"Of course."

The sound of her alarm blares and the world returns to her. Gone again. She's beginning to get used to it all these years later. "I don't understand," her friend Alice had said when she'd told her three years ago of her plan to find him. "First off," said Alice, "before I address your irrational behavior, you only dated for a year. You weren't even engaged! He went to Japan without you for an entire year before coming back! For Christ's sake, Hannah!"

"He came back. That's what matters. He came back for me."

"I don't understand," said Alice. "I mean, Hannah, forget all that. It doesn't matter. He's dead, sweetie. Dead."

The crows caw as the sun rises behind Hannah's apartment complex, its light spreading inch by inch across the buttery wood of her living room floor. She slides her balcony window open and the crows grow louder. She has seen them dart from their perches in the nearby trees to chase small children, to steal shiny objects, just like she had heard crows would do in America, but had never seen before she met Japan's, which are larger, their beaks more hook shaped, the ruffs around their necks shaggier. They are frightening. More raven than crow really. She wonders if Edgar Allan Poe ever saw a raven as terrible as the crows that rule the streets here during spring and summer.

She stands on the balcony, looking out at the fields behind her apartment; and behind the fields, the cemetery; and behind the cemetery, the forest with the temple hidden inside it. The temple bell peals at six in the morning, prompt as always. The crows fall silent while the gong sends out its call. In several months, at the end of the summer, it will be Obon again, but she pushes that thought out of her head as quickly as it comes. *No more of that.* Exhaling heavily, she goes inside to shower.

✳

The morning rushes by. She visits classrooms, greets the students, plays games in which they practice English, until she hears the chimes break their chatter and looks up at the clock to find it is lunchtime. Tired, she fishes her chopstick case from her desk and ascends to the third floor for the next group of eighth graders with whom she will eat this week.

On the way up the stairs, she stares at her feet, too weary to even look up. When she reaches the third-floor landing, another pair of shoes, large and black, meet the tips of her slip-ons. She raises her head and, before she sees his face, she knows it's him by the lanky body sheathed in its suit. "Hey there," he says, so natural. No one here says, "Hey there," as if they'd been raised on a farm somewhere in the middle of America.

"Hey," she says. "What's up?"

"Not much. Where are you eating today?"

"*Ni nen, san kumi,*" she tells him. Second grade, third homeroom. Eighth graders it would be in America.

"Ah, they're very *genki* today," he warns her. "They'll probably talk your ears off." She laughs and he smiles, proud of himself for getting the idiom right.

Lunch begins and ends in nonstop chatter, as he warned her. But she makes it through the endless questions in Japanese and only misunderstands a few of them. It's like

going into battle sometimes. The kids lob questions at her
in Japanese, expecting her to keep up, and she answers them
back almost at natural speed. But once in a while they ask
something that, no matter how hard she tries, she can't understand. She hates when this happens; it always occurs
after she's been on a roll, the conversation building to a
crescendo, as if it's an opera, violins swelling, the boys and
girls growing more excited with each moment of conversation that passes. Then, boom, she hits a false note, says
something that makes no sense at all, or worse, can say
nothing, and their eyes fall to spare her embarrassment.

As she's returning to the office, she stops to listen to three
girls who sit squeezed together on a bench in their maroon
gym outfits, playing the piano. They laugh at Mr. Yoshida as
he passes by, and he shakes his head and smiles, saying,
"Crazy girls!" Hannah laughs with him. What is so funny
about this teacher passing by them? Why do they break into
sudden laughter for no apparent reason all the time? Hannah
wishes she knew the secret to the joy they manifest on a daily
basis.

In the office, Yamamoto sensei sits at his desk reading an
English magazine. She stops to harass him for a moment, to
say he's not allowed to read personal material at work. "No
big deal," he says, taking her sarcasm literally. "If the principal or vice principal asks what it is, I can say it's a magazine
about teaching English. They can't read English, after all."

"But they can tell guitars and drum sets aren't really
English oriented, can't they?"

"*A-no*," Yamamoto says, falling for the first time into a
Japanese reaction. *Umm.*

"Because really," says Hannah, "I don't think the pictures of the punk bands are going to fool them, even if they can't read the words on the page."

He closes his eyes and smiles, nods. Her stomach suddenly flips over inside her. She almost doubles over in pain, but now he's laughing and she's laughing, even though she's in a strange kind of agony for no reason she can think of. She sits down at the desk next to his and continues to laugh even though it hurts and she could really use a moment of silence, where it's just her and her voice and no one else, where the world becomes white space and she the center of that nothing.

It's how Daisuke always was, back when she'd make him laugh at his own foolishness. That smile. Those eyes wincing at his own embarrassment. Now the laughter begins to subside and Yamamoto sensei is talking but she still doesn't really hear him. She says, "Oh, too funny," and wipes her eyes. When did she start crying? Thankfully, they look like tears of laughter, she thinks, when really they didn't come from anything funny at all.

"How long will you allow him to make you cry?" her mother once asked on the phone, several months after she came to Japan and was having trouble adjusting, was having trouble meeting his family. They wouldn't see her, wouldn't acknowledge who she had been. They were country, very traditional, a little afraid of her.

"I have no control over something like this," she had said, and her mother had sighed and told her she had more control over that than she realized.

She gets up from her chair and excuses herself. "Thanks

for the laugh," she tells Yamamoto sensei, and as she's walking out the door he rises from his chair and tells her to wait.

"Are you busy tonight?" he asks. And after a moment of staring at him, not saying a word, she shakes her head. "Good then," he says. "Why don't we go out for dinner?"

She nods and slides the door shut behind her, stepping backwards, her eyes staring at the floor.

⁂

"When should I fly over and join you?"

"I'm not sure. Things are still a little uncertain here. I might want to come back to the States, actually."

"Here? Why? I thought your parents wanted you there."

"They do. But I don't want to be here any longer. I think I've been away too long."

"Almost a year. I miss you."

"Yes..."

She refused to ask if he felt the same way.

"But wait on the flying," he said. "There'll be time for that later."

"I could just come, find work, couldn't I?"

"It would be easier if you found work before you came. Work visas, all the paperwork has to be taken care of before you get here, outside of the country."

"Well, that's what I'll do then."

"By the time you arrange everything, I may be on my way back."

"Or you may not."

"*Uhn.* That's true."

She didn't say anything about his Japanese grunt of
agreement. She had only heard him use it before when he
was teaching her a little of his language, before he'd gone
back to Japan. "So I'll start looking," she said.

"Okay. But take your time. You don't want to find work
on the other side of the country, away from where I live.
That won't help us."

"I'll only take jobs near your town."

"That'll take a long time maybe."

"I have time. I have all the time in the world."

❋

Hannah looks out at the hills and fields that roll and
tuck, roll and tuck, behind her complex, finally coming to
arrange themselves as a grassy knoll where the cemetery
spreads out on their flattened piece of land. A narrow, foot-
worn path winds through the field into the cemetery, then
curves into the forest of bamboo. The path leads to a large
temple surrounded by a burnt-red wooden fence. She has
stood before it many times, has peered through the gates at
the garden and statues of gods in various poses. Every
morning someone at this temple welcomes the sun back
with a slow, steady beat against an unseen bell. She used to
walk these hills often, among the graves that look as if they
are shrines to minor gods, carved and etched with kanji,
surrounded by statues of Buddha or by unrecognizable
icons. This is where his family buried him. She had taken
her time, like she told him she would when he was still here
and hadn't come back to work in America yet. She had followed the plan they made together when they thought he

would be in Japan indefinitely, before he was hired by the bank he'd interned at in New York.

She doesn't go up there often now. She watches from her balcony. Each morning she glances over to see the spires of shrines and gravestones as she drives to work. Three and a half years. Three and a half years of watching. Waiting. No wonder everyone back home thinks she's mad. She's beginning to think she's mad herself, but not for the same reason as everyone else.

She turns from the cemetery and goes to her mirror. Koichi will be coming soon. They'll go to eat at a restaurant and for the entire time she'll feel guilty. This is what it feels like to cheat, she thinks, sliding lipstick over her lips. She clicks the cap back over the stick and rubs her lips together.

And it comes true a little, that prediction. When Koichi arrives he is charming as usual, joking about the other teachers as they drive to the restaurant, telling her stories from his days of studying in Canada and America, what it was like to live in her culture. She thinks of Daisuke as he narrates. She can't help but put Daisuke into the scenarios he's building; she can't help but see Daisuke living in a dorm with a bunch of American boys and girls, speaking his overly polite English, as it was when he first came to America. She sips her wine and gazes at Koichi as if she is truly listening. Once, after they've eaten, while they're drinking coffee, she thinks she sees Daisuke standing at the front counter, paying a bill. She lifts her head, looks over Koichi's shoulder. The man glances over and nods at her, smiling. That unforgettable smile, all teeth. Then he turns to leave.

"Excuse me," she says, standing up, cutting off Koichi

mid-story to cross the room. She evades collisions with servers, as if they are trying to keep her from him, until she steps out the front door and puts her hand on his shoulder as he's opening the door of his car. He turns around to face her, but it's no longer Daisuke. It's a man in a pin-striped suit that she doesn't know at all. He's older and his hair is salt and pepper and he doesn't smile like Daisuke did, but he asks if he can help her. "I'm sorry," she says. "I was mistaken."

Koichi meets her at the door. "Are you okay?" he asks. She can't look at him any longer, so she looks at the buckle of his belt instead.

"I'm feeling strange, actually."

"I'll take you home then," he says. He pays for their meals and they walk to his car.

On the way back she stares out the window at the passing strip malls and shopping plazas, the apartment houses crammed on top of one another, fighting for room. At the occasional family home with a blue- or red-tiled roof perched upon it like a farmer's hat, at the bicyclists and dog walkers blurring behind her. When they arrive at her apartment, she invites him up with her, and when they get inside she turns into his chest and puts her arms around him. A moment passes and she feels his arms go around her back and his mouth touches the top of her head.

She takes him into her bedroom and undresses him until his thin, hairless chest is bare and she can kiss his flesh down to his navel. "Are you sure about this?" he asks. She holds his belt buckle and nods. She doesn't look up. He turns off the overhead light. She takes his hand and pulls him down to her futon. She focuses on his skin beneath her.

In the dark, touching the smooth contours of his body, it's not him she's making love to. It's not him at all.

The next day she wakes alone. Koichi has left at some point in the night. Did they even say goodbye? She can't remember much but climbing on top of him, the almost shocked look on his face as she put him inside her. Then she had looked up at the ceiling and closed her eyes to let oblivion come inside her and do its work.

Her alarm goes off and she slaps at it angrily. Time to join the world again.

The drive to school seems to take longer than usual. The cherry trees have come into full bloom. *When did that happen?* The season seems to have snuck up on her. *What am I doing? How long have I been driving on the same road?* Her head is full of questions that should be easy to answer, but they rush her in a moment as if they recognize she's finally seen them. How long have they been waiting? She pulls off the road near a rice field, leans out the door, and they rush out of her.

At school the front gate is already closed. Damn them. She hates when they do this. Obviously she is late by a few minutes. She doesn't mention it in the office. Not even when Aoki sensei asks if everything's all right. "You look a little sick, Hannah," she says, but Hannah tells her it's nothing.

"Did you see those cherry trees?" she asks Aoki sensei, changing the subject.

"*Sugoku kirei jan,*" says Aoki. Aren't they incredibly beautiful?

Hannah doesn't see Koichi, and after two periods, she asks James during their tutorial if he's seen Yamamoto sensei either. "*Yasumi*," says James, smiling at Hannah with his new Japanese word. Absent.

"Oh," says Hannah. "I didn't realize."

She text messages Koichi from her cell phone later, asking if he's all right. A half hour passes before he replies:

nothing to worry about. thanks though. see you tomorrow.

Just that? She tells herself that, after last night's debacle, perhaps she should be grateful he replied at all.

Later, after she has eaten with the next eighth-grade class, after she has played Concentration and sung Carpenters songs and after she and forty Japanese kids have rowed Michael's boat ashore several times, she drives home. The drive is faster now, normal. She doesn't feel sick at all. In fact, she feels lighter. As if something inside her has either appeared or disappeared. She's not sure which.

As she pulls into her parking lot, she notices a Caucasian family either moving into or out of a house down the street. No. Moving out, definitely. They keep coming out with boxes, not taking them in. Who are they? Americans? Canadians? Russians? A boy and a girl load boxes into the truck. The boy looks at her and nods politely, as if he's Japanese. Then he turns to the girl, says something secretive, and they go back inside the house.

She sits down in her car again, holding her purse in her lap. She looks back at the cemetery in her rearview mirror, wondering why she hasn't seen this family before.

Oh yes, she thinks. *Now I remember.*

She's been looking in the wrong direction all this time. She's been looking at the graves in the hills instead.

She'd heard the crickets chirping that one summer evening, only a few months after she'd arrived in Japan. They rubbed their legs together and sang the moon up into the sky as she stepped along the path, climbing to the grassy knoll where the cemetery was lit with lanterns painted with the kanji of various family names on their paper panels. Some people were already up there, burning incense or cigarettes, praying, leaving bottles of tea and cans of beer as offerings. They sat desultorily among the graves and looked up at the moon or at each other, wearing dark suits and dresses, and called for the spirits of their loved ones to come home.

She'd found his easily. Shortly after arriving several months before, she had walked back to the cemetery and wandered among them until she saw his. There were many kanji on the stone, and she couldn't read most of them, but she saw the ones he'd taught her. What else did it say on the slab where his ashes lay? She wished he could tell her.

His parents and siblings were waiting there. She stood outside the stones that marked the boundary to their family tomb. His sister—it had to be his sister, she was so small and fine-boned like he always said—noticed her before his father and mother did. Hannah nodded and they nodded back before returning to what they'd been doing.

Minutes later they rose and took a lantern with them. She was crying as they came toward her, silently, the tears falling as she stood in the path before them. She couldn't move, so they had to go around. On her way past, his mother had looked up briefly, allowing her husband to go on, and met her eyes. The woman opened her mouth and, with a desperate voice, had said, "Please," before continuing on her way. Her daughter followed, bowing briefly, not meeting Hannah's eyes. Then she was alone and surrounded by glowing lanterns, casting the shadows of kanji upon the trees around her.

One word. One desperate word. It sank inside her like a fishhook. *Please.* Why did she say that? Please what? Why couldn't she have said something else? Why that? What did it even mean?

She found her way home and put herself to bed, but couldn't sleep. The memory of his voice was in her ear all night.

"Do you remember the way we met?" he had asked her. "When I was studying in the library alone and you were trying to get that book down from a high shelf? I heard books fall and then cursing and I got up and went around the corner and found you on the floor, surrounded by books, some half open with their pages fanning. I helped you pick them up and we had coffee together later and talked. And I called the number you gave me and we kept talking after that as well."

"I remember."

"Do you ever think about who we were before that moment? Me, a lonely student, studying law and economics as if that was the only thing my life could be? Thank you, by the way, for breaking me of that. You, a new grad student, sharing a room with someone you barely knew and hardly ever saw."

"Thank you, by the way, for rescuing me from that apartment."

He smiled. "We hadn't known each other before that moment, but even so we'd walked around the peripheries of each other's lives for a long time, I think. We'd probably even been in the library at the same time before, and hadn't known it. And then all of a sudden there we were in each other's arms several nights after that crash and the coffee I bought you. I like to think of you in my arms before that day as well, because that's how it feels when I think about my life before you. You're like a candle in a dark room, throwing light backwards and forwards. And like that, you're now a part of my whole life, past, present, and future. All of them, not just from one point on. Does that make sense?"

"It's very beautiful."

"But..."

"But I'm not sure if I know what you mean."

"Just remember to think about it from time to time. Maybe one day you'll understand what I'm saying."

She hadn't told him that she did know what he meant. Or what she thought he meant. If she had, it would have made her cry. All she could hear was him trying to make an excuse for his absence, for going back to Japan for nearly a year. He had not been present in her life before and someday in the future, even after he came back to her in America; after the towers, he was absent again. All she could hear was him telling her she should be content knowing he loved her and was always a part of her life, even in the future, even if he wasn't there.

But that isn't enough.

Now here it is, after nearly four years of waiting. A knock at the door in the middle of a night spent weeping, and finally knowing why she weeps. She sits up in bed and says with a confidence that later even she will not believe, "Come in." And then the paneled door slides open and he's there, looking down at her. After all this time. She stands and goes to him and stares up into his calm face. He says nothing, but slowly puts his hands in her hair and smells her, kisses her cheeks, her forehead, and finally her lips. She tries to speak but he puts his finger to her lips and shakes his head. She can hear him inside her body as if he lives in her own blood. *Dame da yo*! It's no good. It's useless.

He turns from her and walks out the door, and she watches him from her balcony as he goes up the path to the cemetery in the forest. Leaving her alone again. With more words that she is not allowed to say.

⁂

There are so many things not spoken. *I love you, I miss you, I want you back, don't make me beg.* Keep your problems to yourself. Keep your problems from yourself. Look at each other every day, walk among one another speaking only of the weather or the cherry blossoms. The blossoms that are fanning their petals like butterfly wings at this very moment, the blossoms that will fall in a day or two, littering the ground with their silky husks. Their bodies fallen. Speak of nothing but that.

They never told me if they found his body in the wreckage, she thinks. *They never told me if, during his first Obon, the lanterns they lit so he could see his path clearly had brought him to them.* Did he share a meal with them? Did they speak about the lives they led while he was away? Did he tell them about her? Certainly he did not tell these things to her when he made his way to her door and stood before her as he had in life—beautiful, radiant—only to kiss her cheeks and forehead and lips before turning to walk down the path to the cemetery.

What they don't tell you is what matters most. If only he would have said it, she could have given him up a long time ago, she thinks. If only they would have spoken to her, said one word other than that desperate "please," she might have put him down and walked away. Maybe.

Instead, she is out here on the balcony this morning, staring at the cherry blossoms as they ride the wind, spiraling like a spell on the air, swirling upward, then drifting back to earth to finish their beautiful, brief, heartbreaking lives. Home again, they fall.

Something is going to change.

She just knows this.

In Between Dreams

I'm polishing the coffee table in the living room when I hear the man moan behind the door again. I look up, my hand still gripping the cloth on the table, and stare at the sliding door. I've already spent an hour listening to him recount his memories and dreams this morning before I made myself leave his side to do what I have been hired for. That is, to clean this apartment and take the yen left on the coffee table after I am finished. I'm to leave the bedroom untouched, unlooked at even, and if I happen to hear something strange occur behind its door, I am not to pay it any mind. The yen on the table is a separate amount from what I'm paid by my agency. It's left behind to pay for my ignorance of the man in the next room, the foreigner who tells his memories and dreams like stories. If the owner of this apartment ever suspects I've done more than stand by the door and listen to the sleeping man's mutterings, I'm not sure what would happen. I think he would do more than fire me. That is, I think my life would be in danger.

I should never have taken this job.

Or rather, I should never have slid the door open and peered in on the man that first time, a month ago, as I do now, creeping in on tiptoe to watch him moan in what seems like pain even though he has no sign of fever when I touch the back of my hand to his forehead. His eyes are open (they sometimes are) but he's unable to see. They are so blue I think I could fall into them and drown. His lips are so soft. If I kissed him, I think purple bruises would bloom on them as my mouth left his.

"You're home again," he says. I snatch my hand away from his forehead. "Is that you? Please say something. You never speak to me anymore, except when it pleases you."

I understand most of what he's saying. These simple words and grammars are easy, high school English mostly, unlike when he gets lost in a memory, his words racing, and I can only make out how heartbroken he is, I can only hear the plea in his voice to be released. I don't say a word, though. After all, I don't know what he says when my employer is with him in the evenings. Never trust a sleep talker. If you reveal your secrets to them, they can be your undoing.

"I don't know what to do," he says, "how to live like this. I tell myself you still love me, that you'll come home one day and see the mistake you've made, that you'll wake me from this, that something will change. Something *has* changed. I felt it. I feel it even now. Some time ago—a week? a month? I can't keep track of time any longer—you put your arms around me and carried me through the house like a bride. I know that sounds ridiculous. A bride. It's not as if we can even marry. I never expected that really, but maybe I dreamed something like it a long time ago, at our beginning, before we came to be who we are. An approximation. We could have shared our lives as one. Did that ever occur to you? Did you ever want something more than what we are? You do know what I mean, don't you?"

I do understand a little, but after high school I stopped studying English and sometimes he uses words I've never heard before. It makes me angry. I should have gone to college. But how could I? It's not as though my parents could have paid my way. Still, I might have been more responsible and studied on my own. If I'd done that, I'd understand his English perfectly. And I can tell by what I do know of his words that he is a romantic. Someone who would understand my soul.

He lies on a futon, cradled in a heap of blankets, his cheek on the pillow, his lips fluttering as words flow from his mouth like the gurgle of a stream. If I understood all of them, I'd see myself in that clear water.

"Do you remember the day you introduced me to your parents? You weren't worried at all. And there I stood beside you, the blue-eyed devil, worried I wouldn't understand what your parents and brother and sister-in-law said, worried that I'd shame you. I was surprised you even wanted to introduce me to them. I know that what we are isn't talked about openly here. I know it's best kept a secret. And yet you didn't keep it a secret from anyone.

"Your father spent the night plying me with sake while he told me stories of your childhood. Whenever I understood what he said without your interpretation, he'd hold his hands over his head as if we were playing football and I'd just kicked a field goal. Afterwards he'd pour me more sake and settle into another story, telling me about how silly you were as a boy.

"Your brother and sister-in-law disappeared at some point in the evening with their newborn son. They were taking a bath in the bathroom together, getting ready for bed. You said it was custom for children to spend the night in their childhood home on New Year's Day. But we weren't going to do that, even though your father had asked you in private if we'd stay and have a bath together, too. He was a dear old man. An ex–railway worker, proud of his former career. How I miss him when I think of him now.

"It was New Year's Day, that day. We'd known each other for barely a week, and I somehow already knew I loved you. After I met your family, though, I loved you even more."

Love, love, love. Half the words he says are "love." He doesn't change, and I've been working in this apartment for over a month now, listening to him each time I come. I feel like I know him even though he's never seen me. It makes me want to tell him my story, for him to understand me as well. He makes me want to tell him about the day I went to the mountains and looked into that other stream. How I didn't know where I was going, or why I even went in the first place.

❖

I was eighteen and had been working at the 7-Eleven for two years at that time. I'd finished high school, though. My mother made sure I had at least that much education. She worked like death was always on our doorstep to keep us fed and with a good roof to sleep under, to pay for things my father needed. Always it seemed to be something to do with Father, his medicines, his visits to the doctors, his need to be cared for while I was at school and Mother at work. Always it did him no good. He sat in a wheelchair at the dining room window all day, no matter what treatment they gave him, staring at nothing, saying nothing, hearing nothing we said.

He'd been like that since I was ten. He was one of the unfortunate commuters who, on their way to work one morning over a decade ago now, were poisoned in the sarin gas attack by Aum cult members in the Tokyo subway. A woman watched as he exited his train on the platform where she waited, startled as he fell at her feet, his body flipping about like a fish pulled onto a riverbank. She was the one who called the ambulance to get help for my father.

At the hospital, his doctors told us he'd get better, but the only thing they did was help him breathe on his own again. Afterwards, whenever I knelt in front of his wheelchair and said, "Papa, it's Ai. Papa, please say something," he'd only look over my shoulder at something too far away for me to see.

One spring day after my shift at the 7-Eleven ended, I just decided to get on a train, and walked in a daze to the station. I rode into the countryside and walked through the fields and woods up into the mountains without any knowledge of what I was doing. It wasn't until I arrived at the stream that I returned to myself and knelt by the water and saw who I was again.

My head tilted to one side, I examined the dark curve of hair along my jawline. I was still in my boxy 7-Eleven smock, like it was my uniform for life, not just for work. Even in that uniform, though, I realized for the first time in my life that I was a little bit pretty. I hadn't understood before, but suddenly I knew why boys had always made lewd comments to me in high school, why old men hung around the store every day staring at me while they pretended to page through manga and magazines. One day a salaryman I often saw at the store brought condoms to the counter, and when I handed him his change, he quickly closed his hand around mine and whispered, "Could you help me make use of these?"

I pulled my hand away and shook my head, but I didn't say anything. I went to the back of the store and cried until my coworker found me and said to pull myself together, there are fates worse than working at 7-Eleven, after all. And though it was a bad moment, I knew what she said was true.

And now I saw the softness of my skin in the water, the fine bones in my face, the roundness of my eyes, the shine in my hair as sunlight fell on me. I tried to smile, but it didn't look right for some reason. It seemed more natural if I stared, showing no emotion. Perhaps I had grown so used to making that sort of face that a happy me seemed a complete stranger.

I smile down now, as I kneel beside the dreamer's futon. I try to smile like a lover might, or like a mother as she stands guard over her child.

"It was after meeting your family at New Year's that we decided I'd move from my little apartment in Ibaraki to your apartment in Nagoya. And for the first time in a long time, I was truly happy. I didn't think it was possible to be as happy as I was when I was with you.

"Before we met, I'd decided my life in Japan would be the life of an amnesiac. I'd cast away all of my memories and live as if I hadn't existed before I set foot in Japan. But after we met at that shop window during the winter holidays, after you took me home and we made love, after you warmed me with the glow of your childhood memories, I was able to see warmth in memories of my own past, too. And soon I wanted to share those with you.

"At first you listened when I tried to tell you why I'd come here, but when I spoke of my family, my old friends from college, you became suspicious. Why did I speak of my past so often, you must have wondered, when at our beginning I'd offered nothing but my body, a blank slate upon which you could imagine any past you wanted me to have?

"The truth was, the truth *is,* I wanted you to be able to love me the way I'd come to love you. I wanted you to know who I was and still want me. But I could see you thinking if you acknowledged my past in America, a future without you might still exist for me there."

It was in that moment of staring into the stream, realizing my own beauty, that something even more amazing happened. As I lingered over my features, touching my cheekbones and the curves of my lips as if this were the first time I'd seen anything like them, another woman's face suddenly appeared in the water beside mine. She blinked her long lashes, then smiled, calm and sure of something. Startled, I pushed away from her and landed on my backside. When I opened my eyes, I found her hovering over me, no longer in the water, smiling the most beautiful smile I'd ever seen.

"Sorry!" she said. "Please forgive me. It wasn't my intention to frighten you."

She wore an old blue silk kimono with a pattern of cherry blossoms swirling around white moons, and inside each moon was the rabbit who lives there and watches everything that happens here on earth. He had an evil-looking eye, so I looked up at the woman's face again. She looked familiar, but I didn't know why.

"Be calm," she said, and I was.

She said I was a lucky girl, but I asked, "How am I lucky? I don't have any luck at all."

"That's better," she said. "At least that question is intelligent. Now maybe I can begin to like you a little."

"I don't understand what you're saying. Won't you stop speaking so oddly?"

"It isn't me who's odd," she said. "You're the one. Oh, now don't make such a face. It's not as if we're old friends and I've insulted you. And anyway, it's not just you. It's others, too. Everyone. You see, that's what's so odd, how everyone thinks they're normal and the truth is no one in the world is normal at all. Isn't that wonderful?"

At this she walked away, her kimono dragging along the mossy earth behind her. When she stopped and looked back a moment later, she said, "Ask me a question, one question, and I'll tell you the truth. I have that power."

"What power?"

"To tell the truth."

"Don't we all?"

"Oh, no," she said. "That's not so. I'm sad to say it, but if people all told the truth, the world would be a different place from the one we know."

"But I don't know what to ask."

"Of course you do. Just open your mouth. You can do it if you try."

So I did as she said and opened my mouth. And from my open mouth a question slipped out, quiet as the cherry blossoms that fall in swirls at that time of year.

"Who am I?"

She smiled wider, apparently pleased.

"That question is easier than it seems. But it's difficult to know the answer before everything is over. So I think you may become wise one day if you had the sense to ask it." She kneeled to pluck a cherry blossom from the forest floor, then slipped it by its tiny stem behind my ear. Leaning in closer, her lips brushing my ear, she said, "I must speak low or someone else might hear the truth. And if that happens, it will do you no good. This is the truth, little Ai, *your* truth, so listen well. We wear our masks in between dreams. It's one of the rules of living here. You can't not wear a mask in those spaces of time. But if you want, you can change the one you've been given. All you have to do is be strong and make it so."

Be strong, I want to tell the dreaming man now. *If you are strong enough, you will wake up and walk away from this place forever.*

"I wouldn't have thought you capable of this," he says the following week when I come in to kneel beside him. "How long do you plan on keeping me like this? I must be like a plant to you by now. A pet. Maybe if I stop talking, you'd get tired of me more quickly. But no. It was talking that got me into this, so it must be talking that will get me out. I'll keep my faith in words, even though you used mine to betray me."

The man moans a little and I lift his blanket. I think he may have urinated in his sleep. This has happened before. I poke my head under the blanket and sniff. Yes, he's definitely wet himself. I roll the blanket back so I can pull off his pajamas. "I'm sorry," he says. I want to tell him no, it's nothing, that this isn't his fault. But I can't speak. I must work around him if I am not to be discovered by the man who owns him.

I take the pajamas and put them in the washer. I'll dry them and put them back on him before I leave. "Aren't you sick of taking care of me like this?" he says when I return. I kneel beside him and wipe his penis and thighs with a warm washcloth. I lift his penis so I can clean under it as well. It begins to grow in my hand, slowly at first, then faster. With each pulse it's suddenly a little bit bigger. I feel something stir inside me and am overcome with a mix of desire and shame. I let it go after I finish cleaning him, but it stands up on its own for a while before beginning the slow melt down again.

I sweep the front room and do the dishes. I dust the corners and take out the trash. I wipe down all of the kitchen surfaces. And when his pajamas are dry, I struggle to pull them over his legs and up to his waist. When I'm done I look down at him in his nest of blankets, his lashes soft on his cheek. I wonder how the man I work for could allow such beauty to be shuttered behind closed doors in a dark room, away from the eyes of the world.

"Goodbye, my love," he says as I slide the door to his room closed.

I take the yen spread out on the coffee table, count the bills, then leave, locking the door behind me.

"All you have to do is clean the living room, kitchen, and bathroom. You needn't worry about the bedroom. That room I can take care of myself. It is strictly off-limits. If you cannot accept this proposal, I will ask your agency to send someone else. What do you think? Can you do this?"

I said that I could, but wanted to know if I was in any danger.

"None whatsoever. Simply leave the door to that room closed and never open it, even if you hear something occurring behind it. Even if you hear someone call out."

I shivered, but managed to say, "And how will I be compensated for pretending that door does not exist?" I was being strong like the woman at the stream told me to be. I was making my life happen as I wanted it. No one would ask me to help them use their pack of condoms again, unless I wanted to be asked.

"I will leave some money here on this coffee table for you. This will be above and beyond what you are paid by your agency, and I do not expect you to report it to them. Will that be satisfactory?"

"Yes, that's fine. And we will never speak of this again?"

"You have gotten ahead of me. I'm sorry. What was your name?"

"Miyamoto," I said. "Ai."

"Well, Miyamoto san, you are correct, we will never speak of this again."

It was so easy at first! Why should I care what happened beyond that door? The woman at the stream said to be strong, that I could make a mask of my own liking rather than wear the one I'd been given. That's what I was doing when I came to work for the man who kept the dreamer locked away in his room. I was shaping my future. My future came in the form of yen he left on the coffee table. Each time I took it I told myself one day I wouldn't have to live a life controlled by anyone but me. I'd be strong. That's what the woman had been trying to tell me.

After the woman at the stream told me to forge my own mask to wear in between dreams, she said she had one more thing to give me. She asked me to let her kiss my eyes so I could see my future. So I closed my eyes and felt her hands take hold of my head. Her lips touched each of my eyelids and a spark came to life afterwards, blue-white fire dancing before me.

I saw then. I saw things clearly. I saw my father sitting in his wheelchair, staring out the dining room window. I saw my mother working in the bento factory, her back hunched, slopping curry into the slot of the bento plates as they passed by on the conveyer belt. I saw the dark rings of sleeplessness under her eyes. I saw myself in the 7-Eleven with a salaryman's hand clutching mine, and held my breath, afraid.

"Walk your own way, or be lost to the way someone else has given you," the woman told me. And I opened my eyes to find I'd spent the night sleeping by the stream in the mountains. It was morning. Birds sang in the trees. And the woman was gone.

I walked back down the mountain into the woods and fields and onto a road, and followed it until I found a train station, where I took the train back to Tokyo and made my way to the 7-Eleven. I took off my smock and handed it over the counter to my manager, who stood there with wide eyes. "This is no longer mine," I told him. Then I walked out the door into the bright streets of Tokyo, thinking about the mask I wanted to wear.

It wasn't easy, making that decision. There are so many masks to choose from, and after a while I began to think, which one will do? I could be the *bosozoku* girl, riding a motorcycle, causing trouble with her tribe of wind riders. But that kind of girl is like a piece of broken glass. She can cut if you touch her, but she can also be shattered if you approach without her knowing. I could not be someone with a weakness now. I could be one of those girls who wear Renaissance clothes, I thought, layers of leather and lace, a Gothic Lolita or a Saintly Mary, spending my hours walking the bridge near Harajuku station. But really, those girls, they are too sweet, like peppermints. Not strong at all, I thought.

It's when I passed by a shop window in Shibuya that I saw her. The woman I would become. She was a *kokujin*, her skin the color of chocolate, her hair dyed blonde and dredded so that it piled up on her head like a bush. She danced wildly, wearing camouflage pants and steel-toed boots with a white vest over her black sports bra. She was rapping. Waving her hands, shouting. She was so fierce, so beautiful, all at once I knew this is what I would be, what I was inside already maybe. A *kokujin*. A black woman.

Of course now I wonder, Ai, what were you thinking? How stupid could you be? But at the time it was the best I could think of. When I saw black American women, I saw how strong they were and how, if I were black, too, I could be strong as well. I could learn from them.

So I bought the clothes, the music, the makeup. I dyed my hair blonde, painted my lips red, fitted my arms with bracelets, slipped rings onto each of my fingers. I wore a gold necklace with a charm of fake diamonds that spelled out my name. *Ai.* I took a job in a hip-hop fashion store in Shinjuku and watched the black women in the videos playing on the store televisions, studying them, looking for new ways to be strong.

I bought a temporary tattoo set and drew the word LOVE on my arm in print block letters (I didn't trust myself to write in cursive, I never did get good at that). I surrounded the word with thorny vines so that it looked as if Love, as if Ai, as if I, was the sleeping beauty at the center of the thorn-covered kingdom in fairy tales, who no one but the boldest of knights could ever reach.

I went to hip-hop clubs. I danced with who I wanted. I grew bold. I took men and fucked them. I was the one who did it to them. I didn't let them fuck me. I made them lie down below me and do as I said. I began to drink ridiculous amounts of whiskey. Once I even stopped a man on the street, opened my purse to show him the condoms I kept in there, and said, "Would you help me make use of these?" He held up his hands to wave me off and said, "Excuse me," assuming I would ask him for money, but I said, "Look, I'll be the one to pay." He narrowed his eyes at first, then grinned.

I took him to a love hotel and pulled the salaryman suit off him like the clown costume it is, then fucked him hard until he complained. "It hurts," he said. "Won't you slow down, go nice and easy?"

"No," I said. "I'm paying for you. Now lay back and do as I say."

I'm not sure where this Ai came from. Suddenly in a matter of months the mask I had placed on my face had become more than I'd intended. I hadn't realized that could happen. But all the strength I thought I'd acquired was just another illusion.

One night I went dancing with a man I met in Shinjuku station, some late-twenties jobless guy with a nice smile and a decent sense of fashion. We went to a love hotel and had sex in a room that looked like the bottom of the sea. I liked the looks of him and decided to let him be on top at first, so I could look up at the digital fish swimming across the ceiling.

What an old room that must have been! These days love hotel rooms aren't so tacky. But this room was the old style, tricked out with the gimmicks of love hotels from the eighties and nineties, the flash of spectacle that makes not only sex but love an absurd thing. That's when I realized I'd somehow taken someone else's path on the way to finding mine.

After he came, I grabbed us some beers from the fridge

and tried to make light of the evening. I wanted to make this man into a person now, not just someone I had used to feel strong. I thought I could salvage something now that I'd woken from that terrible dream. But he wasn't interested in making or saving anything that might have been between us. He was all surface, written on by those who'd passed him, like a love hotel diary.

Love hotel diaries are interesting things, filled with the memories of the visitors who came looking for something. Who they are, who they came with, why they came. Sometimes they're silly, sometimes they're sweet, sometimes they're crude, and sometimes they're sadder than a hundred nights spent weeping. But usually nothing out of the ordinary will be found inside them. While I sipped my beer and paged through this room's diary, though, I came upon an entry that stopped me cold.

A man who had come by himself had written the entry. He didn't live with anyone; he had no children, no lovers, not even a friend. He had no reason to come to a love hotel at all. He wrote that he came to that room to think about the lovers who had been there before him, that he imagined himself being one of them, imagined himself having someone to hold. Being in that room helped him imagine what it is like to be loved. He wrote that he stays for an hour, sometimes two, that once he spent the night when he was terribly lonely. He said to whoever reads this diary that he was grateful for the love they shared without knowing.

I couldn't help myself. I cried before I even realized I was doing it. The man I was with asked what was wrong, but I could tell I was making him nervous. I tried to explain but he didn't understand, and then suddenly he got up and was leaving. My heart pounded. *No. Don't leave like this, don't leave me alone.* I stood up and tried to stop him. We had a stupid argument about the name written on the back of his jacket. I couldn't read it well because it was written in cursive, but when he told me what it said I was shocked back to my senses. Who had I slept with? Someone who admired Hitler? I'd seen *Schindler's List.* I knew what that man did.

So I let him pay the room fee and he left, leaving me to gather myself back together in that room alone. I was still crying in the entrance of the love hotel as I looked up and down the neon-lit street ten minutes later, my breath puffing clouds in the cold air. I didn't cry because he left me. I cried because I had abandoned myself months ago, and it was only then I realized what I'd done.

In the morning, I told my mother I was going to leave the hip-hop fashion store where I worked so I could take a job at a cleaning company. "You'll never find a husband that way, Ai," was all that she said.

I looked at my father sitting in his wheelchair by the dining room window and wondered what he would have said, had he been able to say anything. I couldn't imagine. It had been too many years since he'd spoken. I didn't know who he was anymore. I wasn't sure if he was even thinking anything at all inside the silence that surrounded him like a tomb.

That afternoon I went to three cleaning companies and was offered a job after a quick interview at the third one.

Someone had quit that morning and they were in a pinch. "When can you start?" the manager asked me.

"I can start now if you like," I told her.

Two hours later I found myself bargaining with the dreaming man's keeper. How much would it take to keep my mouth closed?

Let's just say the pay for cleaning is much better than selling hip-hop clothes. But the guilt is much, much heavier.

✦

"I want you to let me go," he tells me the following week. "Can you do that? Please. If you ever loved me even a little, you'll release me from this—whatever it is—this spell you've put on me."

Witch, I think. The man who keeps the dreamer deals in some kind of magic. That isn't good. If that's so, he could watch me from wherever he is. He could send a spider to spy on me, a cockroach or a mouse. He could watch me from the other side of the mirror that stands in the corner of this room. A long time ago, I didn't believe in such things. I thought I knew better. But I've seen enough un-likely things in my life to know it's those who don't believe who are truly foolish.

It's an early morning in late summer. The sun is lost be-hind the spires of Tokyo, and beyond them it is lost behind the smog and clouds. An hour ago I was waiting across the street in the shadows of a store entrance, watching, waiting to see the witch leave his building. I decided to start a few hours earlier than usual today. Something has had hold of me for the past few days, and I've spent night after night sleepless, tossing and turning in my futon. A grip of ice is on my throat, choking me. It's how I felt the night I realized I'd been wearing someone else's mask. It's this money I'm taking to keep silent. No good can ever come of such a thing. I don't know why I thought I could justify it with the idea that I was being strong again. Perhaps the greatest weakness in our lives is our desire for control. Real strength is not control. It's knowing when to let go.

I leave the dreaming man and go through the witch's files. I turn on his computer and search through everything in there as well. I go through his address book, bills and letters. He's only been in Tokyo a few months, nearly the same time I've been cleaning his apartment. He moved from Nagoya, a transfer order from his company. But how did he bring the man dreaming in the next room without being discovered? Or did he cast the spell that traps the man here, after coming to Tokyo? I don't know anything, I don't know how to do what I have to do. I don't know if I should even be doing it. *Be wise,* I tell myself. *Come on, Ai, what would someone wise do?*

I could call the police, but I'm only a cleaning girl. Why should I be believed? What if there's an excuse the witch can offer? "This is my sister's American husband. They were in a car accident. She died. He has no other family. I am taking care of him." The police would probably accept it. They're known for swallowing lies like eels to avoid any confrontation that might damage someone's reputation. *Be wise, Ai,* I tell myself again. And that's when I know what it will take for me to really be strong.

I get up and slide the bedroom door open, kick off my slippers, and step over to the futon to kneel at the dreamer's side. He turns his head toward me and his eyes flash open, as they occasionally do. I've grown used to this now. The first time he did it, I scrambled back on my hands and feet like a crab, but after I realized he could see nothing out of those eyes, I calmed down.

"You're still here?" he says. "I thought you'd left again. Won't you touch me?" he says. So I touch his forehead and take his hand in mine. "Won't you kiss me?" he says. So I lean down and kiss him softly on his forehead and both cheeks. "Won't you speak to me, my love?" he says. So I open my mouth, remembering the words of the woman by the stream. You can tell the truth if you just open up your mouth and say it.

"I'm here," I say in my bad English. It's been too long since I spoke it, and I was never very good at it anyway. "But I'm not the man who keeps you. I'm Ai. I'm going to help you. I'm going to take you out of here."

His brows furrow and his face looks worried for a moment. "Ai," he says. "That means love, doesn't it?"

I nod. And suddenly tears roll out of my eyes unbidden. That's it, so easy. He's recognized who I am, who I was all along.

I lean down once more and kiss his lips as I've been aching to do since I first saw him. When I pull away, he is looking at me with those blue eyes and seeing me for the first time, only it feels like I'm the one who's seeing the world again. I've spent months watching him sleep, listening to his dreams without him knowing I was there with him. But now he sees me. Now he raises a hand to his face to feel his cheeks, the stubble on his chin, checking to make sure he's still alive.

"That's right," I tell him. "My name is love. And I'm going to save you."

As I struggle to help him stand I tell myself, *I'm going to save us both.*

Where I Come From

When they brought his mother to the hospital, Danny was sitting up in bed, his face turned toward the window, watching the Tokyo skyline. So it was his mother's voice he heard before he actually saw her. "Oh my God, there you are. Oh, Danny, I'm here. I made it."

When he turned she was already hurrying across the room, arms held out, purse dangling from her elbow, her eyes filling with tears. He couldn't help but raise his brows and smile. As far back as he could remember, his mother had been melodramatic. He was certain that she must have once dreamed of becoming an actress. "What?" she said to him now, though, and stopped with her arms halfway around his shoulders, her face just inches from his own. "What kind of face is that?! Can't a mother hug her own son?"

He hugged her back, smelling home for the first time in two years. The past six months he'd spent dreaming, and now that he was awake again his senses felt sharper, more pointed, than he could ever remember them being. The first few days of his stay at the hospital had been full of tests as the doctors tried to understand what had happened to him, but they'd all returned positive that nothing was wrong.

When he smelled his mother, though, everything he'd forgotten came back in a rush. His father and brother and sister, their little farm in New Castle, Pennsylvania, where he'd
grown up feeding cows, baling hay, and tilling his mother's
garden. A year ago she'd sent him pictures with a note that
said, "You probably remember this garden being nothing
but carrots, potatoes, and cabbage, but now look. Isn't it a
beauty?" The photos showed the garden behind his parents'
house full of sunflowers, their yellow-brown heads raised
toward the summer sky. Danny thought he could smell
them, even though they'd grown well after he'd left home.
What else, he wondered, had changed while he'd been
dreaming?

When he looked down at himself or in a mirror, it
seemed nothing had changed about him personally. Kenji
had thought to move him a little every evening, so he was
still mostly limber and healthy. But Danny didn't bother
telling his doctors or the police his story, how it had happened, how the cleaning girl had found him unconscious.
He pretended to not remember anything. If he told the
truth, they'd just say he was talking nonsense anyway. That
he'd been listening to stories old women from the countryside must have told him, and perhaps he belonged in the
psych ward instead. He imagined the faces of the doctors
and police who had tended to him since Ai brought him in
a week ago. They surrounded him, laughing. He imagined
them going home to tell their wives and husbands or roommates about the American boy in their care, the boy who
thought he'd been trapped in his dreams by a Japanese
curse.

So Danny played dumb. He didn't need to tell them about Kenji, how it had been Kenji who lulled him into another world. Sometimes he wondered if it wasn't his own fault anyway. Did Kenji do it, or had Danny let it be done? But when the police began to question him, and then the woman from the embassy who said his parents had contacted them months ago trying to find him, he decided he wouldn't hold Kenji responsible. He would do what Kenji hadn't. He would let Kenji go. He blinked now, and shook his head a little, trying to focus on what was in front of him.

And now this: "The doctors say they can release you and there's a woman in the hall translating for me, so everything will be okay, but let's be quick. Get your clothes on and let's get out of here. The American embassy says we can get a flight home whenever we want. Oh, honey, I didn't think they'd ever find you. I thought I'd lost you," she said, and clasped him tighter, which made him laugh again. "What are you laughing about?" she said, shaking him a little, then holding him at arm's length so she could examine him. "Well, come on then," she said. "Where are your clothes?"

"Slow down," Danny said. "You just got here. We don't have to leave this instant. We don't even have to leave today if we don't want to."

"Well, of course not!" said his mother.

"Tell me something," said Danny.

"What?" his mother said, suspicion shadowing her face.

"Is there still a war out there?"

"You mean in Iraq?"

"Well, anywhere."

"I don't pay much attention to those things, Danny, you

know that. But yes. There's still a war over there. Doesn't look like it's going to be finished anytime soon either."

He turned back to face the window. It had almost been a fairy tale, his life here spent asleep and dreaming. But he wasn't Sleeping Beauty, and his kingdom hadn't frozen in time while he slept. It had kept on going. It had kept tumbling and tumbling.

"Of course we don't have to hurry," his mother said now. "I'm just saying. Hospitals. You never liked them. I'm just trying to help, that's all."

"Just your being here is enough, Mom," he said, turning back to her with half a smile. She smiled then, too, and caught him in another fierce hug.

When they pulled away she said, "Your clothes," and went searching through the room's closets and cabinets with swift determination.

On the street an hour later, wearing the jeans and T-shirt he'd come in with, Danny breathed in the late summer Tokyo air. It smelled of ozone and gasoline and something vaguely floral. The street was crowded with cars in the early evening, the sidewalks with bikes and pedestrians, and his mother began to complain. "All these cars, all these people. How on earth does anyone here ever get to where they're going?"

"Just follow me and I'll show you," Danny said. "What's the name of our hotel?"

"Where did I put that card?" she said, and began to rustle through her purse. "There it is," she exclaimed, and her hand reappeared with a business card a second later. She looked at it a moment before making a face. "It's all in Japanese!" she said. "What? They think I step off a plane and can suddenly understand the language?"

Danny took the card, turned it over, and showed her the back, where the information was written in English. She pouted, swatting at his arm like a schoolgirl, and told him to keep his remarks to himself and to keep moving. She wanted to get a good night's sleep before flying home tomorrow. They should probably get dinner, she added. Room service at the hotel would be fine. Danny stopped walking. "Tomorrow?" he said.

"Why, of course tomorrow," said his mother. "What? Do you have something left to do here? Did you give your statement to the police about that man? The woman at the embassy told me—"

"I gave my statement," Danny said. "But why are you in such a hurry? You're in Tokyo! Don't you want to see where I've been the past two years?"

"All I know," said his mother, "is that you came to Japan and that man—"

"Kenji," said Danny. "And as I told the police, he's innocent. As far as I know, I was fine the night before the cleaning girl found me. Kenji must have gone to work in the morning without realizing something was wrong. I'm not sure they believed me, but they have to."

"Do *I* have to?" she said.

"What do you mean?"

"We couldn't find you, Danny. No one at your old job

knew where you went. He did something to you. He...
changed you, didn't he?"

"Not like you mean," said Danny. "No, I think maybe I
wanted things that way."

"Wanted things what way?" she said, frowning in confusion. "Wanted us to believe you were *dead*?" She turned
away, making sure her purse was secure in the crook of her
elbow, and started to march away. In her purple and white
floral print blouse and matching lilac pants, she looked like
she was on her way to church for Easter services.

A memory surged to the surface, bobbing for a moment
before sinking back under. "Mom! Wait!" Danny shouted.
"You don't know where you're going!"

He jogged to where she was waiting with her back to
him. She wouldn't look at him, only stared straight ahead
like a soldier preparing to go into battle. "First of all," she
said, "there will be no more treating your mother as if she's
a stupid child. Secondly, if you can provide a reason for why
on earth you want to dawdle in Japan instead of going
home, I won't even ask you to justify what you just told me.
I'll listen, as I have always done, but I swear to God, Danny,
I swear—"

"It's a chance for you to see where I've been the past two
years. There are good things here. And Kenji, it wasn't like
what the woman at the embassy made it out to be. I know it
may be hard to understand but—"

"I've heard enough." She still wouldn't look at him.
People stared as they passed by. Danny had gotten used to
the occasional stare, but usually it didn't happen in Tokyo,
and usually not because he and his mother were standing in
the middle of the sidewalk having an argument. How many

times had she done this in the past? He was embarrassed as he'd been any other time, but this felt worse. She was doing it as if Japan's streets were as much hers as anyone's. "So you want me to see where you've been living?" she said. "Fine. It's important for you. I get it. But, Danny," she said, turning to him, "I think it would be best if we didn't talk about that man."

Danny looked away. Here she was—his longed-for mother—and after only two hours he already wanted to escape her again. "Fine," he said, "we'll not mention *that* man's name again."

"Thank you," said his mother. The next moment her straight little mouth turned into a smile. "Now take me to a restaurant. Someplace with good Japanese food. I can be a tourist for a few days, I suppose."

❋

He took her to a part of the city where the streets were loud with traffic and human voices, and all the buildings were lit so bright with neon it felt as if they were in Las Vegas. With their argument out of the way, his mother became a rubbernecker, turning to stare at Japanese twenty-somethings with rock-and-roll hairstyles and body piercings, smiling indulgently at women with babies or young children in tow. Danny was grateful for the mothers and pregnant women that appeared in their path, who, through their mere presence, gave his mother some link to the strange new world that surrounded her.

He took her to eat at a *tonkatsu* restaurant, which seemed safest. Deep-fried pork cutlets and shredded cabbage with lemon-and-sesame salad dressing wasn't anything too alien. Teaching her how to use chopsticks would be enough for her first night out. He'd hold off on the sushi and eel until later.

After eating, they wandered back to the hotel to find that a package had been delivered for Danny, a suitcase. A bellhop brought it to their room, and after he'd left, Danny's mother stood at the end of the bed and stared at it, wondering aloud at what it could be. When Danny shrugged, uninterested, she opened it herself and made a face. "What's all this?" she said.

"My things," he told her. "From Kenji's apartment." He apologized immediately. "I mean, *that* man's apartment."

"Don't start with me. We had a good night," said his mother. "Is it just clothes?"

"Mostly. And a few trinkets."

"Like what?"

"A puzzle box," said Danny. He went over and took out a small lacquered box. Beneath the lacquer, the wood was painted with geometric designs in shades of brown, gold, and red. "It's from Hakone," he said. "A place south of Tokyo famous for its hot springs and mountain scenery. And also these boxes. Kenji bought it for me when we spent a weekend there last year."

"Interesting," said his mother. But when Danny held the box out for her to look at, she hesitated before finally taking it from his hands to examine it cautiously, as if it might be a bomb. "How does it work?" she asked.

"You have to find the sliding panels in the wood and move them all until it opens. It's hard in the beginning because the patterns make everything look the same, but once you find the sliding panels, it opens pretty easily. When Kenji gave it to me, he said I should fill it with my hopes and dreams."

"That's nice," his mother said, and began searching for the moving panels. "But they sure make it hard enough," she said, sitting down with it on the end of her bed while Danny went into the bathroom to change into pajamas. When he returned, the box was back in the suitcase, sitting on top of his neatly folded clothes. "Too difficult," she said when he looked at her, then picked up the remote control and snapped on the television.

"You have to be gentle to slide the panels open," Danny said. "Too much pressure and they won't budge."

"Sounds like your father," said his mother. She went to the bathroom to change into her nightgown. When she came out again, she turned the television and bedside light off. "Let's get some sleep," she said, and settled under the bedcovers.

Danny lay on top of his comforter and kept the lamp near his bed on low so it wouldn't keep his mother awake. He took the puzzle box into his hands and slowly, surely slid each panel open, one after the other, unfolding it like origami, until the top slid open to reveal the empty space inside. The space Kenji had told him to fill with something special, something entirely his own.

"Turn the light out and go to sleep, honey," his mother's voice, muffled in her pillow, came a moment later.

"I'm not tired," said Danny. He had months of being awake to catch up on.

She gave him three days. Three days to show her some sights and do whatever he wanted. Then they would go home. Five days, he countered, and they settled on four.

The first day, he took her to see kabuki in Ginza, the wealthy shopping district of Tokyo. She exclaimed over the costumes but complained she didn't know Japanese history well enough to understand the point of the play. Danny said it was the story of a love suicide. She understood that, of course, she said, but she wondered why the Japanese killed themselves over love so often. Family problems, social class problems, Danny said. Just like Shakespeare's lovers kill themselves for the same reasons. She asked if he meant *Romeo and Juliet*. He said that was a good example. "Hmmph," she sighed, "I guess I never thought of it that way."

"We have a lot in common," he told her.

"Well, I don't know about that," she said. "I mean, where we come from, love isn't worth suicide."

"Where *you* come from," said Danny.

"What are you saying?" she asked.

"Love can be worth suicide," he told her. "Not always. And not all kinds of love. But if it's a love you've never felt before and doubt you'll ever feel again, and the pain of not having it is too much, maybe then love could be worth ending things."

"My God," said his mother, "if I lived in that sort of world, I'd have been dead ages ago."

"You chose something else."

"If you're implying that I settled, you're wrong, Danny. I chose life. A livable life. There's nothing to judge in that, so you'd best quit before you start saying things you don't know anything about."

He liked her when she got this way. Angry but honest. It was difficult, most of the time, to get her to express a genuine emotion or observation. Often she was too busy playing at being a sweet and overly cautious mother, caught up in being what she thought she should be, rather than being herself. But when he was a teenager at home, late at night, after his father had gone to bed, he used to be able to get her to talk about things with him. Not just about her feelings on their family or their town, but the world and life and what felt more like private memories. Once they had a conversation about President Clinton, before the frenzy of the Lewinsky scandal, and his mother had said, "So many women think that man is good-looking, but I don't get it. I think he's decent enough, as far as politicians go, which isn't far if you ask me, but what's the appeal? He looks like anyone. When your grandmother met him at a rally in Pittsburgh, she shook his hand and said his skin was soft as a baby. You know what that means. Hasn't worked a day in his life."

And another time, "You know I was thinking this morning about my mother's death, how I was seventeen when it happened, only a month after I graduated high school. I was remembering the morning after she died, I got up and walked out to stand in our drive and look at everything. The sky, the trees, the birds on the telephone wires. Everything seemed to be the same as it always was, but my mother was gone and I couldn't help but think of myself as half an orphan. Then four years later, when my dad died, I thought, well, that's it, I'm an orphan, even though I was twenty-one, married, and had my own child. But I tell you, I felt like one, I did. What's the difference between a child losing a parent and an adult? Well sure, there are lots of differences, but I mean, why aren't adults who lose parents orphans, too? There should be a word for that, for anyone who loses a parent. Aren't we all orphans in the end anyway?"

This banal philosophical side was the part of her Danny liked more than anything. But it seemed that part of her faded a little with each passing year. He was afraid of her a little, afraid that someday he, too, would become one particular thing that made all the other facets of himself into strangers.

Danny had spent his first year in Japan teaching English at a conversation school, learning Japanese, and relearning how to be happy. He found that easy to do after a few months away from the voices that had surrounded him back home. The voice of the girl in his Political Thought class who had told him to leave if he didn't like America, his mother's fear that terrorists were on their way over to kill Christians, his father's apocalyptic preparations for a war he sensed on the horizon. One day his sister had taken him to lunch—to get him alone, he realized halfway into the meal—so she could offer him a piece of advice: "Danny," she'd said, "you should get a job and settle down with a nice girl. You can't be a student forever. You're going to have to grow up sometime." But isn't that what being a student is? he'd thought then. Growing up? Growing? But he'd told his sister she was probably right.

And then, during his first winter break in Japan, he'd met Kenji by chance or fate, and somehow—he still couldn't explain it, even to himself—found himself in love. He hadn't thought that would ever happen. He had never assumed that love was a thing everyone found in life, himself included. And anyway, how would he even recognize it, he sometimes wondered, when it seemed love in his country was waving a flag, when love in his family was his sister telling him to settle down and get on with things? His mother, too, had once attempted to explain it all to him, the whole mystery of life. "You dwell on things too much," she'd said. That had been the extent of her evaluation of his worries about the world he found himself living in, the world he'd come to talk to her about one night in his senior year, afraid it was going to end. Stop dwelling, she had told him. Caring too much didn't help anyone. If all that was love, he thought he'd never know how to truly love someone. That it had ended up being a Japanese man he fell in love with had been a shock to him even as it happened. In all the futures that had seemed available to him, he had never anticipated that one.

After he left home, he'd spoken to his family infrequently. He'd called once after he'd arrived and was settling in, and had talked to his mother before she put his father on the line. His father had asked if everything was okay over there, had listened to Danny's initial observations on his new country, had grunted his acknowledgments, then told Danny to take good care before passing the phone back to Danny's mother, who had a roast in the oven, she said, and had to go. There'd been the obligatory phone calls on Thanksgiving and Christmas after that, but nothing more after he met Kenji.

All that had been months ago. His mother was here now,

he reminded himself. He could hardly believe how much she'd aged since he last saw her. She looked like an old woman. Two years before, he'd thought she'd be eternally young. He still hadn't spoken to his father or brother and sister, not even now that his mother was here, and she didn't suggest calling home. Why did their disinterest hurt so much? He should be used to it, he thought, and tried making himself not care, like his mother had advised him, but he failed every time.

His mother slept soundly in her futon across the room from him. They had arrived in Hakone earlier that evening, and come to a *ryokan*, a traditional Japanese inn, instead of a hotel. It was the one he and Kenji had stayed in the previous spring when the cherry trees were in bloom, before they'd argued. He hadn't told his mother this had been his and Kenji's room then, that he was spending his last few days here retracing the love they'd shared, trying to recapture it, to have something, some token to put in the box Kenji had given him when they were here. Even if it was only one memory of a moment when they were happy together, he wanted to fill it with something other than the broken dreams Kenji had left him. His mother could figure all this out if she wanted, that he was leading her across a map that led back to a place where he'd once been happy. But as he looked at her face now, pinched in sleep, he thought, *She'll only understand the parts of me that she wants to see. Every other piece of me she'll disappear.* Like Kenji did. Like Kenji had done to him.

He wondered if he should give up on her, on his whole family, ever loving him. He wondered if he should give up and consider himself an orphan.

The next morning, they left the *ryokan* by bus and went to the nearest train station. From there they went further south, to Nagoya, where they visited a castle full of old samurai armor, and later climbed the carved-out stairs in a mountain on the outskirts of the city to bathe in an *onsen* famous for its healing properties. His mother grew winded several times on the way up, and they had to stop often so she could catch her breath. "All this for a hot spring?" she said as they neared the top, huffing and puffing. "I preferred the one at that little hotel we stayed in."

"*Ryokan*," said Danny. "It's more of an inn than a hotel."

"Well, you can't expect me to learn a language overnight."

Danny laughed to try to take the edge off. "You use English even when you say 'thank you.'"

"Jesus wept, Danny!" she said. "Tell me how you say 'thank you' in Japanese and I'll say it to everyone I see from now on."

"*Doumo.*"

"Do-mo," she said. "Do-mo do-mo do-mo. Great. Easy enough. I'll say do-mo from now on everywhere I go."

She'd get a few Japanese girls behind checkout counters giggling, but that was okay. He wanted to hear her say it. *Just try,* he thought. *Try, Mom.*

At the *onsen* there was a long line at the counter. Danny asked his mother to wait by the lockers where they'd store their things while he paid their fee. Rejoining her a moment later, he explained that she'd wash herself in the shower area first, then go into the hot springs with the other women. He told her not to wear the towel into the water, that it was custom here to remain naked in front of the other women. "You only live once," his mother exclaimed when he showed her to the women's entrance, and he watched her go in, then went into the men's changing room next door.

After soaping up and spraying himself off, he slipped into a hot spring outside on the edge of the mountainside. The wind on his face was cool but the water was steaming. The men in the pool with him chattered, carrying on like old women, Danny's father would have said. One nudged his shoulder and slowly asked in Japanese if Danny understood them. He said that he did and the man drew him into the conversation. They were all middle-aged or older, all smiling, open-faced, and curious. They wanted to know how he liked Japan, how long he'd been in the country, how long he planned to stay, whether or not he had a Japanese girlfriend. They all smiled and laughed about the last question, Danny too. He told them he liked Japan very much, that he'd been here two years, that he was leaving in a few days actually. He said he didn't have a girlfriend. He didn't mention that he'd had a Japanese boyfriend.

Then suddenly the door to the shower room slid open and a uniformed staff member appeared, urging Danny to come with him. "Your mother," the man said, "she is confused and upset. We tried to help her, but she doesn't understand. Please come. She is disturbing the other guests."

He got out of the water and wrapped himself in the towel the man offered, then followed him out to the changing room and into the hall where he'd parted ways with his mother. She was there, huddled on a chair in a white robe. A

Japanese girl kneeled beside her with a cup of green tea, trying to calm her. "It's okay," she kept telling Danny's mother. "It's okay." It might have been the only English the girl knew, but she was using it for all it was worth.

Danny knelt in front of his mother, too, and now saw she'd been crying. "What happened?" he asked, putting his hand on her knee.

"I was attacked," she said, her voice indignant. "I did just like you said. I washed myself on that little stool and then got into that pool of water with those other women, and everything was fine, but then there were these three old women. They came over and started talking to me. They saw I couldn't understand, but they kept talking to me. I tried to be nice, but then one reached out and touched my breast!" She turned her face, red now, away from Danny. "Oh, I don't understand these people!" she said into her shoulder. "Where I come from people don't do like that! They don't just take baths together! They don't touch a stranger's body!"

"Calm down, Mom," he said. "They didn't mean anything by it. They were curious, I think. Did you notice they don't have the same, um, dimensions as American women?"

"That's no excuse!"

"I know. Come on. Let's get changed and we'll get you out of here. It's okay."

She got up, ignoring the young girl's offer of help, and went back into the changing room with the straight-ahead soldier look on her face. Danny sighed, thanked the attendants for helping, and went to the men's room to change.

They checked into a hotel in Nagoya an hour later, a real hotel this time, no longer a *ryokan*. His mother had had enough Japanese culture for one day, and she seemed to appreciate the Western bed as she scissored her legs across its comforter and sighed. As they were getting ready for bed, though, she asked, "Why are we in Nagoya, Danny? There don't seem to be that many sights to see here."

"It's not a huge tourist spot," he said. "But it's a nice city. I met someone important to me here."

"Tokyo seemed nicer," she said. Then, a few moments later, after Danny hadn't replied, "I liked Tokyo."

"We'll be back in Tokyo for another day before we leave," he said, sensing that she was, in her own awkward way, trying to be positive. "I'll take you to eat *shabu-shabu* in Asakusa."

"What's that?" she asked, suspicious.

"Just shaved slices of beef you cook yourself with lots of vegetables and tofu in boiling water, then you dip it in this really good sauce. You'll like it. And Asakusa is one of the oldest sections of Tokyo."

"That sounds good," she said. "Maybe if I pay attention, I can make it for us when we're home again."

❀

The next day, they strolled through several shopping malls and visited a local temple before deciding to have lunch at a ramen shop. Danny's mother had trouble eating the noodles with chopsticks, so Danny asked for a fork. Of course they had some set aside for foreigners, and after that was settled, Danny said, "Mom, why won't you talk about Kenji with me?"

"Oh, Danny," she said, putting her fork and spoon down. They didn't say anything for a while, and he watched her look out the window at people walking past on the street. Finally, she turned to him again and said, "Honestly, I don't know how to talk about that with you. I don't know what you want to hear me say."

"Anything," he said. He could hear his voice grow smaller, and felt smaller, too, as if he were shrinking, aging backwards as he looked at her, becoming a child again under her gaze.

"I don't know," she said, shaking her head, picking her fork up again, adamant that her appetite would not be ruined.

"It's because we were together, isn't it? That's why you don't want to talk about him. That's why your face freezes up every time I mention his name."

She didn't speak at first. Her face froze in exactly the way he described whenever he brought up Kenji. Her blue eyes suddenly became vacant. Her pinched expression fell away to reveal a face lined with worry and age. She looked much older, but somehow more like herself. More like the woman she was when he was a child, the woman he used to think was the most beautiful in the world.

Finally, looking down at the table, she said, "I made you this way, didn't I?" Her voice was small like his now. Each syllable shook as they left her lips.

"No," he said, "you didn't."

"Then how is it? What about your girlfriends? Back home you had girlfriends."

"None of that's changed," he said. "But I loved Kenji, too. I guess it just doesn't matter to me, as long as it's love I'm in. It was a surprise for me, too. You'd know that if we could talk more honestly."

"If you can love either way, why don't you just love women? Why do you have to make everything so hard?"

"It's not me that makes it hard," said Danny. "That's other people, don't you think? And I want to live truthfully, not however is easiest."

"The truth isn't all that special, Danny. What has the truth done for me lately?" She looked up at him, eyes filling. "I did my best to raise you and your brother and sister to be good, honest people, and what did that accomplish? Your brother is my harshest critic, your sister never calls unless she needs something from me, and your father— well, sometimes I'll be doing something and he'll come along and I'll see him and he'll see me, and we smile, but sometimes I feel like after all these years I'm still meeting him for the first time. It isn't just you, you know. I know that's what you think. You think it's just you who doesn't understand other people. You think it's just you who isn't understood. You know your own story so well, Danny, but no one else's. God help me, when you said you wanted to go to college, even though it was going to be tough on us, your father and I figured out a way to make sure you could do that. We helped you get a decent education, but *where*, honey, is your heart? I'm so afraid when I look at you. When I do, I see that I didn't do my job right. I see a scared little boy who will give himself to someone who will hurt him just to keep him, a scared little boy who thinks it's okay to stop living because love didn't work out the way he thought it should, and then I think, Oh God, please give me one more chance to tell him it's not just him. You're not the only person who's alone and afraid. We all are! *That's* the truth and by God I tell you I prefer to live with a few lies if it makes things easier."

"It seems like a lot of work, making up another reality to hide from the one in front of you."

"And what's my other option?" she said, her eyes widening. "Walk away? Walk out on everyone and just make everything that much worse? Like you did?"

She grabbed her purse and walked out, leaving the bell over the door ringing behind her. Danny didn't immediately follow. He sighed, frustrated, exhausted. But only a moment passed before he began to worry, and he quickly paid the bill and ran out and down the side street he'd seen her take.

She was walking fast, already two blocks ahead of him, her shoes clicking on the sidewalk. When he finally caught up, he took her by the elbow and she pulled away. "Don't handle me like that!" she said. "I'm not a cow to be pushed around with some prod! I'm your mother!"

"I wish you wouldn't run away every time I try to talk to you! I wish you could look at me and see who I am and love me, not *tolerate* me or force me to cooperate with your lies about who we are. Why can't we tell each other the truth? We used to be able to do that."

"You want more truth?" she said, choking a little on that last word. "Okay, I'll tell you the truth and nothing but the truth so help me God. When the lady from the embassy talked to me on the phone, when she told me you'd been found and how you'd been found, I cried. I did. Your father took the phone from me when he saw me, and after a few minutes, he gave the phone back and didn't say anything. I tried to get him to come with me, but he wasn't going to leave American soil. No, if you were okay, then everything was all right and I could go, but he was staying. So I came. Alone. Twelve hours on a plane in a seat the size of a dinner plate. And here I am running up and down mountainsides, getting molested by old Japanese women, eating food that still has eyes in it, trying to act like everything's fine. No, I don't want my son to love other men. No, I don't want him to live in Japan. No, I don't want my family to fall apart any more than it already has. I've been fighting for thirty years for our family, and I'll damn well make a way out of no way to keep us one. The truth is, even though things aren't perfect between us, even though we don't have the relationships you'd like, we're useless apart from one another. And your walking away was worse than any lie I ever told. When you abandoned us, well, to be completely honest I thought I'd never forgive you. It was like a part of me died. But I did forgive you. I did. I made my peace as well as a great many excuses and reasons for why you should go and do something like this and how it was a good thing—I suppose that's just wallpapering reality, like you say, but I do it because I love you. And I love you even if you love a man. I just don't know how to get used to it. Okay? That's the truth. That's where I'm coming from, Danny. Are you happy?"

He slowly nodded, then leaned over and kissed her on her forehead and hugged her, her wet cheek against his. And there, without knowing she was standing in the very spot where love had first touched him, she put her arms around him and clutched him to her, as if at any moment he might disappear again. When they pulled away, she looked up and gave him a little twist of a smile. "*Doumo*," she said, wiping her tears away, and offered him her arm.

Day of the Dead

There is no difference, Kazuko thought when she opened her eyes and saw the other side. *There is no difference.* Isn't that what Hitomi had whispered as her eyes fluttered and finally closed? Kazuko had wondered what the girl had meant, had thought surely it was the beginning of a sentence interrupted. What meaning would Hitomi have created if she'd completed her thought before dying? Now that Kazuko's eyes were truly open, she saw it clearly. Between the realm of the dead and the land of the living, there was no difference.

There were the same rice fields, the same towering pine trees and bamboo forests around her, the same blue sky above, the same clouds streaming through it. She heard coughing, choking, and turned to see three men standing around a body laid out on a stretcher. A fourth man kneeled beside the stretcher and spoke to the body. "Mizuno san, can you hear me?" he said.

But no answer came from Mizuno san. Who was that anyway? Kazuko couldn't help but be curious. She walked over to the van and the men around the body. "Excuse me," she said, and tried peeking over their shoulders, but at the same time they shifted positions and she scrambled back a few steps to give them room.

She looked over her shoulder at the narrow strip of dirt path between the boggy rice fields. No one was behind her. The dirt path led across the fields to a paved road as small and narrow as the path itself. Two police cars and two ambulances were parked on the road, one after the other. There was no shoulder to park on, so a policeman stood beside the vehicles, directing the small stream of traffic that came his way. A tiny car slowed to a crawl near the ambulances, squeezing past just barely. The driver stared out as he passed by the scene, then sped up again to continue on his way.

"Mizuno san, can you hear me?" one medic repeated. She squeezed between two of them in their neat jumpsuits, like the little car squeezing through the police cars and ambulances, and this time managed to see.

It was a woman on the stretcher, eyes wide open, lips slightly parted. She coughed, but didn't respond to their voices. Kazuko blinked, studying the woman's face. It looked familiar. She blinked again. Squinted. One of the medics held the woman's wrist, taking her pulse. There was a tiny heart-shaped birthmark on the woman's wrist. Kazuko had seen that somewhere. She lifted her own arm to examine it, saw the same mark, a shadow on the skin just above her wrist. She looked back at the woman's face. The man called the woman's name again and Kazuko recognized her, finally. The woman on the stretcher, coughing, choking, eyes wide open, not saying anything, was her. She, too, was Kazuko.

"Mizuno san," a voice called to her. She looked around

for the medics, but they had all left. "Mizuno san, are you all right?" the voice called again. Kazuko blinked and the rice fields and ambulance faded. She blinked again and saw a man in a dark suit sitting in a chair across from her. She looked down. She, too, was sitting in a similar chair. The man in the suit held a book open on his lap. He tapped a pen against it before closing it to turn to the table beside him and pour a glass of water from a pitcher. Kazuko watched beads of condensation dribble down the silver. The man turned back with the glass and said, "*Douzo.*" Kazuko took it automatically. She drank, and blinked, and set the glass on the table beside her. "We're making progress, Mizuno san," the doctor said. "But I think that you are tired. Shall we talk again next week?"

Kazuko nodded. She knew that she should, that it would reflect well on her. Almost a year had passed since her failed suicide, and here she found herself still walking through that day, slowly, carefully, circling its perimeter, examining what remained: the charcoal burners they'd placed at their feet, the adhesive vinyl Hitomi had taped around the windows to seal them in, the bottle of water they'd shared to drink down the sleeping pills Kazuko had provided. Their last moments together, holding Hitomi's hand while the girl mumbled, "There is no difference," before closing her eyes to make the voyage to the other side. Here she found herself listening to a man who gave her water and said that she was tired. *Hitomi was right,* thought Kazuko. *There is no difference.*

Kazuko walked with her head down, watching her feet move in front of each other. She was wearing a pair of low heels that both accentuated the curves of her calves yet appeared sensible and appropriate. They were what she used to wear at the office to greet customers who wanted to learn English, to greet foreign employees as they arrived to teach English, to assemble trays of tea and rice crackers for business partners, to escort the foreign teachers to schools where her boss had placed them, to help them set up bank accounts and buy household items and see the doctor with them when they got sick, to do so many things, a long time ago—they were good, solid shoes, and now they carried her down the steps to the train station and along the narrow side streets of Tokyo as she made her way home.

Home was a one-room apartment on the outskirts of Ueno. Kazuko had moved there six months ago, after she'd been released from the hospital, after the divorce Yusuke had not fought her on was over. Final and complete. Their marriage had run a course to a different end than the one she'd planned for nearly a year ago. And now, as she climbed the steps to her apartment, as she slipped her key in the lock and turned it, as she stepped out of her good, solid shoes in the entryway and into a pair of slippers, Kazuko couldn't help but feel each breath she took, each action, each step, each thought, each feeling she felt, was not hers alone. She was living for all of them now. They were all still together. Hitomi, Tadashi, Asami. The divorce had not been just for her and Yusuke. When it was over, the others had sighed with relief with her.

When she had first stepped into this apartment six

months ago, she could hear Hitomi behind her saying, "It's awfully small, isn't it?"

"You should have seen my apartment," Tadashi had countered. "Much smaller than this one."

"It's a start," Asami had said, and Kazuko had nodded. It was a start. To what, she thought now as she waited for the tea to heat, she still didn't know.

It was August, but she couldn't hear the locusts like she could back in Ami, the little town where she'd grown up wedged between farms and suburbia. Here in the city she didn't see the glow of fireflies either. This had been the plan. To leave it all behind, to remove herself from all that had been part of her life before, to make a break. Now, though, she noticed what she did not hear and see—the locusts and their awful chatter in the swelter and heat of summer, the yellow lights of the fireflies floating outside her window—and their absences only served to remind her of what she'd wanted to let go of. She would never be able to escape anything, would she?

The phone rang, but she didn't move to answer it. She stared at it on the table across the room and sipped her tea. It was her father. Or one of her brothers. Always one of them would call after her appointments, to ask how things went, to see if she needed anything. They were behind her, too, in Ami and Tsukuba and Tsuchiura City, back home in Ibaraki prefecture. Hometown men, all of them. If their calls were less precisely timed, she might have considered talking to them. To call when they did was a duty, though, an obligation, and Kazuko wanted nothing to do with duty or obligation beyond her duties and obligations to the others—for Hitomi, Tadashi, and Asami—but that was different. Her obligations to the dead took precedence.

When the phone stopped ringing, she moved from the kitchen down the hall to the one room that served as both her living and sleeping quarters. Her futon was rolled and packed away in her closet, so the floor was bare, the space in the room empty and open, waiting for her to fill it. She had left almost all of her things behind in Ami at the house with Yusuke, taking only her clothes, a futon, the essentials. She went outside and sat on a stool on the balcony now, and looked out at the city, at the people moving through its labyrinth of streets and alleys. She breathed deeply, feeling better already at this height, far above everything where the air seemed to reach her more easily. In a day or two, many would leave to return to their hometowns, like salmon traveling upriver to their birthplaces, for Obon, day of the dead. Kazuko had no plans to return, though. She would stay in this apartment with her own dead. That would be enough ceremony for her.

When the sun went down, she decided to go inside and listen to the phone message blinking on the recorder. When the message began, her father's shy, low voice came through the machine. He asked about her session with the doctor, how her job prospects were coming, about whether she was going out and taking walks, getting fresh air and exercise. Kazuko sighed, already weary.

Everything was as she'd suspected. He was doing fine, he told her, as was his summer garden. He'd started taking English conversation classes for fun, too, he said, but not at her old workplace, of course, so she shouldn't worry. He would not want to face her old boss after what Kazuko had done anyway, and Kazuko had asked her father to do only one thing after she'd been released from the hospital, before she left Yusuke months ago: not to speak of her to anyone, to let her suicide remain as it was, to not make her life public for his friends and neighbors, to allow her this measure of solitude. He did that for her, despite the pain it caused him, she knew. She heard it behind every word he uttered, this pain, restrained yet somehow plaintive.

And then there it was: "Are you coming home?" he asked now. "For Obon?" This request, buried between concerns for her health and an update on his own doings, was completed when he added, "I have a present for you, Kazuko, but I'd like to give it to you in person rather than send it. Would you please come home?"

When he finally finished, she deleted the recording, not wanting to leave it behind as a temptation to listen again, to hear the absence of her mother in his message. "Will you go?" Hitomi asked her.

"Of course she'll go," said Tadashi. "She has to."

"She doesn't have to do anything," said Asami. "Not unless she wants to."

"But I do," said Kazuko. "After all, there's this place to keep."

If she could have afforded the apartment without help from her father and brothers, she would have cut herself off from them completely, but their assistance helped to pay for her privacy. So there were still some obligations she couldn't avoid, even if she'd have liked to.

"It doesn't have to be a long visit," said Hitomi in her little girl's voice. *Always compromising,* thought Kazuko.

"You can be home on the evening train of the same day," Tadashi agreed.

But Asami was silent. When Kazuko looked at her sulking in a corner, she said, "Do as you wish. It's what you wanted, Kazuko," and turned to go back out on the balcony and watch the lights of the world below flicker on as night descended.

She would go for a day then, Kazuko decided. She wouldn't bother calling ahead to tell her father either. Despite his having called to ask her to come, she would let it be a surprise for him. It was easier that way, to just appear and disappear when she felt like it, to take part when need obliged her, to drop away from the world when it became too much for her. Her empty apartment, her life of emptiness, was a fold in the fabric of a city of millions. In six months she'd not met one of her neighbors, not in passing in the hall nor on the stairwell. She could hide in that fold and no one would know she existed, but she could see all of them from the balcony whenever she wanted. The distance put everything into focus, made it clearer, easier. She gathered herself in that distance, stored it for times like this, when she needed to take herself out among others. And at Obon, to visit with her father and brothers and sit in the silence that surrounded them when it came to her mother's absence, she would need every bit of distance she'd managed to save.

In the morning she packed a small bag. One change of clothes, one novel wrapped in brown paper, one bottle of green tea, one package of *mochi* cakes to present to her father, one candle, one package of incense, and one perfectly round orange to place on the family altar. Looking down at the orange inside her bag, Kazuko couldn't help but feel it was a miserable offering, but they'd been her mother's favorite, and this one glowed like a setting sun.

As she closed the door of her apartment and locked it, her hand shook a little. The key jiggled in the lock for a moment before she could calm herself and pull it free. She breathed deeply, gathering courage, and stepped down the stairwell into the bustle of bodies, and wove her way through the streets among the other travelers preparing to leave Tokyo for their family homes. The highways would be crammed today, the vehicles moving slow and slick as a river. The trains, too, would be crowded, everyone standing or sitting shoulder to shoulder, eyes on books or cell phone screens or closed altogether. Kazuko did not hurry to become part of the mass she knew awaited her. She stayed close to the storefronts as she walked, under the shadows of their awnings, until she reached a bridge overlooking a pond full of purple and white lotus drifting on its surface, and stopped to look at the flowers and the birds perched upon the pond's inner island before continuing on to Ueno station.

As expected, the ride home was long and cramped. Kazuko held her novel in front of her, but did not read the words that bled down the page in front of her. Instead she peered over the edge of the book at the other riders, using it like a fan to hide her face as she watched the play before her. Men and women stood in front of her, their slim trunks lined up next to one another like bamboo in a forest. On one side of her, a child begged his mother for another piece of candy; on the other, a schoolgirl whispered conspiratorially with a friend.

She and Midori had been those girls, riding trains together in a cluster of limbs, laughing behind their hands. Once they saw an old man with a scrunched-up nose and a sallow complexion scold his granddaughter for not paying attention to others, and Midori had stared so hard, Kazuko had thought he would surely grab his chest and keel over dead from a heart attack. "*Buta*," Midori whispered harshly at the man as the little girl began to cry. *Pig*. Kazuko had slipped her arm through Midori's and held her like that, all the way home, to calm her. Kazuko had never met anyone who could grow angry like Midori. And because Midori was so beautiful, it made her anger somehow beautiful, too. Where had Midori learned to do that? To feel her anger like any other emotion and have no fear of holding it, like a piece of fire, in her small, delicate hands?

"Thinking about her again?" Asami asked as the train shuttled further and further away from Tokyo.

Kazuko nodded.

"What was it about her?" Hitomi wanted to know.

Kazuko shook her head.

"You miss her," said Tadashi. Kazuko nodded again, silently, and Tadashi slipped his arm through hers, saying no more as they rocked and swayed to the train's rhythm.

The train stopped suddenly and Kazuko looked around, realizing that at some point it had nearly emptied. She was in the countryside now. The doors released a sigh of stale air as they slid open for departing passengers, quietly closed, and the train began to move again. In another ten minutes, she would reach her stop and step from the train doors into the waiting memories of her family.

When she walked up the path to the front door, Kazuko found thin strips of pinewood gathered in a small smoking pile before the entryway. A tiny fire burned within their structure, the flames releasing a spiced fragrance on the wind to call the spirits home, alerting them that their families were waiting for their presence. Kazuko kneeled in front of the smoldering wood, allowing the smoke to cover her face, her hair, breathing it in deeply, feeling it rush into her lungs cleaner than the evening air. A lantern already hung by the door, lighting the path for her ancestors. She closed her eyes, feeling slightly as if she were dreaming of coming home instead of actually being here now, scooping the smoke in her hands and bringing it to her face like clean water. She could almost feel her mother's hand on top of her head, ruffling long fingers through Kazuko's hair, the smoke from a small fire of some other summer covering her, saying, "Smells good, doesn't it, Kazuko?" And then Kazuko took her mother's hand and they walked into the house together.

The front door opened and Kazuko opened her eyes to see her white-haired father, shoulders sagging a little, the skin around his eyes pinched with age, standing in the entry. He looked startled at first, as Kazuko thought he would, but quickly a slight smile lifted his cheeks as he called out, "*Okaerinasai*." Welcome home.

The old man took her bag from her shoulder and moved

aside to let her enter, asking after her trip, her general well-being, saying she must surely be exhausted after the train. He allowed her a safe distance, nodding to her, still smiling, grateful for her presence, and waved her ahead of him into the living room. He did not bother her with questions beyond these ones, or pepper her with instructions for the holiday preparations, and said he would take her bags to her room. She stopped him before he left, though, and took from the depths of her carryall the orange, the treats, the incense she'd brought, and offered him a slight smile in return.

When he left the living room, Kazuko went to the *butsudan* in the next room, the altar that held the tablet with the names of their ancestors, and kneeled before it. She gently placed her *mochi* cakes and the perfect orange among the other offerings of fruits and vegetables her father had already laid out, the melon and flowers, the statue of the Buddha, the cucumber and eggplant, which, in the days of her childhood, her father used to cut into the shapes of a horse and a cow for the spirits to ride on their journeys to and from this world. Such silliness, she thought. Had she ever really believed it? She must have.

She picked up the lighter and lit the two candles on the table before the altar. When the candles came to life, she lit two incense sticks in the flames before planting the sticks in a small, ornate box full of ashes and sand, allowing their smoke to curl up in slow ribbons. Then she took up a striker and rang a brassy cup of a bell that sat on a cushion beside the candles. The sound shimmered and quivered in the air, like heat rising over an empty plain. Kazuko struck the bell again, and the echo of the first strike mingled with the second. She struck the bell a third, final time then, before setting the striker aside to clap her hands together in front of her nose and bow her head in prayer.

Okaasan, she began, but did not know what to say other than this word that was lodged inside her like a hot bullet. *Mother*. She tried to find her voice once more. This time, though, she found herself stopped after, again, only one word: *Midori*. What could she say? What could she say to any of the dead that surrounded her? Asami, Hitomi, Tadashi. She called their names in her heart, pausing a moment between each one, then gave up, lowering her hands, opening her eyes again, snuffing the candles with two strong waves of her hands.

There were too many. Too many dead. She carried them all with her. Like the old women in this town who walked hunched over, straw hats shielding their faces from the sun, it was a labor for her. But if she did not carry them, who would? Someone had to.

"A priest will visit tonight," her father said when Kazuko turned and rose from the altar. "He's coming for dinner. Your brothers, too." Kazuko furrowed her brow, but nodded, trying to recall if a priest had ever entered her family home before. Her father was pious, certainly, but services at temple had always been enough for him, for her brothers, for their wives, for her nephews and nieces who ran through the house like crazed warriors or else sulked in front of the television playing video games, the drip-feed of overworked, test-worn teenagers. She was already dizzy with the thought of so many people crowding into her father's home to respond in any articulate manner. Her face must have given her away, because quickly her father said, "Your brothers are coming alone this year."

"Because of me?" Kazuko asked. Her voice was soft and low in her throat, but it was finally there with her. He had asked her brothers to leave their wives and children at home, hadn't he? No, no, he insisted, waving the question away, saying he wanted it to be just the four of them this year, like it used to be. Didn't she remember the old times?

Kazuko nodded, remembering when it had been just her, her brothers, and their parents and grandparents. Her oldest brother, Akira, so well-mannered and serious, like her father, her middle brother, Hiroshi, his total opposite, always joking and wanting to get to the good part of drinking the beer and sake. And Kazuko herself, basking in the light of her older brothers, upon whom her mother had showered so much affection. Kazuko, too, had loved them as her mother had, because her mother did. But they had closed up, closed off, all of them, and spoke few words to each other long before their mother died almost three years ago. They'd become strangers as their childhoods receded. And when her mother was gone, they shared few memories of their common history when it was most needed. When Kazuko most needed it. Kazuko knew this shouldn't upset her as much as it did, that they hadn't necessarily behaved badly, but she'd expected more for some reason. She'd expected more until she realized that more was what her mother had always given, not them.

"I do. I remember." And silently, without any problem finding words now, her back to the altar, she recalled her disappointments. Akira's and Hiroshi's stupid hearts, her father's stupid silence, Yusuke's stupid disloyalty, her own stupid wish to remove herself from all the stupidity of the world. It was a kind of prayer, a litany of what she most hated, and she felt that in a way it might even be something in her that seemed to want to forgive them, to forgive herself, if she could only let herself be forgiven. But what exactly needed forgiving? She still wasn't sure. "It will be good to see them. It's been a long time, hasn't it?"

"It's good to have you home, Kazuko," said her father.

Kazuko nodded politely, then looked away.

She went to her old room, her childhood room, and sat down in a chair at a desk. She'd spent many hours sitting at this desk in junior high and high school, studying for exams. She could almost feel the stress and anxiety from those days come back to her, as if she were now preparing for yet another test, another entrance exam, another hurdle that she would either leap or trip and fall over on her way to whatever life it was she'd been encouraged to strive for. One test ends, she used to complain to Midori when they were girls together, and another begins. She had failed. She had failed utterly. She had even failed at killing herself. Surely there were no tests left to be taken after such a poor performance.

Turning in her seat, she noticed a futon spread out on the floor for her. Her father must have done that, and he'd made it up very neatly. When he'd called and left the message asking her to come home, she'd interpreted this to mean he needed her to cook the family meal for Obon, to clean her mother's grave, which surely needed tending. That was what she had done the first two years after her mother was gone. But the house was already neat and tidy, and now a sweet smell from the kitchen drifted down the hall to her bedroom. What did he want from her?

Then there he was in the doorway, excusing himself. "I'm sorry, Kazuko," he said, "but can I come in?" She nodded and rose from her chair to let him sit instead. "No, no," he said, shaking his head, but she remained standing. He held something in his hands, a parcel wrapped in orange and white cloth, its corners tied together. He held it out for her. Kazuko blinked, looking into his age-lined face, but took it and unceremoniously placed it on the desk to untie the knots in the cloth until it unfurled and opened like a flower to reveal what lay within. Dark cloth decorated with pink cherry blossoms. Her mother's *yukata*, her summer kimono. She brushed her fingertips across it before drawing her hands back to her sides again, shivering a little. "*Otousan*," she whispered. Father. But when she turned to say she could not accept this, what must be the gift he'd mentioned in his message, he'd already left the room.

She found him in the kitchen, chopping mushrooms into thin slices. He looked up from the blade and said, "You look like your mother, but I worry. Do you think it will fit right?"

Kazuko opened her mouth, prepared to tell him it wasn't something that could fit her even if she wanted. Putting it on would be like stepping into someone else's grave. And she'd already tried stepping into her own. That hadn't fit either. It was as if death was always too big or too small. When she saw him blinking innocently as he waited for her answer, though, she held her tongue. "It should fit," said

Kazuko. "But I'm not sure when I'll have the chance to wear it."

"Perhaps at the lantern festival," said her father, returning to his work of slicing the soft flesh of the mushrooms on the cutting board.

"We're going to the festival?" said Kazuko.

"Of course," said her father. "Why not?"

"No reason," said Kazuko, though they hadn't been to a lantern festival in years, and secretly she'd always thought it a bit too much of a tourist attraction. The Great Buddha of Ushiku lit up like the Statue of Liberty, fireworks opening over its shoulders in the night sky. It was all too much, really.

The front door opened behind her, and she heard her brothers before she saw them. "Kazuko chan," they both said. Little Kazuko. And when she turned to greet them, they were coming toward her with their arms full of their own offerings. Akira was casual as usual, in jeans and a polo shirt, Hiroshi even more so, wearing shorts and sandals and a loose T-shirt. After setting their things on the floor in the living room, they came to her and hugged her, one after the other, asking if she was well, how the train home had been, wondering if Tokyo had already come to look like a ghost town before she left it. She was shocked to be touched by them, to be touched at all, and tensed in their arms, tensed at their many questions, but tried her best to answer without hesitating, realizing that perhaps this was the test she'd felt approaching while she sat at her old desk moments ago. And if she didn't pass, she would lose the apartment, lose all the distance she'd managed to acquire.

"I'm well," she told them. "The ride home was long and

sweaty." She laughed a little, making them laugh with her. "And as for Tokyo," she added, "it was emptying as I left it."

"Akira, Hiroshi," said her father behind her. "Come help me finish dinner. The priest will soon be here."

"Let me, Father," said Kazuko as they set to work together. Her brothers barely knew the steps for boiling water.

Her father waved her away, though. "You should rest," he said. "You've come a long way to see us."

"But I want to help," said Kazuko.

"Well, then," said her father, "how about setting the table?"

❀

The priest arrived an hour later, parking his car on the side street entrance to her father's home. Kazuko watched from the living room window as he exited, white *tabi* socks stark beneath his flowing black robes. She opened the door before he could knock, and welcomed him in. The food her father and brothers had made—sushi, tempura, tofu, and cold soba noodles—was spread on the table she'd set for everyone. When the priest came in, her father and brothers bowed to him deeply, thanking him for coming, and after a few quick words about the heat and humidity of August, the priest looked from face to face and said, "Shall we begin?"

Her father nodded, showing him to the *butsudan*, where the priest kneeled, with Kazuko and her father and brothers arranged into proper sitting positions on the floor behind him. He rang the bell on the altar three times, then took up a small drum Kazuko's father had set out, and began to chant a sutra.

In the silence, the priest's voice rose and wavered, quivering like the reverberations of the altar bell in the air, his words a mixture of old and new languages, a blend of both the familiar and foreign. To understand completely required knowledge of not only Japanese but Chinese and Sanskrit, but Kazuko knew he was asking for a blessing while committing them all to the Buddha's care, that he was recounting the story of a monk whose mother died and was reborn into the low realm of Hungry Ghosts, where she was to hang upside down for eternity, how it was only through her son's offerings over time that he won her freedom, and how he won his own joy at having freed her. It was a story about sacrifice and loyalty. Kazuko shuddered as the priest's voice filled the room like thick incense, and was grateful when the sutra finally came to an end. It was only then that she reached up to touch her throat, realizing that she'd been choking on the thick smoke of his voice, his blessings.

"Please have a meal with us," her father offered afterwards, and Kazuko nearly coughed out all the smoke inside her. But the priest said he could not linger. There were other families to attend to this evening.

"It's Obon after all," he said, smiling. "They're waiting for me." Kazuko wondered if he meant the other families or the spirits, but she only nodded in agreement.

"Just a little beer then," said Hiroshi, already pouring half a can into a small glass. Kazuko stared hard at this polite offering. Ordinarily the priest might have taken a drink or two out of politeness, but he declined, saying there were others to attend to this evening, and Kazuko took the opportunity to lead him to the door. Standing between the door and the small fire of pinewood on the walkway, they sent him off together from the front stoop, waving as he started his engine and drove away.

"Why did you have a priest come?" Kazuko asked when they'd gone back inside. "We always went to temple, but you've never asked priests into the house before."

Her father shrugged, spreading his hands before him, as if the answer was in the wide fan of his fingers. "I thought it would be a good change. Why? Is something the matter?"

Kazuko shook her head, but something was definitely bothering her. She placed her hand on her throat again and massaged it a little. Her brothers could obviously sense her frustration, because Akira brought her a glass of beer and said, "Here, drink something, Kazuko chan. Relax and enjoy yourself."

Hiroshi was already shifting to sit on the floor around the table. He looked up at Kazuko and patted the pillow beside his. "Sit down, sis," he said. "I don't know about you, but I'm hungry."

Kazuko sat down beside him in resignation. It was the priest, she thought. It was that story that filled the room like sickly sweet incense. She could manage an evening meal with her father and brothers just barely, but the priest, a stranger, had set her off balance. What did he know about her ancestors anyway? He'd only come for the money her father had placed in a gift envelope on the altar next to the drum. *Being a priest,* she remembered her mother once saying, laughing a little as she'd said it, *what a good business!*

"Pick up your chopsticks," Asami told her. "You're not eating."

"They're watching you," said Hitomi, her voice high-pitched with fear.

"Just a little, Kazuko," Tadashi encouraged, and she felt his hand come to rest on her shoulder. She put her own hand over his and held it.

"Is something wrong?" her father asked across the table, nodding at her shoulder. Cold soba noodles dangled between his chopsticks as he waited for an answer.

"No," said Kazuko, and picked up her chopsticks as Asami had instructed. "Just a little sore," she said, massaging her shoulder. "Probably just tired."

"After dinner you should sleep," said Akira. "Hiroshi and I will clean up here." She blinked at him sitting across the table beside their father. They looked like each other, Akira and her father, only Akira's hair was still dark and shiny with youth. They were stepping very carefully around her, she knew, trying not to disturb her. She wasn't sure whether she should feel grateful or annoyed by these gestures. Akira smiled and teased, "What sort of face is that you're giving me?"

Kazuko shook her head. She grinned to make him feel less self-conscious, and lifted a piece of pumpkin tempura to her lips. "No face," she told him after swallowing. "No face at all, brother."

❋

Morning sun edged its way into Kazuko's room, drifting like a pool of water along the floor, growing larger, wider, inching toward her futon until it finally found her face. She blinked, feeling warmth on her cheeks and eyelids, and threw off the thin blanket she'd clung to in the night. The cicadas that had been so noticeably absent in Tokyo were crying in full force on this morning in late summer in Ami, and their cries were the second thing Kazuko noticed after the sunlight woke her. She sat up, listening to their strange sawing in the pine and bamboo woods near her father's house. A fly buzzed desultorily from window to window, plinking its tiny body against the glass in hopes of escape. Kazuko stood and went to it, slid the window open, and shooed the fly outside.

A soft wind blew in through the window, and she left it open while she got dressed for the day in shorts and a T-shirt. Ordinarily she preferred to cover her body as much as possible, but August was a murderously hot month, the only time of year she allowed herself to dress very casually, to be more like her brothers.

Her father was already awake and in the kitchen, where she'd left him and Akira and Hiroshi early the previous night. Her brothers had left at some point after she'd fallen asleep, gone back to their own homes, to their own families. "*Ohayo!*" her father said now, his voice full of cheer and vigor.

"*Ohayo,*" Kazuko replied, sitting down at the kitchen table to eat the miso soup and rice her father had set out for her. "You've been busy this morning," she said. She took her first sip and said, "It's delicious," before taking another spoonful.

"Yes, busy," said her father, who was washing dishes now. Where had he learned to do all of these things? Surely not from Kazuko's mother, who had done all the cooking and cleaning as a matter of course as long as Kazuko could remember. And not from Kazuko herself, who had done the same for over a year and a half after her mother died, coming over to make sure her father had eaten, cleaning for him, trying to keep him going. She imagined her father perusing websites on the Internet after she'd begun to distance herself; she imagined him worrying he'd never eat a home-cooked meal again, seeking out online recipes, watching videos on YouTube that revealed the secret mysteries of the rice cooker that lived on the counter. "Yes, busy," he said, "because we must go to your mother's grave later."

"But you already left a lantern by the door," said Kazuko. "You've been to the cemetery already, haven't you?"

He grunted acknowledgment that he had. "I was there yesterday to hang a lantern, but the headstone and incense burners need to be cleaned, the old offerings removed and new ones left. I have a bag packed for us. It won't take long if we work together."

Kazuko nodded and stood. This was more like it. The tiptoeing of the night before was over, it seemed, and though it had been a nice change, she was glad. She did better when she knew where she stood with others, what they wanted from her. And even her father wanted things from her. A sign, probably. A sign that she would not try to kill herself again in the future.

Could she give him what he wanted? Did she really want to give away what she'd wanted so badly only a year ago? A way out of the mess of this world. An option. She held her bowl to her lips and drank the last drops of the soup.

"Ready?" her father asked.

"Ready?" Asami asked behind her. Kazuko looked over her shoulder and saw them sitting at the table behind her, where she'd been sitting, staring, waiting for her answer.

Would she stay or join them? *Issho ni.* Together. That had been the plan.

She turned back to her father and said, "Let's go."

❀

Her father wanted to walk, so Kazuko slung the backpack full of cleaning tools over her shoulder. "Are you sure I can't carry it?" her father asked, but she waved him off and told him to lead the way, even though she herself knew every step of it.

They left by the side street entrance, and walked up the quiet road until it began to winnow in width and, slowly but surely, wound into the pine and bamboo forest that bordered her father's neighborhood. The cemetery was only a few miles away, another plot full of stone plinths set up on a hillside behind a suburban development. The sort of thing you found throughout Japan in places that had changed as the dreams of Tokyo spread over the land like pollen on the wind. This wooded hillside was where their family tomb awaited them. This was where Kazuko's mother had gone before them.

Small statues of gods sprouted among the tombstones, peering at Kazuko from various angles. Some fat and jolly, some thin and serious, some contemplative, some sad. Kazuko pumped well water and watched them watching her stony-eyed as she squeezed soap from a bottle into a plastic bucket, mixing it until lather grew like a skin on top. Her father had already taken the brush from the toolbox built into a hidden pocket of the tomb and swept the place before she came back. He put the brush away when Kazuko returned, and picked up the old offerings of tea and sake he'd left on a previous visit, gathered them into his arms, and set them off to the side of the tomb while Kazuko scrubbed off the thin grime that had built up over the past few seasons.

She ran the cloth over the kanji on the headstone, pushing into their grooves, pretending she was engraving them with her fingers. She rang the dirty water out, dipped the cloth in the bucket, and soaked the marble slab she stood on, washing it inch by inch as she backed up and stood on the dirt and gravel, her father beside her. He put his hand on her shoulder, a job well done, and she let it rest there, though it sent a shock through her, this sudden warmth and affection.

Her father replaced the candle in the lantern he'd hung beside the tomb the day before, and lit it before leaving. It was afternoon, but the lantern light glared on the newly washed marble of the tomb, casting shadows of the kanji, painted black on its white panels, onto the stone below. As they turned toward home again, Kazuko looked back and, for a moment, thought she saw a slim figure following behind in their footsteps.

❋

"What do you want to be when you grow up, Kazuko chan?" her mother once asked while they were making dinner in the kitchen, the kitchen her father now seemed so in control of.

"A nurse," Kazuko had immediately replied. She was fifteen. The world spun somewhat vaguely around her, its edges blurry, its details still undefined, but she knew herself. That was the one thing of which she was certain.

"And why do you want to be a nurse?"

"I want to help people," said Kazuko.

"Many people need help," said her mother. "What sort of people do you want to help?"

"Hurt people," said Kazuko.

"Ahh, that's a difficult job, Kazuko," her mother said. "But I think you can do it. Why? Because look at your arm. Look at what I've given you."

Kazuko lifted her arm to look at the heart-shaped birth-mark on her skin just below her left wrist. When she looked up, her mother was holding up her right arm, where a similar shape marked her skin just a little further up her arm, near her elbow.

"That's our mark, Kazuko," said her mother. "That's how you know you're my daughter. We have two hearts, the women in our family. One on the inside, and one on the outside."

"It's ugly," said Kazuko, frowning at her second, dark heart. "I wish I didn't have it."

"What?!" Her mother glared at her, offended. "Why do you say such things? Two hearts is a gift, Kazuko!"

"But at school—"

"Don't listen to them, Kazuko," said her mother. "They don't understand. But you do. You understand because of this. You don't realize yet, I know. But you will. You can't hide your feelings like others, and because of this others can't hide theirs from you."

"Two hearts," Kazuko said, looking at her birthmark closer, trying to somehow like it.

"Two hearts," said her mother, handing her a rice ball to wrap in roasted seaweed. She gently took hold of Kazuko's wrist afterwards, stroked the birthmark with her thumb, and said, "It's good for something else, too. Even when I'm gone, you can look at this and remember this moment, you can remember me telling you this, right now, in this room."

Kazuko had nodded, but said nothing. The world was still spinning vaguely around her. She had no idea how, years later, the memory her mother was creating for her in that moment would come to be an anchor for her now, when the world spun so fast and clear before her that every day was a struggle to remember who she'd once been, a fifteen-year-old girl with two hearts her mother had given her.

She rubbed her own thumb over the heart below her wrist now, remembering how Yusuke, too, had told her she was lucky to have it, how most people only got one. Her mother must have known something Kazuko never learned, though, because the only comfort she took in her second heart was the memory her mother gave her that summer afternoon nearly two decades ago. She had not become a nurse. She had not helped her best friend, Midori, when she needed her most. She remembered that day more clearly than the day with her mother in the kitchen. Midori's voice trembling as they spoke on the phone, telling Kazuko what her father had done to her, how he had hurt her, but that it was going to be okay, not to worry, how she was going to be happy, how she was going to get what she wanted in the end.

Death. Death had been what she wanted. Kazuko hadn't understood that wish at seventeen, but now she knew it well, like an old friend. Death had always been with her, her shadow, even before her suicide, after Midori had made her see it, after she'd recognized it as a possibility.

But death had not wanted her. She held her second heart to her eyes and wiped away the tears that had begun to well there.

"Tomorrow evening is the lantern festival," her father said as they came up the drive. He nodded at the lantern he'd hung by his front door. "That one will need a new candle by evening, too, I suppose."

"Yes," said Kazuko. "I suppose."

⁕

Her brothers came round again later in the day with their families, her sisters-in-law asking after her, asking about Tokyo life. How exciting it must be to live with so many people and so many things to do! Her nephews and nieces climbed into her lap as if they did this on a regular basis, as if she hadn't been absent from their lives for months. She gave them candy she'd packed in her bag, and sent them spilling off her lap to play outside in the sunlight.

She excused herself after an hour, saying she was exhausted by the heat, and everyone said of course, she should drink some water and turn on the air conditioning in her room, that she should rest. She apologized for cutting the visit short, and they shook their heads, told her to go, to go rest properly. It was obvious by the looks on their faces they were afraid she'd do something strange and horrible if they didn't encourage her to rest, to retreat.

She did as suggested and drank a glass of water, turned

on the air conditioning, and unrolled her futon. The side of her face pressed against the pillow, she sighed, closed her eyes, and slept without waking until early the next morning.

"You slept so long!" her father said when she stumbled back out into the living room as if she'd just left it only an hour ago. He was dressed, had eaten his breakfast. "There's fruit in the refrigerator if you'd like some," he said. "Eat it all if you want. We'll buy food at the festival for dinner."

The festival. If she could get through the festival, her visit would be over, her obligations met, and she could return to her room in Tokyo with the others. They sat around the table with her as she ate grapes and strawberries. Hitomi licked her lips like a small child, pouting a little. Kazuko would have given her the fruit in the bowl if Hitomi could have eaten it. Since she couldn't, she ate and enjoyed it for Hitomi, imagined that as she tasted the sweet and tart of the strawberries, Hitomi and the others could taste it, too. Imagined that the burst of grape between her teeth burst in their mouths, too. They sat in deep silence, watching her steadily. Something was wrong with them, but she was unsure what she could say. She knew them better than she knew her own family. They had shared something most people would never experience. They'd shared death. But Kazuko had returned without them. And here she sat, a taste in her mouth they could never share. She choked on their stares suddenly, and ran to the sink, trying to vomit it all up, but couldn't. Her body refused her, as it had refused, at some point, to go further ahead than they had. *Why?* Why hadn't she died, too?

She slumped to the floor, her back against the lower cabinets, and closed her eyes. But even behind her eyelids, she could see them staring at her.

Would she or wouldn't she? She would. She wouldn't. Yes, she would, she decided, and finally unfolded her mother's summer kimono, letting the fabric fall to the floor. Then she draped herself in it, shivering as it slid over her shoulders and arms, cooling her in the heat. She folded the right side over her body and the left over the right, belting the obi tightly.

"Are you ready yet, Kazuko?" her father asked through the door a little later. They were all waiting, her father, her brothers, all waiting for her. Their wives and children had gone ahead in a separate car to the festival grounds at the Great Buddha of Ushiku. They were already there, waiting for her, too. What was taking her so long? "Are you ill?" her father asked now.

"No," Kazuko replied through the door, and slid it open the next moment. Her father's eyes widened in shock, but he said nothing. "I'm ready."

Her brothers, too, were surprised, and complimented her. "I should have worn mine, too," said Akira, and she could tell he was wishing he'd worn his so she would stand out less. There would be others wearing traditional kimono at the festival, but mostly little girls and old women. His and Hiroshi's wives were in jeans or dresses, she imagined. But she didn't care. The kimono had seemed so much like someone else's grave when she first looked at it. When she put it on at the last minute, though, it felt like a second skin, a dark skin patterned with blossoms.

When they arrived at the cemetery surrounding the feet of the Great Buddha, she noticed the long lines of cars parked in the lots and tensed, realizing just how many people would be here, how it would be like Tokyo, an obstacle course, and she would have to navigate it as deftly as possible. The evening was coming on earlier as the end of summer dipped toward autumn, the sky turning violet and dark. Kazuko looked up at the Great Buddha's head, where she knew people wandered inside the museum of his body, looking down through his eyes at the cemetery and the fields and woods and houses surrounding the area before the daily tours ended. Small. So small, she felt as she looked up at him, at the people inside the statue looking down at her.

In fields of dirt between the cemetery and the Buddha's feet, paper lanterns were being lit by elderly men wearing white pants and shirts like housepainters. The lanterns hung from rows of cord suspended between wooden posts. Paper lanterns with family names painted on them. *How silly we were.* Kazuko thought back to a year ago. They'd gone and killed themselves during Obon, and it was only now that she realized. It was just one more item on her ex-husband's list of reasons to be infuriated with her. Her suicide had been an embarrassment for him, but to have done it during Obon, on the day of the dead, would serve to remind him of her forever. For that, she was sure, he would never forgive her.

Consider us even, Yusuke.

Drums were beating, dancers were dancing the *bon*

odori for their dear departed ancestors, cold beer chilling the sweaty-browed drinkers, both tourists and Japanese townies. Multicolored stage lights illuminated the feet and legs of the Great Buddha as the evening swept deeper into night. Kazuko drifted away from her father and brothers and their wives and children. She gathered the distance she had stored up over her months away, placed it around her shoulders like a cloak, and picked her way through the crowd that had gathered for the festival.

Around a small pond, Japanese men and women had gathered together, holding paper lanterns, which they lit, then placed down on the dark water and set adrift as if on a long, lonely voyage. Their flickering lights would guide the dead back to the underworld. When she was little, Kazuko had always wondered how the dead could follow the lanterns across a pond or a lake or down a river. "Why don't the ghosts sink?" she had asked her mother, who replied by saying that ghosts don't have feet, and winked at Kazuko. That had just been more Japanese folklore, she knew now, because Asami, Hitomi, and Tadashi followed behind her on their own two feet, walking in the wake of the steps she made for them.

It was good to know such things, thought Kazuko. It was good to know what had once been a mystery. She felt almost as if knowing allowed her a measure of happiness that, previously, life with all its uncertainties had withheld from her.

She wandered among the crowd of festival-goers, smiling, warmed by their presence. They were complete strangers, and they did not see her as she walked past them quietly in the cloak of her distance. To look upon their innocent faces shining in the brassy firelight and lantern light buoyed her. She admired the dancers and the drum players, she admired the grilled octopus and yakitori, the tented vendor stalls that served yakisoba with slivers of pinkish-red ginger sprinkled over the noodles. If she could have gone unnoticed, she would have stolen a sweet azuki-bean-filled sugar bun from a little boy, who held it down at his side, as if he'd forgotten it.

A group of foreigners were huddled along the path to the Buddha, chatting loudly in English, as if they owned the place. She recognized them, and with a flush of fear worried they'd see her now walking among them. The farm boy from Wisconsin was there with a tall can of beer in one hand, his face flushed, laughing. A Japanese girl clung to his arm, staring up at him, smiling as if she'd won something. She would marry him. They would stay in Japan or else return to America and she would have his children, at least two: a boy and a girl. She had decided this already. Kazuko could see the decision sitting in the girl's mind like an egg in a nest. The girl warmed her decision each day by staring at him and grinning, by giggling at his jokes and covering her mouth when she smiled with her teeth. One day the decision would hatch and she would find herself in Wisconsin in the middle of a snowstorm, barefoot and pregnant in a kitchen with a refrigerator the size of a tank and a counter that ran all the way across one wall and down another, jutting out into the middle of the room, a counter long enough to open up her own sushi restaurant if she wanted. A plugged-in Santa Claus would be lit up on the front lawn, his mechanical arm eternally waving a wrapped present at neighbors and passing cars.

The night grew darker, the lanterns brighter, and Kazuko

wandered away from the crowd, into the marigolds planted beneath the rows of lanterns. She knelt to touch one, concentrated so the others could feel it beneath her fingers. Could they feel how soft it was, a marigold, could they remember? She leaned down to put her nose against it, tickling herself for just a moment, indulging in the fragrance. What did it remind her of? Something from childhood again probably. Another moment she'd forgotten. What was it?

A high soaring sound interrupted her question, a shriek into the night that erupted into an explosion of bright stacks of golden fireworks above the Great Buddha's shoulders. Kazuko looked up to watch them open, unfurling, over and over, a sudden barrage of *hanabi*. "Best fireworks of the year, outside of the Tsuchiura City displays, Mother always said, didn't she?" a man standing at the entrance to the row of lanterns said. Kazuko looked up to see who he was. Did she know him? No, it didn't matter. He was talking to a woman standing beside him, not her. He had not seen Kazuko kneeling in the dirt under the lanterns, smelling a marigold. He continued on, reminiscing, and Kazuko glanced around the rows of lanterns and marigolds as if she'd lost something among them.

"Best fireworks of the year, outside of the Tsuchiura City displays," someone said, mimicking the man Kazuko had overheard, and Kazuko turned in the direction of the voice, a girl's voice, a voice she recognized before she even saw her friend's smiling face looking down at her.

"Midori," she whispered, and her hand flew to her mouth as if she could catch the name and put it back inside her. She had not spoken of her friend in all the years since her death.

But once out in the world again, the name refused to go back where it came from.

"Kazuko chan," said Midori, and grinned as she lowered herself into a slight bow, the cranes on the dark blue kimono she wore swinging forward with her. Kazuko stood to return the gesture automatically. "Kazuko chan," said Midori Nakajima, "it's been a long time."

"Yes," said Kazuko. "An amazingly long time."

"Let us walk together awhile," said Midori. "Tell me what's become of you." She held out her hand. Kazuko took it, linking arms with her as they used to, and they set off together in their summer kimonos, walking carefully, two women of the old world of empires and love suicides and pillow books, sharing court gossip as they wandered away from everyone, down the hillside, away from the festival, to a pond where already a few family lanterns were floating in the dark, glassy water, away from the world and all of its frustrations and rules.

Kazuko took her time telling Midori what had become of her. The words came slowly and sometimes, for long moments, it seemed as if they would not come at all. Especially as she reached certain points in her story—her mother's death, her family's silence over it, Yusuke's lover, Kazuko's friendship with the others, the ones who now followed behind her, their plan, what they had decided to do together. Their suicide. Her suicide.

"So you tried to follow me," Midori said after Kazuko had finished her story. They were down by the pond, where people were beginning to gather now. Kazuko furrowed her brows, unsure. She wanted to cry, but had no tears in her.

"I thought it would be the best way to end things. Like you did," Kazuko said, choking on the knot in her throat. "I thought it would solve everything. I could leave Yusuke and our lie of a marriage; I could leave my father, my brothers, their stubborn silence; I could leave my job coordinating other people's lives. There was nothing left that was mine."

"Then you were lucky," said Midori, and Kazuko stopped walking.

"What do you mean?"

"It was not what I expected," said Midori. "Over there. It was not how I thought it would be. I'm not who I thought I'd become."

"You are my best friend," said Kazuko. "That's the only thing that matters."

Midori smiled. "No," she said, "it isn't the only thing, Kazuko. You don't know this, but death has taught me something I hope you won't learn any earlier than you have to."

Kazuko blinked, not knowing how to answer, and Midori didn't offer any further explanation. Her silence rang like a temple bell between them. Kazuko nodded, silent now, too.

"Listen, Kazuko chan. We have little time left. The lanterns are calling."

"Help me, then," said Kazuko, feeling afraid for the first time since her suicide.

"I cannot help you," said Midori. "What can I do? What can any of the dead do for you, Kazuko?"

"How do I find my way?" Kazuko asked. But before

Midori could answer, Kazuko felt light-headed, weak, as if she might fall and crumple up like a piece of paper, as if an unseen hand held her, was squeezing her tight in her middle.

"Let yourself see it, Kazuko. You already know it. Look. Look how your friends know their way."

Midori turned back to the pond, where the lanterns were floating away from shore, and Kazuko saw them. No longer behind her, sharing her footsteps, they trod gracefully over the still water—Hitomi, Asami, Tadashi—following the lantern lights as they drifted, until they melted into the dark on the other side. "They're leaving me," Kazuko whispered, and tears welled up, finally, rolling out of her eyes, hot and stinging.

"No," said Midori. "They're leaving. There is a difference, Kazuko."

She held her hands out and Kazuko took them quickly, brought them to her chest to hold against her there, where her heart beat beneath her ribs like a bird fluttering in a cage. She was crying in earnest now, shaking her head, sobbing. "You have always known my heart more than anyone," Kazuko said. "But we did not say a good farewell last time, did we?"

Midori shook her head.

"Now you must go ahead of me," said Kazuko, "and so I say it now how I should have then. Farewell, my friend."

"*O genki de*," said Midori, and leaned into a bow.

She turned then, and walked across the water like the others, like all of the dead were doing, and did not turn back to look at Kazuko, to wave goodbye, to linger. In another moment she was nothing more than the mist that hovered over the dark water.

Kazuko turned from the pond and was startled to find herself on a shore full of people. The fireworks had ended. The festival was winding down. Everyone had gathered to watch the lanterns glow as they drifted. "So pretty," a little girl said to her mother, and the mother nodded and smiled. Kazuko looked for her family among the festival-goers, but could not find them until she looked up to the hillside where she had separated from them earlier. They stood up there, on the crest of the hill, her father between her brothers, waiting for her to join them. Her father raised his hand to wave down at her. Kazuko raised hers in return. Then, clutching her hand to her chest, she began the climb back up the hillside, weeping as she took each steep step, to make her way toward them.

A Thousand Tails

When I was five years old, my mother gave me a silver ball and said, "Midori chan, my little *kitsune*, don't let Father know about this. He'd take it from you to sell it, but it's yours, my little fox girl. It's yours, and now you can learn how to take care of yourself."

"You mean I can learn how to take care of the ball," I said. Even then I was not polite as I was supposed to be. I was a girl who corrected her mother.

"No, no," said my mother. "So you can learn how to take care of yourself. That's what I said, didn't I?" She swatted a fly buzzing near her nose and it fell to the floor, stunned by the impact, next to her bare foot. The next moment she crushed it beneath her heel and continued. "A fox always takes care of itself by taking care of its silver ball. Don't you remember the stories I've told you? Well, I'll tell them again, my little one. So listen and you'll know what I mean."

My mother had always called me her fox girl, had always told me she'd found me wandering in the woods and brought me home with her. Father would laugh and say, "Your mother is always bringing home lost creatures. Soon we'll be keeping a zoo!" He'd stroked the back of my head like I sometimes saw him pet our cats: one long stroke and a quick pat to send me off again.

As a child I was often confused by the things my mother said and did, but it didn't bother me. It felt natural that life was mysterious and that my mother hid her meaning behind a veil of stories, as if her words were water through which truth shimmered and splintered like the beams of the rising sun. She taught me that some matters have no clear way to explain their meaning to others.

Children at school often remarked on her. How strange your mother is, they told me. And how alike the two of us were. "Why does your mother speak to herself? Why does she sometimes laugh at nothing? Is she crazy?" a small group once asked me at recess, forming a circle around me. "Why do you sit in class and stare out the window while we're playing *karuta* or Fruit Basket? Why don't you talk to us, Midori? What's the matter? Don't you like people?"

To tell the truth, they were correct. I was a strange child, and they sensed it. It was because, even then, people seemed so odd to me in their single-minded concerns and simple pleasures. I did not know at the time why, at the age of five—at an age before the world had had time to inflict many wounds on me—I felt this way. Somehow, though, I felt somewhere a world existed that was my true home, not the rice fields or the gray mountainsides in the distance, not the rivers and the fishermen standing along their banks, not the dusty fields where other children played games during afternoon recess, not the farm on which I was being raised. And it was not that I felt I belonged in a radiant, carnivalesque city like Tokyo either. It was that I somehow knew I simply did not belong with people.

I knew all that at the age of five. But it was at nine years old that I discovered my true being in this world.

❋

In fourth grade we read a book called *Gongitsune.* This is an honorable way of spelling and saying the name of the fox, the *kitsune*. Many of the new kanji we were learning that month were in this tale, and beside each new character the publisher had printed small *hiragana*, the simpler alphabet, to guide us to the right sound and meaning. I didn't need *hiragana* as much as the others, though. Kanji was easy for me. When sensei introduced new characters, it seemed I could look at them and, almost by magic, they would reveal their meanings to me, yet one more reason for my classmates to be suspicious. So when sensei gave us this story, I read for pleasure, I read without having to study our new words.

Gongitsune was about a little fox named Gon, who found a small village while he was out looking for food, and began to steal from the villagers. One day Gon stole an eel from a man named Hyoju. The eel was supposed to be for Hyoju's sick old mother. And because Gon stole the mother's meal, the old woman died. When Gon discovered the consequence of his actions, he tried to repent by secretly giving things he stole from other villagers to Hyoju. But the villagers saw that Hyoju had their things and they beat him up, thinking he was the thief. From then on, Gon only brought Hyoju mushrooms and nuts from the forest. Hyoju was grateful, but didn't know who brought him the gifts, or why. Then one day he saw a fox

in the woods and, remembering the fox that stole the eel
for his dying mother, he shot, and Gon died. It was only
afterwards, when the gifts of mushrooms and nuts stopped
showing up on his doorstep, that he realized Gon was who
had been bringing them all along.

"And what is the moral of this story?" our sensei asked
after we finished our reading.

We waited with our eyes open, our mouths sealed tight.
We knew that she would deliver the answer the very next
moment, that our input was not important.

"The moral is that there is an order to the world, that
everything is as it is for a reason. Gon's mother dies, Hyoju's
mother dies, Gon is shot while he tries to make amends for
his mistakes, and Hyoju feels guilty after realizing he's killed
the creature that's been helping him. But nothing can be
done about this. Everyone must accept their own fate."

We stayed silent. A few children nodded. But I didn't like
what the sensei said. I didn't think the story was about ac-
cepting fate. I thought it was about how stupid Hyoju was
for not trying to find out who was leaving mushrooms and
nuts. Gon wasn't that clever really. Hyoju, if he wanted to
know, could have discovered Gon at any time. Instead he
chose the human way. He chose the path humans almost always choose. The path of ignorance.

Poor Gon, I thought as I sat at my desk. *Poor little fox.* I
stroked the picture of him struck down by stupid Hyoju's
bullet, his fur glowing white as moonlight. And there, in
that moment, I realized it was Gon's tribe that I belonged to,
not the human family. I was a *kitsune,* I realized. I was a fox.

✦

Every *kitsune* has a silver ball that contains part of their essence. Why hadn't I understood this when my mother gave it to me years before? I'd thought she was just telling me another of her stories, the kind she was always telling me, the kind that I hadn't really, until that day, believed. The silver ball holds a piece of the *kitsune*'s spirit so that when they change shape they're never entirely separated from their original form. It made sense now. It all washed over my mind like a clear spring rain, and I stood and walked to the back of the room to gather my things. Sensei turned around when she heard me shuffling the backpack onto my shoulders and cried out, "Midori chan, what are you doing?"

"Going home," I said. I slid the door of the classroom open and walked down the hallway. Sensei rushed and caught me by my shoulder as I was walking out the front entrance, but I shrugged her hand off and stared up at her, making the most defiant face I could summon, and said, "Never touch me in such a way again."

She slowly took her hand off my shoulder. Her face dropped, all the muscles relaxing, and in this way she revealed the fear I'd instilled in her. When you are a *kitsune*, you can use your powers to persuade and affect human emotions. It's a simple trick really, especially because most humans have little control over their own emotions anyway. So even so soon after realizing what I was, I knew how to use one of the powers that is a right of all *kitsune*.

At home I put my school things away and pulled my futon from the closet, unfolded it, and sat down, folding my legs under me. I took the silver ball from a box of toys, and rolled it around in the palms of my hands, pressing it against my cheek occasionally. It was as warm as my own flesh, and when I held it to my ear I heard a pulse and a thump, a heart beating over and over.

When my mother came in from hanging out the wash, she found me with the ball held against my ear and said, "Midori chan, what are you doing home already? School isn't over."

"I left," I said.

"What?! Why did you leave?" she asked, her face creased with worry. It was the face that I would watch over the years as it became her final mask, it was the face that would make her an old woman before her time.

"I was sick," I lied. "I phoned, but you didn't answer. They had me lie down in the clinic, but I left when no one was looking. I wanted to come home."

"Oh my," she said, and left the room to call the principal, to let him know I'd arrived home safely. When she returned a little while later, she said, "Midori," and her voice dripped with disappointment. "You trust me so little that you lie to me now?"

I nodded, but did not say any more. After all, why was I in the care of these people anyway? Simply because my mother had found me lost in the woods one day and brought me home? They were my jailers, for all I knew. Such was my thinking at that moment.

"Well then," she said, "now that you've gone and done it, you'll have to clean up your own mess at school. But don't tell Father! If he knows, I'm not sure what he'll do."

"I won't tell," I said, taking the beat of my own heart away from my ear finally. "But you must tell me more about myself," I said. "About my true nature."

"Your true nature?" she said. "What do you mean?"

"I am a *kitsune*," I said, "aren't I?"

She frowned and laughed a little, and put one hand against her face and shook her head. "Midori chan, I should never have told you that story. You're getting a little old for that now, aren't you?"

I stared at her, my face burning, but did not answer.

"Midori," she said. "Really, you are an impossible child."

My mother—or my human mother, as I came to think of her more often after that day—suddenly had very little to tell me. So for the second time that day, I snuck away. Out the back door I went, taking a small trail that lay between my father's cabbage fields and a persimmon orchard. It was autumn and the persimmons were growing to ripeness, their golden-orange globes fattening day by day, weighing down the tree limbs. Mother always picked baskets of them to bring back and cut into slivers for dessert.

When I reached the end of the persimmon orchard and cabbage field, there was a small road that led out to the main road in town. On the other side of the road was a forest of bamboo and pine trees. I looked both ways, and when I was satisfied that all was safe, I hurried across the road, into the forest.

I was not certain where I was going, but I stepped with certain strides, as if I knew the path like the inside of my heart. The forest floor was mostly clean. Only a few branches littered the ground. Light filtered down through the treetops like shafts of molten gold. When I finally stopped, I stood in a clearing before a tiny house on a small wooden platform beneath a fir tree. The house's miniature double doors were locked, and there were little steps leading down to the platform it sat upon. Coins and colored strings and bottles of tea had been left on the steps. It was an old shrine, dilapidated, the wood gray and moldy. A home for the spirits of this place. I looked around, staring up at the canopy of trees surrounding me, and thought, *Yes, I remember. These woods are my home.*

My father's father had made this shrine many years ago, to honor the spirit of this land, and I was that very same spirit. My mother had found me lost in the woods and brought me home with her. This land belonged to me. I was a *kitsune*, as I'd realized, and this was the land to which I was bound.

How, then, had I come to be a human child? That was a much more difficult story to put together. But, oh, I was one smart fox.

My father had worked this land for many years, as had his father before him, with a decent enough crop each year, until suddenly one year a blight plagued his cabbage and persimmon and anything else he tried to grow. He was baffled, but he never thought to honor the spirit of the land as his father had. It was my mother who must have reminded him. She was always saying how he'd forgotten his ancestors, how he'd forgotten the spirits of the land. Yes, I thought, she had to have been the one to remind him of this shrine his father had built years ago.

So he restored the shrine to appease whatever gods may have been roaming nearby, and soon the land gave forth again. But this only angered him more. He didn't like that his land did not truly belong to him. So he waited and watched until he saw a small fox visiting the shrine every evening, at dusk, sniffing around the steps where he'd left his offerings. "A *kitsune*!" he shouted through the house that night. And soon he was plotting. "They are the trickiest of all," he told my mother, "but their weakness is that they're in love with their own cleverness."

This is true, unfortunately. This is very, very true.

So he began to leave even more offerings at the spirit house, until its steps were full. I could imagine him as he left the door of the shrine open one evening, and sure enough, when the little fox came by, it stood on its hind legs to pull itself up the steps, knocking off the other offerings to see what had been placed inside. And when the fox poked its head through the doorway, my father jumped out from his hiding place and pushed the fox in the rest of the way. Then he barred the door, locking it. The land would be under his control as long as he held me in his power. But it was my mother who would find the silver ball.

Days later, she visited the shrine to tidy it up. She couldn't stand the idea of what had happened, and wanted in some way to let the *kitsune* know that she was loyal to it. She could not speak of her feelings to my father for fear of being thought disloyal, or to others for fear of being thought crazy, so while she arranged offerings on the steps and chattered to the spirit locked in the house about how she couldn't help it even if she wanted because he had the key, she noticed a silver ball sitting on the forest floor, just beneath the platform the house stood upon. She knelt down and picked it up, and that is when I told her how she could help me.

She would bring me into this world as her child, so that I could eventually free myself. Do not worry, I told her through the ball. I will be the source of my own liberation.

I did not see my human father as my enemy, as some may think would be my natural feelings toward the man. Instead I thought him very clever to trap my spirit. Not clever enough to remember a *kitsune* has tricks up her sleeve even in the worst of conditions, but clever nonetheless. I also felt indebted to him, for it's a rare opportunity for those born in the spirit realm to receive the chance to be human, and it's through human suffering that one can enter nirvana most easily. I decided to welcome this entrapment as a step on the path to eternity. The Buddha himself is said to be like a lotus flower, growing upward from the mud at the bottom of a pond, for the time he spent in the world allowed his bright wisdom to flow forth. Instead of despising my conditions, I would learn from others, I thought. Now that I knew my position in the world, I could carry on with life, with fate, more easily. I would grow into a young woman and try my best to please my teachers and parents.

Later, when I returned from the woods, I told my mother not to worry. That all would be well. I told her I would apologize to sensei and make everything right at school again, that Father would never have to know what had happened. She stroked my cheek and said, "Now that's my good girl, Midori. That's my good girl."

❈

When I went back to school the next day, sensei didn't say anything to me. She pretended as if nothing strange at all had happened. I could have allowed her to remain in fear of me forever, but I decided that, as I was a human for the moment, I would go to her and apologize for my behavior, as humans do.

"Sensei," I said, "about yesterday, please excuse me. I'm so sorry. I myself don't even know why I acted in such a way. I am truly sorry."

"Midori chan, I was so surprised!" she said. "But it's all right. This sort of thing happens sometimes. Especially in the fall, when the wind from the mountains is bearing down on us." She looked out the classroom window then and said, "Winter is coming."

We did not speak of this matter again, and I appreciated her easy forgiveness and the way she turned the discussion away from the matter of my guilt to the change of the season. I decided I would not give her so much trouble in the future. I would do my best to be a model student.

The chime for class to begin sounded and all of us took our seats. I listened intently and volunteered to help in any way possible that day. After lunch, it was time for all of the students to clean the school. I was on hallway duty with a girl named Kazuko. She was from a good family in town. Out of all the children in my class, she was the only one who never made fun of me or my mother. But she was so quiet I wasn't even sure how her voice would sound if she said something. Usually we wiped our section of the hall floor facing each other on hands and knees, her feet braced against the wall behind her, mine braced against the wall behind me, saying nothing. We had never spoken before, but on that day, while we wiped the dust and dirt away, Kazuko stopped working and looked up at me. I looked back and smiled. It was the first time I had tried to be friendly to someone. When she smiled back, I was thrilled. I had done this thing right.

"Yesterday," she said in a voice like a trickle of water, "what you did was amazing. I couldn't believe it. I thought, This can't be! But you did it! You walked out and sensei couldn't do anything about it. You're so strong. I envy you."

"It wasn't anything," I said, shrugging. "I regret it. It was too much. I apologized to sensei this morning."

"That's what's even more wonderful," she said. "You showed her how you felt, and because it was rude you apologized—but you weren't afraid. It's all the same, don't you see? You have no fear. I wish I was more like you."

I wanted to reach out and touch her face, to stroke her cheek like my mother stroked mine. *I have a friend,* I thought. "I wish I was like you, too," I told her. "Why don't we teach each other how?"

She grinned and nodded, her bangs bouncing on her forehead under the red bandanna wrapped around her head. "We'll be good friends for sure," she said.

"And even when we're no longer near each other one day," I said, unable to stop myself even then from predicting the future, "we'll never be alone again."

From Kazuko I learned many things. How to tell a girl that her hairstyle was pretty, how to tell a boy that he was smart or funny, how to tell a teacher that they have been a great help to me, how deep I should bow according to a person's status, how to seem excited about playing silly games like Fruit Basket when the foreign teacher from Australia came to teach us English. And later, after we began to grow fast and went to junior high, how if I wore my hair in two braids and smiled with my teeth I was the cutest girl in our class, how if I pretended to daydream while sitting at a picnic table in the school courtyard during afternoon recess, others would think I was poetic.

When I went to Kazuko's house, her family was so normal. Her mother was always cooking or cleaning or mending clothes; her father was always working or, on Sundays, watching sports on television; her older brothers constantly arguing while they played video games in a back bedroom. I could hear them back there even with their door slid shut. I learned from Kazuko and her family how to be human. I learned what it felt like to love others, to be loved, at least a little bit, even though I was not a member of their family. And from all that, I learned how to feel a great absence in my life when I was with my own mother and father, in my own home, wondering why I could not have the kind of life Kazuko's family gave her.

My self-pity never lasted long. I couldn't allow it. I knew why my mother and father couldn't love me in that way. My father because his wife didn't give him the son he longed for. My mother because when she looked at me, I could see in her eyes his disappointment pressing down on her. None of us could give the other what they needed. We were doomed from the beginning.

So in the end the universe had exacted a price for our cunning behavior. My father thought he'd tricked me by trapping me in the shrine, and I thought I'd tricked him by becoming his daughter. But all of our trickery was for nothing. Since my spirit was not truly trapped in the shrine, my father's crops were still often blighted. And for me, what I'd thought would be an escape from the spirit world was instead an education in the sorrow of mortality. I learned how everything slips away in the moment we hold it. I learned from the beat of my human heart how we are forced to live in a world that will inevitably fade.

This is not enough, I thought one day as I was hanging the laundry on the line for my mother. *This is not enough,* I was thinking still, when suddenly I heard a strange choking sound come from the nearby kitchen window. I dropped the sheet I was hanging and ran inside shouting, "*Okaasan! Okaasan!*" There was a pain in my heart before I even reached the kitchen, a throb in my chest as if someone had reached inside my chest and squeezed hard. When I arrived I found her on the floor, one arm across her chest, the other stretched out on the floor beside her body.

This is not enough, I had thought.

And Death replied:

"But this is what you have."

❖

I was a third-grade student in high school that spring, seventeen years old and preparing to go to college in Tokyo with Kazuko. We had remained friends throughout the years, drawing closer and closer until we were more like sisters. My mother knew of our plans to go to university together in Tokyo. There would be trouble with Father, she'd told me, but she would take care of it. There was no need to worry.

Now she was gone and I wasn't sure what would become of the plans Kazuko and I had made together. Over the years my father had grown to dislike me more and more, especially when it became apparent he'd have no son to inherit his blighted farm, in which he took a spiteful pride. And with my mother dead, he'd taken to drinking sake every night until he was drowned in his and its misery. When he drank, his dislike for me grew into a hatred that brought forth curses that shook the walls. That spring, I often found myself running from the house, my hands clapped over my ears to shut his voice out behind me. Without my mother to protect me, I didn't know how to proceed with my plans to leave. I'd become so human that I'd forgotten I could challenge his belligerence with the strength of my own will. I'd become such a proper Japanese girl that I'd forgotten I was stronger than him.

One day, soon after our graduation ceremony, I told him my plans. "I'm moving to Tokyo with Kazuko," I said. "We're going to room together and go to college."

"College?" he said, as if it were another planet. "College? How can you think about college? Your mother has died!"

"She died three months ago, Father."

"I need you here," he said. I could see his muscles tense with frustration. "Besides," he said, "you've graduated. You don't need to go to school any longer."

I could hear the rest of his meaning unspoken: that I did not need to go to school because one day I'd marry a man who would take care of me. That, until then, I'd help him take care of this home.

"I'm sorry, Father," I said, "but I've already decided. I'm going to Tokyo. You must learn to take care of this house on your own. I want a different life than the one you see fit for me."

I felt the back of his hand strike my cheek before I actually saw him moving. For a long stretch of time, I could feel the knobs of his knuckles pushing my face to the side after his fist struck. I saw a bright flash of light behind my eyes and my jaw rattled. I thought I was seeing a dream, the way I sometimes dreamed my teeth were all crumbling and falling out of my mouth. Soon they would all be broken and fall out covered in blood, I thought, when I felt them scrape against each other. There was no pain immediately, but as soon as the white flash of light faded and my vision returned, I felt the sting and the piercing flow of blood flooding through my cheek. What's more, I saw his hand rise again, come down at me again, moving toward me like the scythe moves toward a stalk of rice.

My cheeks, my mouth, my nose, my shoulders, my chest. His rage was like the rage of a demon as he pushed, grabbed, shook me. I cried, pleading, but he could not hear me. When his rage was spent, he stood above me, crying like a child, his hands over his face. "Why this?" he said. "Why this?"

I stood up slowly, gingerly, my head bowed, one arm held in front of it to protect me from further blows. "Why can't you be a good girl, Midori?" he said as I walked past him to my room. I passed a mirror on the way and caught a glimpse of the bloody meat of my face. I stopped for a moment to get a better look. My bottom lip was split and my cheek was swelling so that it seemed it might tear open. I was fascinated. The blood seeped out, and in my blood I saw a glimmering. When I looked closer, it seemed like tiny

beads of mercury, and then I remembered the silver ball my
mother had given me years ago. I'd put it in a toy box and
hidden it at the back of my closet after I became friends
with Kazuko and no longer needed the comforts of my secret origin.

Now I crawled on my hands and knees to the back of my
closet to find it. When I opened the lid, the ball seemed to
glow, faintly illuminating the dark. I picked it up and heard
the same heartbeat inside it I'd heard nearly ten years
before. That was me in there, I remembered. Kazuko had
made me feel so human that the silver ball had become
something I dreamed about over the years, and forgot each
morning when I woke. I had become someone else. I had
forgotten myself.

I fell asleep in the closet, listening to the silver ball's
heartbeat, feeling its warmth in my hands. When I woke
several hours later, my father had fallen asleep on the floor
in the living room. I crept back to my room and picked up
the phone to call Kazuko. When she answered, I was already crying. "*Ne, ne*, Midori chan," she said, "*Doushita
no*?" What's the matter?

Through clenched teeth, I told her what had happened
after I told my father our plans. When I finished, she said
she was calling the police. I told her not to, that I would take
care of this myself, but within a half hour the police were at
my house and my father, crying, was explaining how his
wife had just died and now his daughter was going to leave
him to go to college in Tokyo. "I didn't intend to hurt the
child, you see, it just happened, she is abandoning me."

I stayed in my bedroom and when the police officers
were done speaking with my father, they came back

through the hallway to my room and knocked. I slid the door open, lifted my face to them. They were both men. They squinted at the sight of me. Then, as if shaking off a bad dream, they regained their stiff composures. They said in kind tones that my father was having a difficult time right now, and that I should be a good girl, take care of him now that my mother was gone, that I should help him. "There's a university right here in town," one of them said.

"That is the agricultural college," I reminded them. "I already know as much about farming as I want to."

"You can go to secretarial school," the other suggested.

I nodded. "You are right," I told them. "Thank you for your help."

They excused themselves from my room and I watched their backs as they went down the hall, back to the living room, and talked more with my father, telling him to control himself, or else they would return and that they'd not be so kind the next time. Minutes later they were gone and he was in my room, angry again. "What person of importance do you think you are?" he said. "Calling the police on your father!" He shook his head as if I were the one who should be ashamed. "Such willfulness, even as a child," he complained. "I blame your mother."

"I did not get my willfulness from her," I told him, staring straight into his eyes.

"Bah!" He threw his hand in the air, as if he were throwing away trash. "No good has ever come of you, and nothing ever will."

When he had passed out for the second time that evening, I called Kazuko again. I thanked her for being concerned, for being my friend, but said that I wouldn't need her help any longer. "Midori chan," she said, "you're acting as if we're never going to see each other again."

"I won't be going to Tokyo with you," I explained. "But please don't worry. Really. I'll be fine. I'll be more than fine. I hope you'll be happy, Kazuko."

"Midori—"

But quietly I disconnected.

For a few days I kept to my room, barely coming out to eat, barely sleeping more than three hours in the night. My father knocked on my door from time to time, and called my name weakly from the other side, but I didn't answer, and eventually he'd drift away. The phone rang sometimes, but neither he nor I moved to answer it. It was probably Kazuko calling. *But I've already said goodbye,* I thought. I held the silver ball in my hands, cradling it against my body while I considered my fate. There was a reason for everything, I'd been told, but I was not at peace with this. I was finished, I decided on the fourth day. I was through with this world. It was time to reclaim my proper identity.

I took the silver ball and placed it inside my mouth, holding it there, a pearl in an oyster, and finally swallowed it with much effort, choking, my throat swollen with it until my body filled with its terrible rhythm and I fell—that *body* fell to the floor, I should say, but I remained standing above her, looking down at the girl I'd been for nearly eighteen years. Midori Nakajima. *Such a pretty child,* I thought, kneeling down to look at her more closely. Even with bruises, she looked like an angel. "Goodbye," I said, and kissed the flesh that had been home to me for so long. "Goodbye," I said, and walked out of that room and out of that house, into the woods to the shrine, where I broke the lock he had placed on the doors so many years ago, and reached inside to retrieve my true skin.

❊

It's been a long time since that moment of discovery. I can still remember in detail, and still wince at the memory, how I reached into that old, rotten shrine in the forest and found nothing but dust, the dried husks of insects, and empty air. And then what? Then I looked around the forest with my eyes wide open without a story to go along with it. It was a forest of bamboo and pine trees with an old shrine at the heart of it, and me standing in the middle of it, my hands empty, and no way to undo my choices.

I ride the trains at night now, staring out the windows at the lights of passing cities and towns and villages, thinking back to that moment, the point that I'd thought without any doubt would be my exit to salvation. I'd thought so far ahead in the story, had imagined all of it happening in a particular way. *Midori,* I think as I stare at my face in the glass of the train window, *you silly girl.* I truly had been a *kitsune* in spirit, clever as an old nine-tailed fox, cleverer maybe, clever enough to have grown a thousand tails over my brief history of living. But the only person I'd managed to trick with the stories I'd been telling for so long had been me. A *kitsune.* Indeed.

I walk the streets of Tokyo sometimes, and wander through its parks and subway stations, watching all the people that fill the city with their fragile bodies, their feathery breath, their fleeting dreams. The buildings are so tall that when I look up I get the sense of falling backwards, as if I'm flying. When I look down again, though, the streets still surround me, the neon glares in the puddles, and the people continue doing whatever they're always doing. Laughing, arguing, reminiscing, cursing the day they met each other, holding hands, walking together, remembering their childhoods, their school days, and then, when they come to an unfamiliar intersection, they realize they've forgotten their intended destinations, and look around wondering how they got here.

I like looking at their faces, at their smiles and frowns, at their brows furrowed in confusion. And when they return home for the evening and the streets begin to grow empty, I go down into a train station and select a destination. There are so many paths to choose from, and no one ever tries to stop me. But I always travel alone. That's the price of my ticket.

In fifteen years, I've seen everywhere the trains of Japan can take me. I've climbed Mount Fuji in the dark of a stormy night, lightning cracking the sky open around me, and when I reached the top I saw the sun rise clear and bright. I've visited Nara, where the deer roam through the cemeteries and parks like lost children, and I've been to Kyoto, the old capital, where the trees are already beginning to change colors as the summer closes and autumn draws near. At the Golden Palace, even weak sunlight is more than enough to set the walls of that place aglow. I lingered in the shadows of its great walls on days when my spirit's body, instead of growing bent and wizened, grew thin and light as the flame of a candle. I looked up at the golden phoenix perched on the rooftop and wished that one day it would show me a different sort of trick than the one I played.

I've stood upon the wooden bridge of Kiyomizu Temple, where the water is purer than anywhere else on this planet, and held my arms out like the wings of a crane, looking up into the sky and waiting for Buddha to make me light enough to fly up into the blue air, to see Japan grow smaller and smaller below me until I am so far above everything that I can see people walking the busy streets like ants tumbling through their tunnels, living obliviously or else noticing far too much, living contentedly or in frustration, unhappily or ridiculously happy, as they always seem to be doing. People. Higher and higher still I'll go, until the island I call home is a stone surrounded by water. I'll wave with both hands as Tokyo and Nikko and Sapporo and Osaka and Nagoya and the rice fields of my youth fall away from me. "*Sayonara*, Japan!" I'll shout, and even then I'd fly higher.

But, no, this is just another story I tell myself, even now. I never did leave that bridge, or any other high place I've visited. I can stand on tiptoe and reach, stretching my arms out like a beggar, but the sky will not open for someone who does not truly want to leave.

In fifteen years, I've seen so many things, enough things to last a lifetime. But I don't want to stop watching people on their way to their destinations, loving and saying goodbye to each other as they go wherever they must go.

I don't travel far from home any longer. After a day spent walking along the Sumida River, watching a foreign family taking pictures of each other in front of Tokyo Tower, after an evening of wandering through the brightly lit game centers and their bubbling noises of winning and losing, I take the train home, back to Ami, of all places. It's a long ride, but it's never long enough if you ask me.

I sit and watch my fellow travelers while they read novels and newspapers, drink coffee or beer, and send messages from their cell phones to someone they're leaving behind in the city or to one of their friends sitting beside them. Sometimes I'll stand and hold on to a strap in a crowded car, swaying back and forth with my eyes wide open while everyone else has closed theirs tight, pretending they're not among so many others, trying to be alone.

Back home in Ami, the streets are quiet and you can hear the wind blow down them and around the tiny houses, on its way to wherever it is going. I walk along the banks of the slow moonlight-rippled river, along the rice fields on the outskirts of town. I stand in front of my father's house and watch his hunched shadow pass by the frosted windows. The farm often gives good crops now, though it's nothing to do with me so much as the man who rents his fields from him. I stand in front of the gate of the schoolyard where the other children once asked if I didn't like people, and sigh at the memory of the obstinate silence I gave in return. It's strange to remember I used to think I'd do anything to leave here. Now I can't get enough of people. Now I can't get enough of this place. The moon is always right in front of me or just beyond the curve of my shoulder. I can hear the cicadas scream all day in the summer, their soft whisperings in the night, and they are a kind of consolation, the closest things I have to living. I could give it all up again and walk away knowing what that really means this time, but I won't. Not yet at least. Just a little bit longer, I tell myself. Just a little.

The fireflies glow off and on in the mist-covered fields, calling out, *Here I am,* waiting for another light to appear in the darkness. *Here I am,* one calls to another. *Come find me.*

Here I am.

Acknowledgments

I wrote this novel while living abroad for two years in Japan. A lot of people helped me write it, both in Japan and here in America, whether they know it or not. Thank you, Beth and Kevin Butters, for inviting me to come over, and for always being there. Thank you, Matt Komatsuzawa, for giving me work, and thank you to my coworkers in Edosaki, with whom I spent the majority of my days in Japan, for welcoming me and trying to make life in a new country easy. Thank you to my many students, who probably taught me more than I taught them. Thank you to Yoshio Kobayashi, for inviting me to spend Christmas with your family in Tokyo when I was alone. Thank you to Masako Yasuoka, Akiko Tada, and Hiroko Iwase for our Wednesday night lessons, laughter, and dinner. Thank you to my adopted Japanese mom, Fusako Tabata, for her open heart, and for making me a part of her family (Akira, Akihiro, and Motoi) in Sapporo. Thank you to my mom and dad and my family in Ohio for everything they do for me whether I'm near or far. Thank you to my colleagues and friends at Youngstown State University, for all the support, and to my students for all their excitement and infectious energy. Thank you, Maureen McHugh and Barbara

Gilly, Christopher Rowe and Gwenda Bond, Scott Westerfeld and Justine Larbalestier, for well-timed gifts and packages from home. Thank you, Mary Rickert, for our constant conversation, even overseas. Thank you, Kelly Link and Gavin Grant, for books and CDs in my own language. Thank you, Sharyn November, Ellen Datlow, Terri Windling, and George Mann, for bringing out various pieces of this puzzle. Thank you, Katie DuForny, for navigating Thailand with me, the mumps, and for coming to Ohio. Thank you, Jody D. White, for your beautiful friendship and for our much-missed karaoke sessions. Thanks to Peter Boatright, Karina Wakabayashi, Jana Poukka, Erin Ludeman, Andrea Ball, and Mona Quinones, for fun times in the Far East. Thank you, Matt Cheney, for all the long-distance phone calls. Thank you, Rick Bowes, for making sure I made it to Japan in the first place. Thank you, Chris Schelling, for your valiant support. Thank you, Juliet Ulman, for moonbeams, rose hips, and the really good beat of working together. Thank you, Brooke Slanina, for your always welcome laughter and your loyal friendship. Thank you, Tadashi Mizuno, for all your words, and for helping me find in Japan what I thought I'd lost in America. And thank you, Tony Romandetti, for being here when I got back.

About the Author

CHRISTOPHER BARZAK was born and raised in rural Ohio and has lived in a southern California beach town, the capital of Michigan, and the suburbs of Tokyo, Japan, where he taught English in rural junior-high and elementary schools. His stories have appeared in many venues, including *Lady Churchill's Rosebud Wristlet, Trampoline, Interfictions, Nerve, Salon Fantastique*, and *The Year's Best Fantasy and Horror*. He currently lives in Youngstown, Ohio, where he teaches writing at Youngstown State University. *The Love We Share Without Knowing* is his second novel, following *One For Sorrow* (Bantam Books, 2007).